FINAL CHANCE

FINAL CHANCE

P.I.V.O.T. LAB CHRONICLES™ BOOK THREE

MICHAEL ANDERLE

LMBPN Publishing
PMB 196, 2540 South Maryland Pkwy
Las Vegas, NV 89109

First US Edition, November, 2020
(Previously published as a part of *Too Young To Die*)
eBook ISBN: 978-1-64971-326-1
Print ISBN: 978-1-64971-327-8

THE FINAL CHANCE TEAM

Thanks to the Beta Readers

John Ashmore, Theresa Holmes, Nicole Emens, Larry Omans,
Allen Collins

Thanks to the JIT Readers

Allen Collins
Angel LaVey
Billie Leigh Kellar
Dave Hicks
Deb Mader
Diane L. Smith
Jeff Eaton
Jeff Goode
Kerry Mortimer

If I've missed anyone, please let me know!

Editor
The Skyhunter Editing Team

CHAPTER ONE

"I feel like a new man," Nick announced as he came into the lab. This had become something of a ritual since they'd first relocated to the new premises.

Jacob studied him quickly. "You look like a new man." He refocused on his work for a moment before he looked up again. "Damn. We joke about this, but you really do look like a new man. In fact, you look good."

"Well, I think we can deduce from the exchange that I've slept enough and Jacob hasn't," he announced.

Amber snorted into her coffee. She didn't look up from her spreadsheets and a careful list she had made in a notebook.

"Amber," he said. "You also haven't slept enough. I can answer all the money questions you have in there. We have unlimited money now." He gestured broadly. "Hell, any one of us could tie up every loose end in there and still have money to spare."

She leaned back in her chair and grinned at him. "We do not have unlimited money. No one has unlimited money. For your information, I am making sure that I pass Diatek's accountants a full list of our debtors as well as a complete accounting of our current situation. I merely want to be careful."

"She's only doing that because she was making a mess drooling all over the equipment," Jacob quipped. He looked into the lab with a contented smile. "I can't blame her, of course. Will you look at that? It's gorgeous, isn't it?"

Nick put his armful of things on his desk—the last empty desk in this section of the lab—and settled into his chair to study their surroundings.

Their old lab had been a small warehouse-esque room in a facility that absolutely was not built to be a lab. While it had seemed like crazy luxury to the three founding members of PIVOT when they first rented the space, it wasn't remotely in the same league as this new premises.

The lab was divided into five unequal parts. On one side of the room, set up a few feet from the rest, was a long, thin area partitioned by panels of glass. Four desks were positioned along the wall, which allowed the PIVOT team and Dr. DuBois to work while looking out over the floor. A mirror area on the other side of the room held servers, although the glass there was misted slightly from the powerful air conditioning.

The main floor was comprised of two sections. The first was the line of pods, each with its own set of monitors to show the vital signs of the patient inside. Only Justin's pod was illuminated right now, but he could easily imagine how it would look when there were more patients there. On the other side of the room from the pods were all the tools and toys they could possibly want arranged around several black workbenches. It looked like what one would get, he thought, if you asked an engineer to draw a candy store.

DuBois was in that area now and gestured enthusiastically to a group of Diatek scientists who had been assigned as his assistants. Nick was pleased to see that they looked interested in the doctor's passion—as well as amused. Between his mannerisms and his genius, the man often reminded him of a cross between Albert Einstein and Doc Brown if either of those two had eaten inordinate amounts of popcorn. His desk was piled with bags of it, in fact.

The last area of their new offices, set behind more panels of glass emblazoned with the Diatek logo, was a comfortable seating area where the families of the patients would be able to watch the work in the lab without sitting on work stools. Mary and Tad Williams were there right now, and both also looked better rested and showered.

That was the kind of setup you got, however, when you were bought out by one of the Defense Department's top private contractors. Diatek had rocketed to the top of its industry without ever going public, instead assisting the Department of Defense and the US intelligence agencies with projects Nick frankly didn't want to think about too hard. Anna Price, the founder of Diatek, was a chemist—and Nick could come up with more than a few guesses of what kind of things she provided to the government.

Price, however, had another side as well. As a young woman, she had lost her daughter and her husband within two years. Her daughter had been left comatose after an accident similar to the one that had injured Justin Williams, but where Justin's parents had been able to turn to PIVOT for help, Anna Price and her husband had found no support. They sold everything they had, only to run out of money anyway. Price started Diatek, determined that she would find a way to make sure no other families had to go through what she and her husband had endured. Two years after their daughter was taken off life support, however, her husband had committed suicide out of grief and guilt.

He could not imagine what she had gone through, and he felt bad for judging her contracts with the Defense Department. If it weren't for her efforts and the money from those contracts, after all, she would not be able to help PIVOT with its work.

Still, the woman unsettled him. She unsettled all of them, he thought. With no family of her own left to save, she was wholly devoted to her goals in a way even the consummate workaholics of PIVOT could not be.

The young engineer shivered as he booted his computer up. They had made the final decision to allow Diatek to buy PIVOT out, and he could only hope that had been a good idea.

Mary watched as the members of the PIVOT team set up. It was enlightening to see DuBois work with a team of assistants. When he was on his own, his genius tended to manifest in unsettling ways. She recalled an instance where Justin was in mortal danger in the video game and DuBois tended to be fascinated rather than worried and simply munched on popcorn as he watched the vital signs spike.

It turned out that the man was also a good teacher. He had spent a solid hour and a half walking his students through the various monitor readouts on the pod and now waved his hands as he explained something in the area of the lab with the workbenches. Mary could not begin to imagine what they were talking about—she probably wouldn't have any clearer an idea, she thought, even if she could hear the speech—but the assistants were enthralled.

The group trooped to another of the pods and one of the assistants took their shoes off and climbed inside. The others, under the doctor's direction, began to hook their colleague up.

Beside Mary, Tad made a frustrated noise. She looked at him.

"Is there a problem?"

"Another email came in." He looked up. "I didn't read it and only saw the title. They want me to…uh, do something that current technology would make very difficult."

He forced a smile but it was impossible not to see how exhausted he was, and her heart ached for him. She'd had very little sleep as she tried to stay up with him, but he'd had even less.

He had spent almost the entire night with his aides in DC going over PR strategies.

Two weeks before, a reporter had been tipped off about Justin's treatment. The resulting questions to him, shown on live television, had triggered a media storm. It was his first term as a senator and he stood up to many of the big lobbyists in Washington and sponsored bills across the aisle to limit the power of pharmaceutical companies.

His work should be the focus of the interviews he was asked for, she thought. Instead, the media painted him not as a principled new senator but as a renegade who had no principles at all and no respect for medical ethics. They either didn't understand that Justin's treatment was well-backed by research or didn't care. Mary couldn't decide which made her angrier.

The man who had stirred all this up was Dru Metcalfe, a lobbyist for several pharmaceutical companies. One of his main clients had been responsible for getting Dr. DuBois's seminal work blackballed from FDA trials. It was his research that PIVOT had stumbled across and melded with their own pod technology to enable Justin's brain to heal from the damage caused by the car accident. By engaging him inside a virtual world, PIVOT and DuBois drew him slowly back to the real world.

Meanwhile, thanks to Dru Metcalf, Tad was bombarded by inaccurate interview questions and hate mail. The other party was only too happy to jump on this as evidence of their opponent's immorality, and Tad's party, angry about his reaches across the aisle, made no effort to defend him.

Mary was seriously considering taking boxing lessons so she could kick some ass. She was not pleased by this situation.

Plus, in her opinion, no one would guess that a woman in a pink skirt suit and pearls could beat them up. She clenched one hand into a fist and made an off-season New Year's Resolution to learn some kind of martial art. She could look it up later.

Right now, he needed her. She took his hand and squeezed it.

"The team wants me to come back to DC," he said. His gaze was fixed on Justin's pod. "They have ideas for PR stuff to do. They want to drum up support."

"That sounds like a good idea," she said. "Do you want me to come with you?"

He shook his head. "I won't ask you to do that. You'd do nothing but sit in meetings."

"I could give interviews," Mary pointed out.

Tad looked at her and considered the suggestion quietly. "I suppose you could. I'll float that idea to them. For now, though, you stay here. The fewer people who have to go into that snake pit, the better." He gave her a pained smile. "At least Price is letting me use her jet to go back. I'll be able to work on the plane." He lowered his head into his hands. "And I'm sure the media will get wind of the fact that I'm using her jet and it will turn into something about how I didn't sell out to the lobbyists, I sold out to a crackpot who promised me they could cure Justin."

"That's a terrible way to talk about DuBois," she said and her lips twitched.

Her husband was startled into a bark of laughter. He looked into the pod section of the lab, where DuBois ran one cheese-stained hand through his wild hair. "Oh, that man. I have to say, he really grows on you."

"He does." She smiled. "Okay, you go. I'll stay here and…well, get DuBois to wash his hands. And his hair. Dear Lord. And you…" She stood and took his face in her hands. "You remember something—you didn't simply throw Justin's life away on a whim. You saved him from a situation where lobbyists were in charge of his life or death, and you found people who truly wanted to help him—and who had shown they could. The truth will come out, I believe that. For now, remember that you found the best care for your son."

Tad crushed her close in a hug. When he spoke, his voice was broken. "I miss him so much, Mary. He's right there, but I can't speak to him."

"You will," she promised. "We'll get him back. Now, you go to DC and fight for all the families that don't have PIVOT and Diatek helping them."

He squeezed her hand and nodded.

"And when you need to smile," she reminded him, "remember those videos of me in the game."

That drew a reflexive and genuine guffaw. He had persuaded DuBois to show him the readouts of Mary in the game, filtered through with basic graphics, and he had teased her nonstop since then about how she should be his bodyguard now. With a tender kiss, he left with his shoulders a little straighter than they had been an hour before.

Mary watched him walk away with a smile that faded as soon as he was gone. She had to keep believing that they would get Justin back. If she thought for a moment that they might lose him, she would be lost as well. She had spoken to him in the game and had seen his humor and his strength.

He was in there. She fixed her gaze firmly on his pod. He was alive and he was in there. They would get him back.

Dru had just showered when his phone rang. He put his razor in its usual place and his jaw tightened. The ringtone was familiar and he took a moment to compose himself before he moved to the bed and answered.

"Mr. White. Good morning, sir." He kept his tone hearty.

"Yes." Raymond White, CEO of IterNext, wasn't a very talkative man. He also wasn't a happy one in general, especially when one of his employees failed him.

The lobbyist had failed him for the past five months. What was supposed to be a routine operation had gone sideways when, instead of falling in line, Tad Williams had decided to go rogue. It was the longest a senator had ever held out against the man's trademark combination of bribery and blackmail, and Dru was absolutely determined to not let it be the first time he failed entirely.

"Well?" White asked. He didn't waste words.

"We're making progress, sir," he assured him. "The media is doing its job wonderfully. The exposé piece on the PIVOT offices is coming out this morning. There are four journalists waiting outside Williams' offices. He'll have to go past them when he gets back from California."

"You said you had him," the CEO reminded him. "You said he would need you to get out of legal trouble. What happened with that?"

He sat on the bed and tried not to snarl. It wasn't his fault that had gone wrong. How was he supposed to guess that the founder of PIVOT would be stupid enough to jump on the grenade to save the rest of them? You went in, you threatened legal action, and people fell in line. It was how it worked. Sometimes, they countersued and you let the lawyers go at it for a while until the other party cracked, but you always won. When you had deep pockets and enough lawyers, it always worked.

Despite the failure, he still believed he could have worked on Jacob Zachary if he'd had the time. Unauthorized human experimentation would haunt the man's career forever if he were convicted. He could have gotten him to flip in a few days if he had access.

What no one had expected was for Anna Price to swoop in. Diatek had no goddammed interest in this bill. They were in defense, for the love of Christ, not pharmaceuticals. They had all the contracts they could ever want.

Now, PIVOT belonged to Diatek, all charges against Zachary had been wiped, and interfering with anything they did was likely to land someone in a prison that didn't technically exist.

Dru had lost significant leverage.

He sketched the details for White, hopeful that the man would offer some connection to Price, preferably something they could use.

Instead, his boss said simply, "Price is a dead end. And I told you to get Williams on board, not PIVOT."

"Yes, sir." Dru fought the urge to yell down the phone line. "He's close to cracking."

"You've said that for four months and the bill is coming to the floor in two weeks," White said crisply. He was spelling it out, which was an extremely bad sign. The man hated spelling things out. "I expect to have the votes by Friday. Do I make myself clear?"

"Perfectly. Sir."

The phone went dead and he put it down slowly and took a deep breath.

He dressed mechanically. Better than anyone, he knew what happened to people who disappointed Raymond White, and it wasn't pretty. What might happen to Jacob Zachary's career was nothing compared to what might happen to him. The CEO didn't like to be concerned with details unless someone close to him screwed him over. Then, he went all out.

Dru wouldn't merely be out of a job, he would be completely discredited. By the time White was done, his own family would believe he was a pathological liar with a drug problem. His ex-girlfriends would believe he had cheated on them, his other clients would believe he had spilled their secrets, his landlord would have evicted him, and his bank accounts would be empty.

It wasn't something he had worried about before now because he had never anticipated failure. He didn't fail—it was his entire hook as a lobbyist. Never once, before now, had he not delivered the promised results.

Which meant it was very clear what he needed to do now.

Bribery hadn't worked for Tad Williams. In retrospect, Dru

thought he should have let the senator bask in his relief for a few days before he made the ask. That chance was gone now, however. Blackmail also hadn't worked. The man's wife must be a saint if the thought of doctored affair photos didn't even faze the man.

The current strategy had brought him a little closer, though. It hurt Williams deeply for people to accuse him of being a bad father who was endangering his only child. Still, he wasn't cracking.

Would it be too much to ask for to have at least one skeleton in Tad Williams's closet? Dru put his tie on with a grimace. Only one. That was all he asked for.

Since he wouldn't find one, however, he had to get creative.

CHAPTER TWO

Kural drained his mug of beer and laughed heartily. "Okay, I should go now while I can still remember the way to my tower."

"Jus' keep goin' uphill," Lyle advised. He wiped foam off his beard after a long drink. "Ye can get a few more in before ye forget that."

The wizard laughed again. "I'm sure I can, master dwarf. Nevertheless, I have a great deal to do and so I shall leave the three of you to your drinks. Any of you are welcome at any time —especially my two apprentices, of course. Zaara, if I could speak to you for a moment?"

Justin watched as she followed him outside.

"Eh." Lyle clapped him on the arm. "Anyone likes a little o' the exotic, an' a sorcerer is always exotic. She'll come back, though."

He stared at his companion.

The dwarf, thinking he hadn't understood the point, elaborated. "See, sorcerers can summon all kinds o' strange things. Ye're telling me if a lovely female sorcerer appeared, ye wouldn't be even a little interested? Powers ye couldn't even dream of, eh?"

"I, uh…" He decided to take a sip rather than respond to the challenge. It was too much to try to explain to Lyle that he felt stupid being jealous of a collection of pixels over a different pile of pixels.

Thankfully, he was saved from more well-meaning advice when Zaara returned. She was unusually subdued and gazed into space for a while. The conversation ebbed and flowed around her until finally, she looked at her companions and saw the question in their eyes.

She shrugged. "He asked if I'd like to come back and be his apprentice—*really* be his apprentice."

Justin shut his mouth on several uncharitable comments about Kural's motives. He had no reason to expect that this was all an attempt to flirt, and Zaara did have a talent for magic. She could be as powerful as the wizard one day if she trained at it, he had no doubt about that.

"What did you say?" he asked as neutrally as he could.

"I told him I don't know," she admitted. "I've missed my magic studies. I want to learn to be able to do the things he can do—or your mother." She smiled.

He shook his head with a rueful smile. His mother had persuaded the scientists to let her into the world of the game, and she had proved to be a very able player. Aided in part by the invulnerability buffs they had given her, she had unleashed a truly amazing amount of power at one point.

The joke, of course, was that she had been startled into it by a spider.

Hopefully, there were videos of that somewhere. While he'd lived it, he really wanted to see it again. His mother had never been outright disdainful of his video games, but she also hadn't really understood them. He would never have guessed that she would be quite so good at playing them. Even if she weren't invulnerable, he would bet she could actually get good, given enough time.

Justin refocused on Zaara. "You know, if you want to do

this—"

"And leave you two alone?" she asked tartly. "You'd be dead within a day. Lyle would run his mouth off—or if he didn't, he'd charge blindly into the fight you found. You have a remarkable talent for finding trouble, Justin Williams."

"I don't know what you're talking about," he said with great dignity. "In fact, I think you're confusing me with you. Who's the one who came to threaten me away from Sephith?"

She rolled her eyes.

"We were…" He looked over his shoulder and pointed. "Right over there, weren't we?"

"Yes." Zaara raised an eyebrow and sipped her beer. "Except, to set the scene, we really should have you ogling a bar maid."

He flushed a deep red and choked on his mouthful of beer.

"You know, she's still here," she said in a whisper. "And I hear you're the hero who defeated Sephith and a demon army. If that's not a strong opener, I don't know what is."

"I'd be willing to bet you don't know what a strong opener is," he retorted, but a smile tugged at his lips. "And there's no reason to be superior simply because your suitor is a sorcerer and mine are bar wenches."

Zaara laughed. "Wrong. My suitors are nobles who might as well wear their pants on their head for all the sense they have."

"Not Kural, then?" Lyle rumbled. He didn't seem to notice Justin kicking him under the table, but he was on his eighteenth mug of beer.

"Kural," she said, "is three hundred and ninety-seven years old."

Her companions both stared at her open-mouthed.

"And I'm given to understand he prefers the fae," she added. "He says if you live long enough, you tend to not want humans anymore."

"Uh…huh." Justin wasn't quite sure where to go with that.

"Anyway," she continued. "We should talk about our next

adventure. Hildon gave us quite a few leads."

He retrieved the scroll with a nod. After their confrontation with the demon, the bandit leader and his army had withdrawn to their new headquarters to restore it and recover. Although they had spent their time together on the roads, they seemed to have had enough adventure after fighting off a force of undead demon-creatures and losing two of their fighters in the process.

When he left, the man had gifted them a list of places they had considered looting. Justin had immediately crossed the monasteries off but that still left numerous targets.

"Where do you think would have an ancient dwarven key?" he asked rhetorically. "The first two were around here, so logically—"

"Logically, the third one should be close," Zaara said with a smile.

"I intended to say, logically, my luck would be that the third one is at the bottom of the ocean," he responded.

"Nah," Lyle said. He drained his beer. "Someone'll have it." He wandered off to get more beer, returned, and drank half the mug before he looked at them. "What?"

"Were you simply being optimistic?" Justin asked. "Because that's not like you. And if you know, how do you know?"

"It's a dwarven artifact," the dwarf said as if that explained everything.

He motioned for him to keep talking.

"Do ye really not know about dwarven artifacts?"

"Let's skip ahead and assume Zaara and I know nothing." He fought the urge to scream.

"Oh. Well, when ye live in mines 'n other dark places, ye learn real quick that ye can lose jus' about anything," Lyle explained. "So anythin' of value is made to find its way back into someone's hands. 'Course, the trouble is, like as not, it'll find its way to someone who hates ye, but at least someone will know where it is."

"Huh." He considered this. "So…we should be able to find it?"

"Should," the dwarf agreed. He shrugged. "That's the legend, anyway."

"Aaaaaand there goes my hope," Justin told Zaara, who laughed.

Any reply she might have made, however, was cut off when the tavern door was thrust open and voices shouted in the doorway. He looked up with interest. Brawls in this town were rare after so many years under Sephith, and he was interested to see what could inspire one.

Wheat? Mud? Cows?

When the people came through the hallway and into the tavern, however, Zaara whispered, "Oh, no."

His heart sank. He recognized the man amongst the armed guards. It was Mayor Hausen, her father.

"Oh, hell," Lyle said and dived under the table.

"That man!" Hausen shouted and pointed at Justin. "He kidnapped my daughter!"

"What?" Justin and Zaara said at the same time.

"Sir." The man who had argued with the mayor was short with dark hair, the former cartwright of East Newbrook and newly made mayor. "There must be some mistake. You told me your daughter was abducted by Sephith, sir, and I regret to inform you that—"

"She's right there!" the other man yelled. Several of his guards moved toward her and stopped when she unsheathed her daggers and fixed them with a death glare.

"Oh." Mayor Killian, who had made a big deal of announcing that "the Saviors of East Newbrook" would sleep and eat for free from there on out, looked both relieved and confused. On the one hand, he didn't have to tell Mayor Hausen that his daughter was a mindless husk left by Sephith.

On the other hand, he didn't have the faintest idea what was going on.

"Sir," he attempted after a pause, "that woman is one of the saviors of our valley. She participated in slaying the vile wizard Sephith."

"Because she was abducted by this man," her father said dramatically.

"I was not," Zaara protested.

"She arrived some time before the gentleman," Mayor Killian interjected.

"You sent me to rescue her," Justin added.

"And did she return?" Mayor Hausen asked. "No. My only daughter, my darling child, was taken from her betrothal to Lord Howard and forced into a life of banditry."

"Lord Howard?" she demanded, outraged. "I told you I would never marry him. I told you I would rather eat cow dung than marry him. I told you I would rather—"

"Now, out of a fear of her captor, she lies," the man said dramatically.

"This is ridiculous," Justin stated to no one in particular.

"I don't want to go back," she said dangerously.

"Shh, my darling, that man can't hurt you anymore. Come over here." He beckoned.

"No," she said flatly. "I wasn't abducted and you sent several adventurers to their deaths under false pretenses. I came to free East Newbrook from Sephith—which you should have done yourself, except you—"

Something hard struck Justin on the back of the head and he fell as stars burst through his vision. By the time he came to, his wrists were bound with rope and Zaara was yelling something. The two mayors were engaged in a hissed argument while Mayor Hausen's lackeys held Justin up, his head lolling.

"Fine," Killian said eventually. He turned and cleared his throat. "Justin Williams, you stand accused of abducting Zaara Hausen and forcing her into a life of banditry. As mayor of East Newbrook, I will allow both you and Mayor Hausen to make your arguments to a jury, who will then decide the truth of the matter."

"What about my arguments?" Zaara asked dangerously.

"Both sides will be permitted to call you as a witness," he answered wearily. "Master Williams, I must ask you to accompany me to the town jail."

"My father will have his thugs kidnap me the second Justin is in there," she said. She held one of her daggers up. "Although I would warn them strongly against trying."

"You will come with us and stay in my house," Mayor Killian said. When her father began to protest, he held a hand up. "Sir, you have invoked the law of this town. That law states that I may take any and all measures to ensure a fair trial. Mistress Hausen, Master Williams, come with me if you please. Mayor Hausen, the innkeeper will see to your needs."

The two friends walked out of the inn, both struck mute. Justin didn't know when to start speaking.

Zaara did, however. As Killian handed him over to the guards, she darted between them to give him a hug.

"I'll get you out of this," she told him fiercely. "I promise."

"I..." He nodded. "Thank you." This seemed like a bad dream and he knew he didn't want to spend several years of recovery time in prison, even if it wasn't real.

"I promise," she repeated. She looked over her shoulder at him as she left with Mayor Killian.

"Sir," one of the guards said awkwardly. He clearly didn't want to clap the Savior of East Newbrook in irons but he had his orders. "This way, please."

With a sigh, he set off for the jail.

The prison hadn't been structurally well-maintained, enough so that he was fairly sure he could bludgeon his way out if he needed to. That was comforting, he thought as the guards put irons on him.

"Hey," Justin said.

They stopped and looked nervous.

"You know Zaara would have slit my throat if I tried to abduct her, right?" he asked. "I wouldn't take my chances with that one."

The men guffawed at that. It was better than the plea for mercy they'd expected, and they left with a nod to him.

He leaned back and tried to remain positive. No matter what strings Mayor Hausen could pull, he was relatively sure he could get out of there one way or another. He had begun to try to decide where to sleep when one of the piles of straw moved.

Reflexively, he yelled. The pile of straw did too. Footsteps sounded as the guards pounded back.

"Is everything all right?" one of them asked.

"Yes. I, uh…" He wanted to sink through the floor with embarrassment. "I didn't realize there was anyone else in here. I, uh—oh shit. Never mind. Nothing." While apologizing to the man in the pile of straw, he had noticed that he had only one arm.

The guards backed away, clearly trying not to laugh, and he turned to see the man looking equally amused.

"If there's a bright spot to having lost an arm," he told Justin, "it's people making that face when they notice."

He shook his head and sat quickly. He couldn't tell if he should apologize or not, all things considered. "How did you get here?" he asked finally.

"Old misdeeds," the man said poetically. "I used to be a bandit, once upon a time. I worked for a man named Hildon."

"Oh, Hildon." He smiled. "A brave man."

"Diff'rent Hildon," the man said. "Must be. No good bandit is brave and Hildon's a good bandit. He's as craven as they come."

Justin resolved to share this assessment with the leader in question at some point. "And what's your name?"

"Ah. Batholemew." The man nodded. "Anyway, I ran off to Insea for the tournament, lost my arm…came back here, and had the bad luck to be recognized while trying to get back to Hildon."

"Ah," he said. His mind caught up with him a moment later. "Insea?"

"That's the nearest city," his cellmate told him. "The king's city. Where are you from that you don't know that?"

"That's a long story."

"Well." Batholemew looked around the cell. "I think we have the time."

The AI laughed in the background.

Justin waved airily. "I'm not in the mood to tell my stories tonight. Tell me about the tournament—and the city. Let's say I'm from quite far away. Assume I know nothing."

"Anyone can assume that," the AI told him.

He rolled his eyes and decided he wouldn't miss this AI. Or maybe he would, but only a little. Still, it would be nice to not have it interrupt otherwise normal conversations.

"Insea has everything," Batholemew said, his face aglow. "It's on the River Gelatia, so there's an abundance of trade. If you want silks, you can buy 'em. Do you want spices, animals, glass, paper? Anything, you can get it in Insea. That's if you have coin, of course, but coin is like water there. It comes and goes. A man can be a noble one day, a pauper the next, and a famous poet the day after that. I never met a people more used to the way the wheel turns."

"Huh." He leaned back and considered this. "What does it look like? Paint me a picture."

"I was right-handed," Batholemew quipped. He gave a bark of laughter at Justin's look. "You're going to hear all the jokes—I don't get an audience for 'em often."

"Right." He grinned. "Well, work them all in, I guess. I should warn you, though, I've traveled with a dwarf. I might have to retaliate with bad jokes of my own."

"Ha. Well, you asked about Insea. It's a strange city built long ago by the fae. It'll never fall to ruin, no, but it's not…made for humans if you catch my meaning. Everything's a little too tall. It's carved from a block of stone."

Justin nodded, then frowned. "Wait, all of it? From one block?"

"That's the way of it. There's not a crack or a join in the whole city. Streets, houses, castle, arena, everything. Some say Insea's where the dwarves learned to work with stone—that they were the apprentices of the fae and they left to find their own mines beneath the mountains."

He gaped. His mind couldn't picture it at all.

"The stone's beautiful," Batholemew told him. "Some of its milky-pale, some's golden like the first light at dawn, and some's almost a rose color. You stop seeing it after a while, but I still dream of it, even now."

"That sounds beautiful," he murmured.

"Oh, it is."

"And the tournament?"

"Oh, the tournament." The man rested his head on the stone, a smile on his lips. "A chance at the greatest treasure in the world."

Justin sat bolt upright. "Treasure?"

"Oh, yes. The king throws his treasure stores open for the tournament and the winner of the grand prize takes home something of incredible worth. Of course, they usually sell it to one of the nobles, but ten thousand gold in your pocket is nothing small." He raised an eyebrow.

"What's the prize this time?" he asked.

"Oh, no one ever knows ahead of time. The last one I was there for, it was a rope of the most beautiful pearls you ever saw. My friend had a glimpse and he said each was the size of a strawberry and a deep purple like dusk. The time before that…ah, yes, a golden statue of one of the elven gods with diamonds for eyes. No one has ever been disappointed, I tell you."

"Ah." He leaned back and his mind rolled furiously. "I wonder what the king has in his storerooms."

"No one knows that," Batholemew said with a laugh, "least of all the king. Some say the whole tournament was devised so he could clean out the storerooms and get some goodwill in the process. It helps the city, too—people come from all over to see the tournament and fight. The inns are always busy and so are the blacksmiths. Poets come to sing songs about the contestants. There was a song about me, you know."

"Really?" He smiled.

"Yes. Well…it said there was one contestant with a nose like a turnip." His cellmate shrugged good-naturedly. "But I was in a song. Everyone knew who I was that week."

Justin tried not to laugh too hard. "You know, I used to study dwarven artifacts."

"Oh, the king has those for certain," the man said emphatically. "Remember when I said people think Insea was partly built by dwarves? Well, one of the reasons why they think that is because there are so many dwarven artifacts there. A whole academy is devoted to them, and rooms in the palace. Not that I, er…"

"Ever considered robbing them?" he asked slyly.

Batholemew cleared his throat and didn't answer.

He laughed. "Well, then. A palace full of dwarven artifacts. A tournament with the king's storerooms thrown open. Huh."

"Are you thinking of seeking your fortune?" The man looked critically at him, then into the area beyond the cell. "Is that your sword and armor?"

"Yes."

"You might have a chance, then." He sounded doubtful. "Of course, that's if you ever get out of here. What landed you in this mess?"

His irritation returned and he blew out a breath. "Did you hear about the people who defeated Sephith?"

"Ah, yes. It doesn't make much difference to me in here, of course, but everyone else seemed happy."

"Well, one of them is a woman named Zaara. She's the daughter of the mayor in Riverbend, beyond the valley. Another one of them…uh, is me."

"Oho!" Batholemew chortled. "And you got her in the family way, did you? Piece of advice, friend, get the deed done and marry her. There's a sight worse you could do than an adventurin' lass."

"I did not get her in the family way," he protested, mortified. "No, her father didn't want to admit to anyone that she ran away to kill Sephith, so he came here and accused me of kidnapping her. I didn't, everyone knows that, but he got Mayor Killian to arrange a trial."

"Then it don't matter much who knows what, do it?" the man asked.

"Wait. What?"

"A trial's a place for the rich to grandstand," his cellmate explained. "Everyone knows that. You'll spend the rest of your life in a cell like mine, you wait and see."

"No. No, I need to get to Insea. I need to get to the king's storerooms." Panic began to rise and cloud his thoughts.

"That's as may be, boyo, but if her father wants you locked up…well, you just wait, that's where you'll be."

Justin lowered his head into his hands. The future, which had looked so bright only a moment before, now seemed insurmountable.

"Cheer up," Batholemew told him.

"Oh? Why?"

"I still have a good few jokes about having only one arm. You haven't even heard the best one yet."

"This is it," he said, the words muffled. "I've survived a car crash and a coma and this is what will kill me."

CHAPTER THREE

Mary was eating a very belated breakfast when DuBois found her in the seating area.

"Mrs. Williams." He smiled broadly at her.

She swallowed her mouthful of eggs. "Hello, Doctor. It's wonderful to see you in these new facilities. Your team looks very engaged and happy."

"Yes, yes, they're remarkable." He looked at the group. Some of them were chatting but they all did so as they worked. They looked as focused on their diagrams and experiments as the members of the PIVOT team did on their computers. "I wanted to ask you if you've had any word from the young woman you mentioned—Tina."

Her smile disappeared.

"She's not injured, is she?" the doctor asked. His mind seemed to spin off in another direction. "Hmm, if she initially seemed fine but now she's having symptoms, would it make sense to…no, we didn't test for that. Too much of a risk—"

"No, no." She shook her head. "I'm sure—I have no reason to think she's ill, no. I haven't…called her yet."

DuBois gaped at her. "You haven't called her yet?" he asked faintly.

"No." Mary felt a deep, squirming sense of guilt.

"Because?" He shook his head. "Mrs. Williams, Justin's recovery may require someone in his age group. I truly believe that linking Tina specifically could help him become ready to wake up."

She made no reply. Instead, she looked at her eggs, although she no longer wanted to eat them.

"Mrs. Williams." He sat down next to her. "It is clear that you do not want to contact this woman. Could I ask why?"

"Yes, why wouldn't I want to call her?" She flared in response. "The woman whose reckless driving put my son in a coma, the woman who brought all this down on us—why wouldn't I want to talk to her? Why wouldn't I want to call and explain that I couldn't help him but she could?"

The words came out before she had time to stop them and she froze. Mortified, she focused stiffly on her hands.

"Ah," DuBois said softly.

Mary pressed her hands against her eyes. She didn't trust her voice in that moment.

"So, perhaps..." he said. His words trailed off thoughtfully. "It is as if, in order to save Justin, I had to rely on those who blacklisted my treatment. I think I would be angry about that." He patted her knee absently. "And yet, I think you know what you would tell me, even if the patient were not Justin. You would tell me that my goal—to save my patient's life—was more important than my anger."

She put her hands down. This was perhaps the least cutting way he could have said this, and she was grateful. She managed to nod.

"I will," she said. "I hate that I hurt him and she could be the one to help."

"If you blame her for his condition, why shouldn't she be the one to make it right?" DuBois asked rhetorically.

"Well…that's a good point. But…" She reached for his arm as he stood. "I want to go into the game. I want to help. I can't simply watch, doctor. I *can't.*"

"Mrs. Williams," he told her gently. "I told you that—"

"I wouldn't have to see him, would I?" she persisted. "Maybe there's another way I could help him. Some way that he couldn't see me and wouldn't know I was there but I would know I helped. I could be helping—smooth the way."

DuBois considered this. "You know, I think there might be a way," he said finally. "Yes. Yes, I think so. I'd have to run it past the team, of course."

"Run what past us?" Amber asked.

Mary now vaguely remembered all of them heading out for lunch—goodness, her breakfast *was* late—and they had already returned. The other woman held a bowl of noodles that smelled amazing, and Nick munched on a wrap of some kind. Jacob set a sandwich awkwardly beside her plate of eggs. He had clearly gone out of his way to get her something to eat as well. She gave him a nod of thanks.

The doctor gave them an overview of her request and his idea. To her surprise, it was quite an interesting one.

"Remember," he said, "we have the option to have each of our patients exist in the same world. Each would know of the deeds of the others, although they might not know those people were actual people."

"Are you up for this?" Amber asked her. "Because I think it sounds seriously cool. You could be a crazy legend—the death sorceress who trained Zaara the Great. Or whatever she ends up being called."

Mary smiled. "A legendary sorceress. I do like that. I'm not sure about the death part, though." She frowned. "But…how will I get her away from Justin?"

"Well," Nick said, "we may have an opening. Give us a few. Well, maybe a half an hour or…I'm not sure how long it will take. Sorry."

"That won't be a problem," DuBois said. "Mrs. Williams has a call to make." He gave her a surprisingly steely look.

"Fine," she muttered. She scooped a last mouthful of eggs into her mouth. "I'll call Tina. But I won't be happy about it."

"Okay," he responded serenely.

Tina realized she'd stared at the book in her lap for forty-five minutes without reading a single word. With a sigh, she closed it and put it beside her on the porch swing.

"Are you all right, dear?" her mother called from inside the house.

She shut her eyes and prayed for patience. Her parents had already been almost unbearable before the accident and now, they took it to an unimaginable level. Her father was absolutely furious that she'd had the accident and her mother coddled her as if she were a baby.

Frankly, she preferred her father's company at this point. However angry he was at her, it couldn't come close to how angry she was at herself—and it felt good, actually, to have someone hate her. She still hadn't heard from Mary Williams, and the thought of how angry and heartbroken Justin's parents must be tore her up inside.

All she wanted was for them to yell at her and say all the things she thought about herself.

She didn't expect her phone to ring and lurched into an ungainly sideways leap to stare nervously at the device as if it might bite her. The number was unfamiliar but it was from the area, which meant a glimmer of a chance that the impossible might have happened.

Tina's heart pounded. She picked the phone up and was shaking so hard, she had to make several attempts to answer. "Hello?"

"Hello?" It was a woman's voice. "Is this Tina?"

"Yes?"

A long pause followed. "This is Mary Williams," the woman said.

"Oh, my God," she whispered. "Oh, my God. Oh, Mrs. Williams, I am so sorry. I am so sorry, you cannot imagine—"

"I know." The woman's voice sounded strained. "Please do not apologize to me. It is Justin who deserves your apology."

Tears came to her eyes and she squeezed them shut. "I know," she managed to say in a croak. "And someday I hope I can—"

"Yes." Mary sounded brisk now. "Justin's doctors have requested to meet you. They believe you may be able to aid in his recovery."

"They do?" She stood up so fast she got a head rush. "Oh, my—"

"God, yes." The caller's tone was now impatient.

"How could I help?"

"The doctors can explain that," she said finally after another long pause.

Tina briefly considered the possibility that she was planning to murder her. Mary must have been thinking the same thing because a moment later she said, "Please understand, there are concerns around patient privacy. Justin's doctor is a man named Jean-Luc DuBois."

"Like Captain Picard?" Tina asked excitedly.

"What?"

"Jean-Luc. Never mind. Um. Yes, I can help. What hospital is Justin at?"

Another pause made her feel a little uneasy. "Ms. Castro, I need to know that you will share this address with no one," Mary said sternly.

The murder vibes had begun to increase alarmingly now. "Uh…maybe it would be best if I didn't come."

"Tina," the woman said pleasantly, "my son is in a coma because you were driving ninety miles per hour on a residential street. If I could, I would rather live the rest of my life without ever hearing from you or acknowledging you again. Trust me when I say I did not respond well to the doctor's suggestion to bring you in. However, they believe your presence might help Justin wake up, and I am determined to do whatever it takes to make that happen. Even allowing you near him again."

"See," Tina said, "that sounds a hell of a lot more honest. I'll be there."

"Really."

"Yeah. And for the record, when he comes out of that coma—"

"I think I know where you're going, Ms. Castro, and I warn you not to say anything of the sort," Mary said crisply. "I will thank you to take responsibility for your own actions before you criticize mine. When, God willing, Justin is out of his coma, I may be willing to discuss your opinions. Not before."

"Right." She swallowed. "Right. So, you need me to come somewhere."

"Yes. The medical staff would like you to stay for several days to…speak to Justin. The head of the facility will contact you and send a car. Her name is Anna Price. And Tina, you cannot imagine how much it pains me to say this—thank you."

Mary hung up and the young woman smiled ruefully at the phone. The chances that she would be murdered were slim to none, she estimated. She could tell from the woman's tone that the thank you had been hard to say and she would never have said it if she didn't have to.

Tina retrieved her phone and her book and headed inside to pack. When she passed her father on the stairs, he glowered at the sight of her smile.

"What do you have to be happy about?"

She looked at him, unperturbed by his belligerence. "I might be able to fix it," she said finally. "Mrs. Williams called me to come see Justin. I might be able to fix this."

CHAPTER FOUR

The clang of the jail door woke Justin the next morning. He sat, winced at the pain in his neck, and spat out a piece of straw that had lodged in his mouth.

Straw from the floor that certainly wasn't anywhere near clean. He looked at it, winced again, and hoped his brain wasn't powerful enough to make him sick based on the reasonable certainty of fake microbes.

Multiple footsteps approached and his heart began to pound —all the more when the group reached his cell and he saw who it was. Mayor Killian looked deeply apologetic to see him on the floor and covered with dirt, Mayor Hausen looked triumphant, and Zaara looked furious.

Screw the crick in his neck. He scrambled to his feet and brushed himself off as quickly as he could.

"Master Williams," Killian said. He smiled at him now. "I am relieved to say that the charges against you are being dropped."

"Yeah, well—wait, what?" He broke off in confusion. "Eh?"

The man looked at Mayor Hausen. On his other side, Zaara folded her arms and glared at her father.

Hausen looked at them both and a somewhat sulky look

31

settled on his face. He cleared his throat and sighed. "Hrm. Yes. Due to several factors, I have—"

"Ahem," his daughter interrupted meaningfully.

Justin, suddenly entertained, looked at him.

Her father was clearly not happy at this state of affairs. He sighed again and gave him a pained look that was clearly supposed to be somewhere in the realm of friendly. "After speaking to my daughter," he said reluctantly, "it seems I was, er…"

"Father." Her voice dripped with poison.

"It seems I was…wrong." The last word seemed to be dragged out of him.

"And how were you wrong?" she asked sweetly.

He darted her an annoyed glance before he cleared his throat and focused on the prisoner. "Zaara has informed me that she left Riverbend of her own free will and remained here in East Newbrook with…you…in order to help the people of this town escape another of Sephith's lackeys. As my daughter assures me that she did all of this without duress—and, importantly, as she is unharmed—I have decided to drop the charges against you." His gaze bored into him.

Against his better judgement, he felt a stirring of sympathy for the man. Sending a rescue party after Zaara under false pretenses had been wrong, but the man had come to find his daughter—a woman he was afraid for after she didn't come home. He wasn't lying when he said that the most important thing to him was her safety.

"Thank you," Justin said as courteously as he could.

"Father," she said. "The matter of the mission."

Mayor Hausen gave her a stricken look. When he looked back, his shoulders were faintly hunched. He cleared his throat. "Ahem. Yes. As a condition of your defeat of Sephith and my daughter's rescue, two things were promised. First, the freedom of Lyle Stout and second, ten gold coins were promised. I regret to inform you that the coffers of Riverbend will only support…five."

"I'll take three," Justin said promptly.

"I—wait, what?" Hausen paused, confused. Beside him, Zaara frowned, Mayor Killian had his head tilted to the side quizzically, and the guards stared with their mouths open.

"I won't bankrupt the people of Riverbend," he said. "Three of us worked together to defeat Sephith—myself, Lyle Stout, and Zaara. Each of us will take one gold coin in recognition of this effort. I would forgo payment entirely, but please understand that my armor is my livelihood."

Hausen, now with no moral high ground to speak of, cast about for something to say. At last, he managed to speak. "That is very generous, Master Williams. There being no objection from the members of your team—"

"None," Zaara said. "I'll speak for Lyle."

"Um," the man said. "In that case, your money will be provided to you at the inn before my daughter and I leave for Riverbend."

Justin's smile slid off his face. He looked at her and saw her regret. She gave him a sad smile and a nod and he now understood that his freedom hadn't come only from facts but from a bargain.

"Now that Sephith is defeated," her father said, "Zaara has no reason to stay in East Newbrook." He looked meaningfully at her. There was no malice in his voice and instead, Justin could hear the echoes of fear.

He understood but he still hated it.

"There's still a great deal more injustice in the world," he reminded them.

"Yes," Zaara said. "My father and I have agreed that, in the future, I will inform him of my plans to fight against individuals like Sephith. He will help me assemble a team so he knows I am not fighting alone." She gave him a half-hearted smile. "I don't suppose you have a pressing injustice to fight now—"

"Zaara," Mayor Hausen said warningly.

"I'm joking," she said. "Of course. I know Mother and Yannick would be glad to see me."

"And have you home, Zaara." There was genuine softness in the mayor's voice. "All of us would be happy to have you home."

Justin swallowed and looked away.

"Yes," she said softly. She cleared her throat. "Justin, I'll…I'll be at the inn to say goodbye to you and Lyle." She left, her footsteps a touch too fast, and her father followed.

"Master Williams." Mayor Killian sounded relieved. "The guards will remove your irons. I hope there are no hard feelings."

He gave him a hard look. "What would you have done if he had insisted on the trial?"

The man had clearly considered this already. "You would have been convicted," he said.

Stunned, he gaped at him. Killian didn't sound sorry at all.

"And then," the man continued, "regrettably, due to an unfortunate clerical error, you would have been released soon after Mayor Hausen returned to Riverbend." He gave him a smile and a nod before he left.

"Huh," he said.

"Don't worry," the guard said. "If he hadn't done the right thing, we would have."

"What must it be like to have friends?" Batholemew asked rhetorically from the corner.

"Shut up," the guard said. "He saved us from Sephith. You robbed my aunt at knifepoint."

"Details." The prisoner made a show of going back to sleep but opened one eye to look at him. "Don't forget what I said about Insea."

"I haven't," he assured him. "Good luck, Batholemew."

Zaara was waiting for him in the inn. Three mugs of beer

were on the table in front of her, laid out as if for her, Justin, and Lyle, but she had drunk all of them already. She wiped the back of her hand across her mouth as he sat.

"Sorry. I don't want to go back."

"So don't," Justin said. He was surprised by how urgent his tone was. He leaned forward. "We'll go right now. Grab Lyle and sneak out the back. We can disappear."

She shook her head sadly. "I thought of that. Trust me, I considered it." She hiccupped and swayed slightly.

"New plan," he said, "we hide in the basement while you sleep that beer off."

"I don't want to do that to my family." She managed a shaky laugh. "My father may be an ass, but he was really worried about me. My mother was too. My brother...well, who knows." She gave a half-smile. "I'm joking. He and I get along fine. I made Father agree to let him marry Annika when we get home."

He frowned and thought back. "The barmaid," he said as he remembered. "That's right. She said the mayor thought his son could do better than a barmaid."

Zaara raised the empty glass to him with a wry smile. "That's my dear father, all right. But he wants Yannick to be mayor after him, so there's no reason for him to marry outside the village. And he would do well as mayor, he really would. He—" She broke off. "You don't care."

"I care," he said quietly.

To his surprise, she smiled at him. "Yeah. Yeah, I know you do. The thing is, Justin..." She steadied herself. "The thing is, you need to go home."

He wasn't sure how to respond so simply said nothing. The innkeeper set three more mugs of beer down and left quickly as if to escape the awkward silence.

"That's why you need the three keys," Zaara said. "Isn't it? You never said as much, at least not straight out, but Lyle and I both knew."

"You told Lyle about where I was from?" He groaned.

"Yes, I did. And the dwarves made those keys, Justin. They're the ones who made it so the bearer could use the door. You've heard him talk. Dwarven artifacts have power woven into them, so him knowing your goal might help him remember things he wouldn't otherwise."

"Okay, I hate to admit it, but you have a point. Still. He'll make fun of me for this, you know."

"Everyone already makes fun of you," the AI said.

"Weak," Justin muttered.

"Yeah, I think I'm losing my touch. I can do better. Hang on."

Justin sighed. To Zaara, he said, "Yes. I don't…know…that it's why I'm finding keys, but I suspect so. I think they're tests I have to pass to show that I'm ready to go back."

Zaara studied him. "When you get back, what do you think you'll do?"

He groaned, picked up a mug of beer, and drank a few gulps. "I don't know," he admitted. "My world isn't like this one. You can't simply go out and do things to help people."

"You can't?" She sounded deeply confused. "Are you sure? But…is everyone happy? Is there no injustice there?"

"Well, no—I mean, yes, there is injustice."

"And war? Poverty?"

"Well, yes."

"So why can't you help people?" She looked like she was trying to put two and two together and failed miserably. "I'm not confused because I'm drunk, am I?"

"A drunk woman, and here I am talking about life plans and injustice," Justin said philosophically.

"Huh?"

"Nothing. Uh…in my world, you can't simply pick up a sword and go kill a wizard. Things are more complicated than that. Sometimes, injustice is in the laws or stuff like that."

Zaara shrugged. "So don't kill any wizards with swords then. We were talking about injustice, not stabbing."

He opened his mouth, closed it, and nodded. She had a point. "It's not that easy," he said finally. "You don't always know that what you're doing is the right thing. No matter what you do, someone will tell you that you hurt people."

She smiled at him. "That's not only your world, you know. There are people here who will tell you that Sephith was doing important work. He was trying to learn how to resurrect people."

"Oh." He felt a stab of regret. "And we killed him."

"Yes." Zaara took a sip of the new beer. "Exactly like he killed thousands of people trying to discover how to resurrect them afterward."

"Oh. Right."

"You have to make the best decisions you can," she told him. "Here, in your world, wherever you are. And part of why I agreed to go back..." She sighed. "Well, it was so I could help you find the last key. I didn't tell you this at the time, but when Kural asked me to be his apprentice, I said what I wanted was to help you get home. He was already looking for the key, and now he knows why. And he said I can help him. He gave me this." She withdrew an orb from a pouch at her belt. It looked like clear glass but somehow, the inside was as black as night.

The pause that followed was both awkward and heavy.

"I always knew you'd have to go back," Zaara said finally and her voice broke. "And so did you."

He cleared his throat and looked away.

Lyle saved the moment when he clapped Justin so hard on the back that the young man smacked face-first into the table. He barely managed to get the mug out of the way and picked his head up, stars dancing in front of his vision, to squint at Zaara.

"Ow," he mumbled.

"Well, ye've some dwarven skills to learn yet," Lyle said philosophically. "I can't send ye home with no manners, now can I?"

"Uh-huh." Justin rubbed his forehead. "Or the same nose, apparently."

"Good point." The dwarf sat. "Hey, who drank all the beer?"

"Surprisingly, that was Zaara." He nodded at her.

"I always knew you had it in ye," Lyle said with a nod of deep respect. "But what's this I hear about you leaving?"

"I'm going back to Riverbend," she explained. "It was one of the ways I got my father to agree to Justin's release."

"Ahhhh." The dwarf nodded. "Has anyone suggested simply making a run for it?"

"Justin did." Zaara managed a smile. "I'll go home, though. My father agreed that I can go adventuring and learn magic. I only need to not run off without telling him, and—I quote—'giving your mother a heart attack.'"

"Mothers," Lyle said. "I remember the first time I fell down a mineshaft. My mother carried on about it for days. Or so I'm told. I was asleep for most of that. Knock on the head, you understand. Still, I came out of it fine."

Justin, who had choked on his beer, nodded seriously. "Ah. Yes."

"So, where are you two going?" she asked.

"I thought perhaps Insea," he told her.

"My people's first city," the dwarf said. "Grand place. I've never seen it meself, of course. Why would we go there?"

"The tournament," he explained. "I hear the king throws his coffers open for the prizes, and he has quite a few Dwarven artifacts. I thought perhaps the third key might be there."

"O' course, there's the small matter of winning the tournament first," Lyle pointed out.

He waved a hand dismissively. "Insignificant."

"Very minor," Zaara agreed. "Hardly worth mentioning. Well, when I was on your team, of course. Now, you two are screwed."

"Now, listen here," he protested. "I've gotten out of plenty of scrapes without—well, we have good combat skills—uh…hmm."

"It's all right," she said. "Other than being quite a fine hand with knives and spells, I can distill most of my use to the group into one simple piece of advice. Don't do stupid shit."

"That's it?" he asked blankly.

"The trick is getting you to follow that advice," she explained.

"Oh. Yeah, we're screwed."

"Shpf," Lyle said eloquently. "I, for one, am well-versed in careful battle plans." He saw his companions staring at him open-mouthed and bristled. "It just so happens that the element of surprise is a good tactic—and charging at someone with yer fists gives ye the element of surprise."

"You'll die," Zaara told Justin.

"Yeah," he agreed. "Yeah, I will."

"We'll find another teammate," the dwarf said. "It'd be easier if Miss Zaara would come along with us, o' course, but if she's determined to go back to Riverbend, I won't risk my life by trying to persuade her otherwise."

"A wise choice," she said serenely. "And I'll make you two a deal. If you get to the final, I'll make sure the last key is the prize."

"What if it's not in the treasury?" Justin asked.

"I didn't say if it was in the treasury, did I?" she gave him a steely-eyed smile. "You hold your end of the bargain up, and I'll hold up mine—come hell or high water."

"Come hell or high water." He clinked his glass with hers. "Lyle?"

"'Til magma swallows us all," the dwarf said seriously.

"Dude, that's intense."

Lyle gave him a grin. "It's a shame ye won't be able to see the dwarven cities before ye leave. Ye'd have a fine time. And dwarven women…ah, let me tell ye about them."

Zaara caught his eye and gestured to indicate a luxurious beard. The two of them stifled their laugher behind their beers as he waxed poetical about the charms and talents of dwarven women, insisting that the ability to make a cast iron pot or find a chunk of ore was a valuable trait in a wife.

"'Course, ye'd have to hold up yer end of the bargain," he told Justin. "But don' worry, I'll teach ye to smelt ore an' find her a vein to mine."

"Is that a double entendre?"

"No." The dwarf sounded offended. "Get yer mind out o' the gutter, adventurer. This is a serious matter. I'm not about to let ye marry a kinswoman if ye can't find her ore to mine. Are ye crazy?"

"I…sorry." He rested his chin on his palm. "Please, go on."

Beside him, Zaara smiled as she sipped her beer. "You know," she said quietly to him and hiccupped. "If I have to leave, I'm glad I could spend another hour drinking beer with you two."

Justin watched Lyle for a moment to gauge the detail with which the dwarf explained mining techniques. "I'd say you have a good four before he's finished."

She clinked her mug against his. "Even better."

CHAPTER FIVE

Anna Price did very little with her life except work—something that became clearer by the day. When Tad first saw the shower and pull-out bed in the private jet, he thought it was an incredible luxury.

Then he realized it was because she combined her travel time with her showering and sleep.

On her recommendation, he showered before taking a nap. It did, indeed, ease some of the tension and allow him to relax. He was surprised at how much wearing old, rumpled clothes had affected his mood.

The thoughts were short-lived, though, and he almost fell asleep on the way to the pull-out bed. He barely made it before passing out for the remainder of the flight, only to be woken by a gentle touch on the shoulder from the attendant.

"We'll be landing soon, sir."

"Thank you." He changed from the provided pajamas into a new suit. On the one hand, the nap had made it painfully clear how much he was behind on sleep but on the other, he could now at least function.

Kevin, one of his aides, met him at the plane with a car, a breakfast sandwich, and a very large coffee. From the taste of it, the coffee had been laced with more than one espresso shot. He ate while the other man briefed him on several routine bills that were coming up for vote.

Once he had agreed with the recommendations from the aides—or, in some cases, asked for additional research—they were almost at the senate building.

"We made sure there wouldn't be word of you coming back today," Kevin said worriedly, "but some of the reporters are bound to recognize you. Alice suggests you simply say, 'I'll give an official statement tomorrow.'"

"And what will be in that official statement?" he asked.

"I'm not sure. We thought that would give us some time to decide."

Tad felt close to despair. "Does politics always work like this?"

"Mostly," Kevin said. "It's rare that there's not a crisis of some kind. But remember, this isn't a time-sensitive crisis. The accident happened a while ago. Simply because they know something about his treatment now doesn't make it imperative for you to share details immediately."

"I know, Kevin. But thank you." He sighed as the car pulled to a stop. "Ready?"

"Absolutely, sir."

He squared his shoulders and stepped out of the car when his driver opened the door. "Thank you, Bill."

"Yes, sir. Nice to see you again."

"Same." He smiled at him. "I hope your daughter is well?"

"Yes, sir." The man's gaze flicked to the stairs, where several people were already yelling in their direction. "Would you like me to walk with you, sir?"

"No, thank you, Bill. There's no need to have coffee thrown on you this early in the morning." He sighed. Most of the people there did not look like reporters but rather like protesters. "You get out of here and I'll see if I can get any of them to throw the coffee directly into my mouth."

"An admirable goal, sir." The man's mouth twitched.

The walk up the stairs, as much as he wanted to be amused by it, was hellish. People screamed Justin's name at him, along with accusations that made his blood run cold. He was in the pocket of the gun companies, was allowing military experiments to be run on Justin, and was a terrible father who didn't care at all for his son's life or happiness. By the time he reached the doors and swept inside, his heart pounded and he wanted to snarl accusations in response.

The first person he saw, by chance, was Charles Snelling. As one of the junior members of the other party, he had been one of Tad's most vocal critics—on everything except a recent bill, where the two of them had collaborated to limit the power of pharmaceutical companies. Their sparring had always been good-natured and the brief alliance had amused them both.

Still, he was wary. "Senator." He hoped Snelling wasn't in the mood for a fight because he would most assuredly get one if he was.

The man looked past him to the door, where the last of the violent shouts died away as the barrier swung closed. His mouth tightened and he paused. "Senator Williams, believe me when I say that of all the things I may think about you, I do not believe you would ever recklessly endanger the life of your son." He cleared his throat awkwardly and offered the tentative smile of someone who attempted a risky joke. "Your opinions may generally be horseshit, but you're a good man."

Tad burst out laughing. He'd needed that and without hesitation, held his hand out for Snelling to clasp. "What do you say we shake it up next time? Go out together and confuse all of the protesters?"

Snelling nodded. "Oh, and by the way, my aides will set up a meeting later. I have a bill I'd like your support on. Or, as is more likely, your pointed comments."

"I'll do my best to oblige." He smiled and headed down the corridor.

More protesters were clustered outside his door and Kevin swept him inside before he could make out what they were saying. They'd taken the time to set it to meter and rhyme, he could tell, but he definitely tried not to know what they accused him of.

"If I hear that stupid chant one more time..." the aide muttered. He guided him into the main room. "The senator's back, everyone."

"Welcome, sir." A few of his aides waved at him.

"Good morning, everyone." He checked the clock. "Afternoon. Good afternoon. So, what's on the docket, then?"

They exchanged slightly nervous looks.

"On the way in here," Tad said conversationally as he took his seat, "I was accused of turning my son into a cyborg for the military. That has set the bar rather high for ridiculous things to say. You're probably fine."

A few of them laughed.

"We're working on your public image," Alice said and took point. "We'll work with you to draft a public statement but in the meantime, we also need to garner positive publicity for you."

"Do we?" he asked wearily. "Elections aren't for two years and I clearly won't win, so..."

She gave him a stern look. "We will have you back on track soon," she said, "but what we need is for you to not get pressured into resigning between now and then."

Tad sighed. He leaned back in his chair and nodded. "Continue."

"We've compiled a list of fundraisers and events for you to appear at," she said.

"No. Absolutely not. I didn't come here to rub shoulders with the elite, I came here to—"

"To do things like tackle child cancer?" Alice suggested delicately. She pushed a dossier down the table and the other aides passed it along. "Or, perhaps, provide technological help for farmers?" Another dossier joined the first.

He looked at them, then at the group of aides. "So that was why you were all nervous. Don't you think child cancer charities is laying it on a little thick?"

"It's a bipartisan issue," Kevin pointed out as he brought him another cup of coffee.

"It has nothing to do with any of the current bills," he protested.

"Which is another reason it's good," Alice pointed out. "There isn't any especially heated rhetoric, merely an opportunity for you to speak to donors, make a donation yourself, and be seen to give your time for a worthy purpose."

Tad sighed.

"We know you don't want to spend your time this way," Kevin said, "but Alice has done good work to compile this list. We have high rollers from all walks, including several who have backed experimental medical procedures before. Senator Yaczwinski actually used one, and she'll be at the benefit for—"

"Okay, but if so many people have backed experimental medical treatments," he interrupted wearily, "why can't we set up an interview where I explain what's going on and tell the truth? That will clear things up nicely, won't it?"

After a pause, all the aides began to snicker. Within a few seconds, every one of them was doubled over, holding their sides.

"The truth!" Kevin gasped.

"It'll clear things up," Tom agreed. "Oh, man."

Alice tried to remain calm, but she looked like she might break a rib trying not to laugh. "Um, sir." She could not seem to find words to say. "While I appreciate your...um..."

"Childlike naivete?" Kevin suggested.

The woman darted him a look before she focused on the senator. "It's risky to put out a statement before we have a good idea of what people are thinking," she explained. "Ronan and Bridget are compiling the data from calls and opinion polls, and they'll help us craft the statement for tomorrow."

"I should have known," he said and sighed. "Telling the truth was too simple and too ridiculous a plan in this town."

"Mm-hmm," she agreed.

"You know who should make a speech," Tad muttered, "is Dru Metcalfe."

"He'd only lie through his teeth," Kevin pointed out. "He's notorious. Apparently, he's worked with ninety-five percent of the senators currently here."

"And how many did he run off?" he asked bitterly. A few people shuffled their papers anxiously and he sighed. "I'm sorry. It turns out it's a little stressful waiting to find out what lie will come down the pike next."

"If we could nail Metcalfe, that would be amazing," Alice said wistfully. "It would be so on-brand for you, too—expose the corruption and show how he's swayed public opinion before. We could have you on record saying how you understand why people were so horrified—" She shook herself. "It's best to have manageable goals, though."

Tad knew a lost fight when he saw one. He pulled the dossiers close and read through them. The team had done good work, he had to admit that. They'd successfully found events that would be populated by members of both major parties, and if he could make donations at some of them, he'd gain valuable credibility.

He had come to have his actions speak for him, he thought despairingly, not his donations—and not lobbyists.

"Senator?" Alice spoke again. She was smiling slightly.

"Yes?" He frowned.

"Smear campaigns are very common," she said. "Perhaps I'm

out of line, but it seems like you hold yourself responsible—as if you messed up or left an opening. Remember that no matter what you did, Metcalfe would have created a smear campaign for you. We knew when we signed on that you wouldn't be popular with lobbyists. We're not surprised to have this meeting."

He smiled at her. "Thank you." He looked around the table. "You're all more sensible than I am, then. I thought this would be smoother sailing than it has been. I thought all the drama would be in the senate chambers."

"That's merely the tip of the iceberg," Kevin said. "The very smallest, tiniest tip of a gigantic iceberg. Trust me. And you've made our jobs so much easier by not going out drinking and hiring call girls and so on. You getting your son medical care? Now, that's the type of public relations situation aides dream of."

Despite the hollow pit in his stomach, he laughed. "I never knew that bar was set so low. All right, everyone. Prep me for these events, please."

Mary paced around the tiny seating area. She was bemused by her own anxiety. On a normal day, she would be happy to not leave the house at all and the downstairs wasn't really larger than the lab. However, after being stuck near Justin's pod for weeks, she was about to climb the walls.

Tina's imminent arrival didn't help to soothe her nerves. Originally, she had seen a couple of pictures of the girl—pictures she now realized had been carefully curated by her mother to give the impression of a dutiful, obedient daughter. She had found her Facebook page, and the profile picture there clearly showed both tattoos and a certain devil-may-care attitude.

When a car door slammed outside, she stood quickly. What was she feeling? Nervousness? Anger? Hope?

Tina arrived, walking in with Anna Price, and she had a small moment of amusement at how uncomfortable the younger woman looked. She wore jeans and a hoodie, and she looked overawed by her companion's suit and the general security in the lab.

The CEO pointed to a few people and items, murmured to her, and nodded to Mary and left. She was always sure to know what was going on in her facility, but she was also ready to get back to work at a moment's notice. Mary began to wonder if the woman slept at all.

The newcomer edged closer and looked a great deal more nervous now. "Mrs. Williams. Hello. It's good to—ah, thank you for—I mean—"

It would have been nice to say something and put her out of her misery, but she didn't feel incredibly nice at that moment. She waited and offered the same pleasant smile she had once given to Tad's grandmother.

That old biddy had been a piece of work, and if she could survive that, she could certainly survive this.

"I'm sorry," Tina said finally. She looked Mary in the eyes. "I've thought about what you said—about taking responsibility for my actions before talking smack about yours."

"I'm fairly sure I understand what that means from context." She nodded. "I'm glad you're here." She managed to get the word "glad" out without her voice going crazy. "Has Ms. Price briefed you on what's happening here?"

"She said someone named Dr. DuBois would explain it," the girl said.

"That's me," the doctor said from behind Mary and made her jump. "Tina, is it?" He shook her hand. "It's very nice to meet you. To be very brief, Justin is varying between an involuntary coma and a controlled one. For the past two decades, I've studied the theory that electric stimulation of certain areas of the brain might help the brain heal itself after trauma, and the team at

PIVOT has developed a technology that lets a user experience an entire virtual reality. Justin is presently immersed in a game of sorts."

Her jaw dropped. "Wait, that kind of thing is real?"

"It's new," he said. "Justin is the first patient to try it. As my employer will doubtless have explained to you, there is a great deal of confidentiality to be maintained."

She swallowed. "I…we'd seen the news coverage about the allegations. You know, the experiments you were running on Justin."

"There are news stories?" DuBois asked.

"Did you think Amber tackled that journalist for fun?" Jacob asked him. He came to shake Tina's hand. "Hi. I'm Jacob Zachary, the founder of PIVOT. My two co-founders over there are Nick and Amber. We developed the pod technology that Justin is currently using, and Dr. DuBois has helped us adapt it to the needs of a trauma patient."

"And Amber…tackles people." Tina seemed more than a little nervous.

"Only when they break in and try to steal secrets," Mary said serenely. "As you've seen, there is considerable curiosity about Justin's treatment."

"How did word of it get out at all?" the girl asked, confused.

"That's not the most important thing right now," the doctor interjected. "Come, I'll show you the lab."

He led Tina to a station to wash her hands and put booties on over her shoes before they walked into the lab itself, and the rest of the team trailed after them. They went first to the pods, where DuBois opened one that was not in use to show Tina its features.

"This headset creates the input that allows your brain to perceive the game world," he explained. "Much of the game is accomplished via the power of suggestion and allows the brain to fill in details with its own memories—the smell of flowers, for instance. We've found that senses beyond sight and sound take longer to develop in-game, but we don't have a large enough sample size to tell if that's unique to trauma patients."

She touched the inside of the pod nervously. "People are shut inside?"

"Yes," Jacob said. "But don't worry, it's not frightening. Mrs. Williams can assure you of that."

Tina looked at Mary, wide-eyed. "You did this?"

"Yes." She forced a smile. "I was the first one to interact with Justin in the game world."

"Oh, I—*oh*." Tina's eyes went even wider. "Oh, you want me to do that, don't you? You want me to go into the game. In…one of the pods." She gulped.

"Precisely," DuBois said. "The game has stimulated Justin's survival and social instincts, both of which are important pieces of restoring him to a waking state. I believe that what is most necessary now is for him to engage with a more proximal piece of his situation—someone related to the accident."

Tina suddenly looked miserable.

"He knows about the accident," Mary explained. She couldn't help but feel a little sympathetic. "We made the choice to tell him why he was there so he would understand and use caution in the game." She hesitated, but her sense of responsibility induced her to add, "He asked about you as soon as he understood where he was, and he's very glad that you're all right."

"Oh." The girl put her hand at her mouth and looked even more miserable. "He's not angry?"

"He's not angry," Jacob assured her.

"I wish he were angry," she said in a small voice.

Mary felt some of her tension ease. "Remember why you came," she told her. "It was to help. Dr. DuBois has very good instincts for this kind of thing and he believes that it will help Justin to come back to a waking state if he can interact with you."

Tina simply stared, her expression worried.

The doctor broke the tension of the moment with his usual efficiency. "Come on," he said jovially. "Let's get you into a pod and start you on the tutorial."

CHAPTER SIX

Tina's heart pounded as the lid of the pod closed over her head. She wanted to do nothing more than throw all the harnesses and electronics off her and sprint out the door. Although she had never been claustrophobic before, she sure as hell felt that way now. She would hyperventilate and they wouldn't get her out in time, she thought desperately.

In a split-second, she was outside again. A weight seemed to lift from her chest and she took a deep breath as she registered blue sky. The ground beneath her feet and the walls to either side of her were made of a translucent, pinkish stone that seemed to glow faintly. It was like something out of a dream.

Unfortunately, the nice parts of outside ended there. Pink stone or no, she was undoubtedly in a back alley. The ground was textured to look like cobblestones with grime between them. There were no birds chirping except for a few bedraggled and murderous-looking pigeons nearby, and a couple of rats gnawed at something.

"Hello," a voice said, seemingly in her head.

"Fuck!" Tina jumped and looked around. "Who was that? Where are you?"

"I'm Evy," the voice said. *"I have created this world."*

"Oh." She settled and took a breath. "Um, hi."

"Hello. Would you like a tutorial?"

"Yes. That would be very nice, thank you."

"How polite." The voice sounded pleased. *"I have someone for you to meet. He could stand to learn a thing or two about manners."*

"Uh…huh."

"First things first." Several screens popped up in midair, each with a differently colored background. One showed her in flowing robes with fireballs in each hand, another showed her in chainmail and with a sword, and the third had her in leather armor and armed with two daggers. *"How would you like to engage in combat in this game?"*

"Oooh. This is hard." Tina tried to tap her chin and failed miserably. It took a few moments of flailing wildly before she was able to control her muscles enough to do so—or whatever impulses her nerves were sending. It made her head hurt if she thought about it too hard. "Did…did you see that?"

"Yes." The AI sounded like it was laughing. *"It's very common."*

"Well, at least there's that. You know, I've always liked biker jackets. I think I'll go for the leather armor and the daggers."

"Are you sure you wouldn't like to base your choice off of combat aptitude instead of aesthetics?"

"I can shiv a bitch if I need to."

"Noted." Two old, rusted daggers appeared in her hands. *"If you would, please, 'shiv' one of the rats for me."*

"Wait, I don't get nice, pretty daggers? And I'm still wearing… what is this, a burlap sack?" She looked at herself. "Okay, answer me one thing. If I follow the tutorial, will you tell me how to get the nice armor and the really sharp daggers?"

"Yes."

"Good." Tina edged closer to one of the rats, which promptly scurried away. She sighed, circled behind it, and tiptoed closer, only for it to scurry away when she was still a few steps away. She thought for a moment, then charged at high speed.

That didn't work either.

She sank into a crouch and considered her options. She had two sheaths, one on either hip, and she put her knives away before she crept closer to the rat again. With barely a moment's thought as to how stupid she would look if this failed, she threw herself at her quarry. It darted away again, but not before she managed to grab its tail.

"Ow, fuck!" She had not expected it to hurt so much when she landed flat on her face. "Damn this game and its realism. Ow, stop biting me! Fuck." She flailed to avoid the teeth and thunked the rat on the ground, then drew her knife and stabbed it.

It was far more realistic than she'd expected and she clapped a hand over her mouth. Blood had spattered on her face.

"Oh, God," she said, her voice muffled. "Oh, I don't think I'm cut out for this. Holy shit."

"You're doing quite well," the AI said. *"You've shown creativity in your approach, and you're mastering the movement controls very—"*

"I have rat blood all over me!"

"There's also that." The AI sounded bemused. *"You know this isn't a real world, right?"*

"It looks real." Tina glowered at the rat.

"Well, if it helps, rats are carriers of disease and you're helping the citizens of this city lead happy, healthy lives. Speaking of which..." A glow appeared around her hand and the bite mark went away. *"Given that this is the tutorial, I won't let you get any debuffs."*

"Can I ask a question?" She pushed up and rotated her shoulders to work out the new bruises. "What were those numbers I saw floating up when I fought with the rat?"

"Ah. Do you see the red bar at the top of the screen? That is your health. You want to keep it from reaching zero. At present, you have seventeen of twenty health—or, as they are often referred to, hit points."

"Charming."

"You lost a point from falling and two points from the bite. Those will heal over time. You will also find that you lose points when you exert energy. However, as in the real world, the more consistently you do so, the more energy you will begin to have."

"I don't know how you're hoping to sell a video game that's like going to the gym," Tina quipped. "But, okay. I level up at things."

"Yes. For instance, watch this."

RAT SLAYER, Level 1 flashed on the screen, followed by **JOKER, Level 1**.

"Huh. Okay. So, what next?"

"Next, you kill two more rats."

"Oh, no."

How she managed to make herself kill the rats, she wasn't sure. She did it, however, and even managed to talk the AI into removing the spatters of blood, which earned her **SILVER TONGUE, Level 1**.

"Now what?" she asked.

"Now, you explore the city." The AI made the end of the alley flash for a moment. Tina could see people walking up and down a main thoroughfare with carts and market stalls. *"Don't worry, they don't bite. Most of them, anyway."*

"How reassuring," she said. She raised her eyebrows at the crowds. "Everyone is better dressed than I am."

"Yes. You will want to perform small tasks from the market board, which will give you the funds to upgrade your wardrobe. Expect some snide comments in the meantime."

"Gee, thanks." She strode to the mouth of the alley. "I don't suppose you'll tell me where the market board is, will you? Of course you won't. In fact—oh, holy shit. Justin!"

The journey to Riverbend took two days, which was about how long Zaara needed to get over the truly monstrous hangover she'd brought on herself.

Her father was not particularly amused by that. He hadn't wanted to stay in East Newbrook for another day, but her carousing had lasted for several hours and she had lost track of how many beers she had consumed.

It was enough that Lyle had been proud of her, which handily explained the hangover.

She was half-afraid that her father would go back on his word when they got home, but on the second day, when they could see Riverbend in the distance, he turned to her and said, "I know you didn't have to come back. I also know I can't keep you in Riverbend if you don't want to stay."

Half-sure that the hangover was playing tricks on her ears, she stared blankly at him. "I'm…sorry, what?"

He gave her a rueful smile. "When I got to East Newbrook and saw you drinking with those men, I wanted to think they had brainwashed you somehow. You don't understand what it was like with your mother asking me when you'd be home and trying to find a way to send people after you when they might not go if they knew you'd left on your own. And then we received word that Sephith was gone, but we still didn't know if you were okay. I arrived and saw you and I was so angry that you could joke and laugh when we were sick with worry."

Zaara stared at her hands while guilt twisted in her belly. "Father—"

"Even when you were as drunk as a dwarf in that inn, you wore your daggers better than any guard I've ever had," he said ruefully. "And I remembered you running off every chance you had when you were little. You'd climb onto the roof and leap off or escape on market day. Did you think we didn't know about your magic teacher and your sword fighting lessons? We knew but we thought it might give you enough of a taste of adventure to stay home."

She cleared her throat awkwardly.

"There's nothing I could do that would keep you in Riverbend," her father said. "I'm sure you could pick locks or burn a jail cell down—and what kind of father would I be if I trapped you?"

"Then why did you make me come home?" she burst out.

"I didn't." He looked steadily at her. "You offered, Zaara, and you drove a hard bargain and made me agree to let you go adventuring again. Do you really think you'll make a noble marriage if you're known to be a highwayman?"

Zaara shrugged.

"I think you came back because you felt bad about leaving the way you did," he guessed. "You know you have an obligation to your family. Everyone does—to their family and their town. So what I'm asking you to do is find a way to fulfill that—and not only adventuring but something that will last for your children and their children."

She had thought about those words all through her tearful reunion with her mother and an ale with her brother at the inn. For some reason, she lingered around the house, helped carry pails of water, and brushed the horses. She took a long walk around the town and greeted the people she hadn't seen in months.

Finally, she went to her room and retrieved the orb Kural had given her.

The spell to activate it was simple and he appeared soon after. He looked tired as if he had not slept since she last saw him—which, she thought, he might not have.

"Zaara." His gaze took in her surroundings. "You're home, are you?"

"Yes." She explained the situation, then added, "I think I've decided what I want to do."

"Is it, 'return to East Newbrook and be a wizard's apprentice?'" he asked hopefully. "Because, let me tell you, I could use your help."

"Oh." She thought about that for a moment. "Hmm. Maybe my plan won't work, then. I wanted to stay here and be your apprentice."

"Oh, really?" He leaned back in his chair. "Explain."

"You protected the people of East Newbrook," she began. "Everyone in the valley knew you would resolve disputes and protect them from armies, everything like that. You could heal people and make sure the crops grew well. My father spoke to me about leaving a legacy for my community, and I think this could be mine. I want to build a wizard's tower here in Riverbend and protect my people."

Kural considered this with a somber expression. "Are you sure?" he asked finally. "To be a wizard is to live for nigh on a thousand years. My mentor was over eight hundred years old when he trained me, and the woman who trained him was still living at one thousand two hundred."

"So?"

"So you will not only see your parents grow old and die, but your brother as well, and his children, and their children," he explained gently. "There is a reason so many wizards settle in a different place than where they were born. There is joy to be had in a long life and much wisdom, but there is also grief, Zaara."

"I know." She swallowed. "But I want to do this. I wanted to be your apprentice when you asked before. I've wanted to learn more sorcery for years. And...I want my name to be remembered." She colored with embarrassment. "I used to get so disgusted with my father for saying that he wanted our family to be remembered, but I want the same thing. As a wizard, I could train my successor and know that I was leaving Riverbend in good hands."

He smiled. "You're forgetting how strongly the winds of fate can blow, Zaara. I'll help you, I will—but this will not make you omnipotent. People will still make their own choices, even ruinous ones. There will still be storms and droughts and wars that are out of your control. Remember that."

Zaara nodded. "Every life has powerlessness and grief and every life has loneliness. Kural, you trained me and you know me. You know I can do this."

"I do." He nodded. "And, as it happens, I have a solution to your problem that does not require me to spend as much time teaching."

"Oh?"

"Yes. A new sorceress has arrived in Insea, a woman of some renown. I heard whispers that she is seeking the sorceress who slew Sephith."

She sat bolt upright. "Wait…really? You knew this and you didn't tell me?"

"I was waiting for you to contact me—and for more confirmation. It is clear that her search is for you and it seems, from what I hear, that she is trustworthy. Or as trustworthy as a wizard can be." Kural smiled. "So, while I confirm that, I will give you a skill that will let you train with her without leaving Riverbend and will help me keep a promise to Justin."

"Oh?" She leaned forward, interested in what he had to share.

"It's called shadow-walking," he explained. "It will let you be in another place…almost entirely. You will be able to explore the king's storerooms—"

"And look for the third key," she finished.

"Precisely." He nodded. "If it is there, I believe I can convince the master of ceremonies to make it the prize for the tournament. However, I do not have the time to search for it myself and the shadow-walking would hone your skills."

"Teach me!" Zaara bounced in her seat. "Please?"

"May I say," Kural interjected, "that a little bird told me you want to be a death sorceress and I'm not entirely sure you have the proper demeanor for that."

"I know." She rolled her eyes. "Anyway, I can't be that if I take care of everyone here. It'll only be…you know, a hobby."

"Quite a hobby to pick," he said in open amusement. "Very well. Here is the spell."

CHAPTER SEVEN

The journey to Insea involved pleasant weather and deeply unpleasant terrain. The King's Road was the only thing that made the exercise bearable, providing an evenly paved path through increasingly difficult hills. More often than not, one side of the road or both plunged into marshland or cliffs, which meant that Justin and Lyle needed to walk far into the night to find a place to rest.

The dwarf was of the opinion that the road had been made this way to ward off any invading armies, while his companion argued often—and loudly—that the road was this way because the elves couldn't take a hint when they found a site for their city.

"I bet the whole place is cursed," he said on the third day. "How much clearer a sign can you get that something doesn't want you to get to this place?"

"On the contrary, I very much want you to get there," the AI said crisply.

"What, so I leave the game?" he muttered.

"No, so you stop bitching about this damned road. On the other hand, you being gone forever does have a certain appeal."

He rolled his eyes and focused on his lunch. When he looked up, Lyle had a strange smile on his face. "What? What is it?"

"So, the city is cursed?" his friend asked.

"I'm not saying it's definitely cursed. I'm only saying it's awfully coincidental that—what? Why are you smiling like that?"

The dwarf grinned like a loon. "So, there's no reason anyone would want to go to Insea?"

He folded his arms and waited for him to explain the joke. Lyle, for his part, clearly wanted to hold out but beckoned him to follow as he climbed the next rise. The road, for most of the past day, had been a series of rolling hills that made Justin's calves ache until he had cursed the doctor, the makers of the game, and everyone involved in this all too realistic simulation.

Now, he sighed and walked to the top of the hill, fully expecting to see another twenty identical hills stretched before him. Instead, the ground sloped away and the road wound through beautiful fields and gardens until it reached the city.

"Wow." Justin exhaled an awed breath.

Insea was everything he had imagined but so beautiful it made his heart ache. He had never been one for architecture but he had to admit there was something inspiring about the way the buildings gleamed in the sunlight. Distant spires and arches, solid walls of translucent stone, and everything in the city seemed almost lit from within.

"Ye sat down for lunch too soon," Lyle said, with a grin. "I noticed just now when I was stretching me legs."

He sank into a crouch, cursed his legs again, and laughed in wonder. "This is gorgeous."

"And you wondered why they moved heaven an' earth to build a city here," the dwarf said smugly. He thought for a moment. "Well…the elves were never ones to let practicalities stand in the way of being floopy, pretty bastards, 'specially when they could get someone else to do the work for them."

"They must have paid well," he said with a laugh. "Otherwise, I don't see what the dwarves got out of it."

"A blessin' an' a curse," his companion said philosophically. "We got our hands on that gorgeous hunk of rock an' all the training we'd need to make our own cities. Since then, we've chased the dream of finding a place half as beautiful as Insea—or, Elfholt. That's what we call it."

Justin began to pack his gear up with newfound energy. "Batholemew seemed to think it was only a legend that the dwarves built it. I was joking when I mentioned them but it seems like you're sure."

"I grew up hearing tales of Elfholt," Lyle said and shouldered his pack. "A city that shone like the sun, made from the most gorgeous rock you ever saw, carved by tools and magic alike, of elven design and dwarven make. No one ever told me where it was—it's a legend to us, too. But now I've seen Insea…that's it. I knew at a glance." Wistfully, he added, "This is the first time in years I've wanted to go home. I want to show me da' this."

"You can," he told him as the road led him down the long slope toward the city. "You can go home as the hero who slew a wizard and won the tournament of Elfholt and bring your family here to live in style."

Lyle responded with an unwilling laugh. "None o' them ever knew why I wanted to leave. Dwarves don't leave. For this, though…"

"So, why'd you leave?" Justin asked.

"I went…what's it you humans say? Stir-crazy, that's it. Dwarves don't even have a word for it, see. A few leave every generation. I found that out when I did. Their families cover it up. I couldn't stay—an' I had siblings, so it's not like my parents were hard up." Lyle shrugged. "Oh, they were angry, though. Still, I wasn't the eldest, so it's not like I was s'posed to carry on the family name."

Justin tried to imagine Lyle as a family man and village elder, and his brain shorted out. "Huh."

"I reckon they might forgive me if I showed 'em Elfholt, though," Lyle said contentedly. "And, after all, I promised ye a dwarven bride."

"I told you, I need to go home." That was the most diplomatic way he could find to get out of this insane marriage plan his friend was concocting.

"Don't do yourself the disservice of leaving afore ye see dwarven women," the dwarf advised. "But, first things first. We have to win that tournament."

"Uh-huh. Yes." He tried to hide the horrified look on his face. "Yep, that's a good place to focus first."

Justin expected a huge crowd of visitors trying to gain entry to Insea and was pleasantly surprised, instead, to see the gates standing open and no guards at all. When he expressed his astonishment, his companion guffawed.

"Oh, the king's craftier than ye'd think. No one's seen him in years. Everyone knows Insea has no guards an' everyone knows it's never been conquered."

"Wait, seriously?" He couldn't imagine a place as beautiful as this—with storerooms so full that the king gave away treasure to adventurers—going unconquered. "So, is the king elven?"

"Maybe?" The dwarf shrugged. "That's the guess, anyway. No one really knows. The city never has drought or famine, no riots, the nobles are merely the families that have stayed rich for generations."

"And no one ever sees the king?" He had stopped but now hurried after Lyle. "You're seriously telling me no one is curious about this? A city that runs itself? Like...an AI?"

"Good luck explaining that one to him," it snarked.

He rolled his eyes.

The dwarf, luckily, seemed to not have noticed. "Oh, people are curious, all right. There are always a few new theories floating around. Some people say Insea is the city of the gods an' they move around here unseen an' keep people safe." He shrugged. "Me, I wasn't too interested in a place where nothin' ever goes wrong, ye ken?"

Justin, who was having dreams of living in a beautiful stone city that never got dirty and never had famine or war, suddenly felt very boring. He shook his head and followed along the boulevard, keeping an eye out for shops. The blacksmith of East Newbrook had improved his armor before he and Lyle left the town, but he'd advised him to get a new sword belt, new boots, new leathers for under the armor, and a proper shield.

There was a truly astounding amount of weaponry and armor on sale for a city that never saw war, but the multiple signs advertising tournament gear explained that.

He chuckled. "Maybe the king knows there's a war coming and the tournament is a way to make sure the populace is all trained up."

"Ye've got what it takes to be a prophet," Lyle said with grudging respect.

"A prophet?"

"Ye know, one o' those on street corners, yelling about the secret cabals an' the end times."

"Oh…where I come from, we call those conspiracy theorists. Or crackpots."

"Ha, crackpots. I like that." The dwarf looked around critically. "Business don't seem to be too good. That's interestin'."

"Not for a week," one of the shopkeepers said. He was a lithe young man with boots of deep-red leather, and he sat glumly on his stool. "Not since the sixth win for the Twins."

Lyle leaned on the man's table. He raised an eyebrow for more details as he pored over the daggers on display. "Twins?" he asked.

"Sure. Ah, you're new here." The shopkeeper clearly tried to decide whether to spill the gossip or keep his mouth shut in order to drum up more business. The first instinct won out and he huddled closer and beckoned them forward. "The Twins have won the tournament for the last six weeks. They must be as rich as the king himself by now but no one knows who they are. No noble house has claimed them and no one knows where they live or where they've put the treasures. And they always wear masks."

"A kind of Battle Royale Daft Punk," Justin mused.

Lyle and the shopkeeper stared at him.

"Nothing," he said hastily. "Go on."

"Well, anyway." The shopkeeper eased onto his stool again and shrugged expressively. "With those two winning every week, no one seems to think they can win so they don't spend money anymore. No one comes to look at my wares." He gave a theatrical sigh.

"Oh, yeah?" The dwarf gave him a smile that displayed all his teeth. "I bet ye've had to lower yer prices, then."

Justin watched, his lips twitching, as Lyle and the shopkeeper launched into a round of spirited negotiations—one invoking the power of dwarven might and the possibility of defeating the Twins to bring business back and the other insisting that if his prices were any lower, it would be highway robbery and he would starve in the gutter.

"Justin!" a voice called.

He spun, not at all sure what he expected.

Of course, what he hoped was to see Zaara again.

What he did see, however, was Tina with her Valkyrie tattoo and eyeliner. Her short nails were covered in deep-blue polish and she wore Level One clothes that reminded him vividly of his first few hours in the game. They were even covered in mud.

"Tina." Before he could react properly, she barreled into his arms for a hug.

"Oh! I'm sorry. I got alley grime on your armor." She pulled away, then frowned. "Also, running full-speed into plate armor hurts. I keep forgetting this game can do that. Wait, before you say anything, I'm fine. Your mother said to make sure to say that first and I forgot. I'm okay. I only came into the game to see you."

Justin relaxed. "Okay. Okay, you're all right, that's good." He looked to where Lyle and the shopkeeper had escalated their bargaining. The dwarf now loudly beseeched the gods to look down on "this most miserable and ill-equipped of their servants," while the shopkeeper uttered pleas to "his dearest friend" to see reason. "Uh…let's go over here."

Tina waited while they trailed away, then looked at Justin. She swallowed and looked at her feet. "Justin…I'm so sorry."

"I'm not," he said and to his surprise, he realized it was true. "Tina, seriously. I've had a chance to experience a life I would never have otherwise. I'm scared sometimes that things will go wrong and I'll die, but…this place is amazing. I was already scared all the time. I let myself retreat into my room and my games and I never did anything I could be proud of. I tried but I wasn't who I wanted to be."

She stared at him, confused. "Justin, I almost got you killed."

"I know—and, I guess, maybe don't do that again."

Her laugh sounded a little strangled.

He chuckled. "That night when we went on the date, you made me ask questions about why I lived my life the way I did. I had become used to being the disappointment and I told myself that it didn't matter what I did because my parents wouldn't ever be proud of me. The thing was, that was where I focused. I never concentrated on what would make me proud of the life I lived. Here, I've the chance to change lives." He looked around at the gorgeous city and felt something shift inside him. "And I'm looking forward to bringing that back to the real world. Our world."

———

"Holy shit," Amber whispered.

She realized she and DuBois were clutching each other's hands as they stared at the monitors. For the life of her, she couldn't recall how that had happened and from his embarrassed glance, neither could he. They withdrew their hands at the same time and cleared their throats.

"Ah…" He looked around and gestured at the team. "Everyone. Come see. Come see."

At Amber's urgent wave, Nick and Jacob dashed closer from their position at another pod and the assistants crowded around.

"Oh, wow," Nick said. Mary appeared, trailing wires from her headset and haptic rig. "What's going on?"

One of the assistants answered her. "He wants to wake up. He's still healing but when he's better, he'll be ready to come home."

Justin and Tina, both with trembling chins and unsteady voices, decided to abandon meaningful talk for the time being. After much throat-clearing and pretending to look in different directions, they settled in to watch the negotiations.

The theatrics did not disappoint. After much beating of chests and bemoaning the futures of brides who had not yet been married and children who had not yet been born, the dwarf and the shopkeeper hammered out a deal and Justin ushered Tina forward to look at the daggers. Lyle and the shopkeeper chatted like old friends as she brushed her fingers over the blades—and even cut one of her fingers.

"Ah, this set." The man pulled himself away from his discussion with Lyle. "The lady will be most pleased—"

"If you talk to her directly," she finished sweetly.

He had been looking at Justin but glanced at Tina, then at Justin, then at Tina again.

"I wanted to suggest, perhaps, something not combat-oriented. My lady does not look accustomed to the use of weapons." He clearly struggled to not mention the burlap shirt.

"I've fallen on hard times," she said and fell into LARPing with ease, "but I'll have you know that in my city, my skills are well-known and I will also make my name known in…in…"

"Insea," Justin muttered.

"In Insea," she finished. "Now, your wares have surprised me with their quality. Suppose we strike a bargain." She leaned forward. "You give me the name of a good leatherworker and the daggers at cost and in return, I will mention your name to my friends and not force you to bargain with this man again." She gestured at Lyle.

"Who is this?" the dwarf asked Justin.

"I'll explain later," he muttered. He folded his arms and looked at the shopkeeper. He was enjoying himself more than he had expected to with this exchange. "You won't get a better endorsement than hers," he said loudly. "I had to beg her to come to Insea for the tournament. For weeks, she told me it wouldn't be enough of a challenge. Only when the Twins rose to prominence did she think she had found a worthy adversary."

People had begun to gather to watch, and he had to stop talking so laughter wouldn't escape him.

To his amusement, Tina took up the thread without any prompting. "I lost my family to a warlord," she told the shopkeeper and made sure her voice carried. "It took half his mercenaries to defend him from me, and with the winnings from this tournament, I will go back and avenge my loved ones."

The people nodded and murmured.

"Now," she said and smiled magnanimously. "To win the tournament, I must have the best weapons money can buy. I have looked at many stalls, but nowhere have I seen blades so sharp as this. Surely we can strike a deal, shopkeeper."

The people of Insea clearly liked good theater. They clapped and a few sighed and murmured about the new challenger's dramatic story. The proprietor, meanwhile, settled into negotiations with goodwill, apparently viewing emotional manipulation not as an inconvenience but instead, as an essential part of a good sale.

Ten minutes later, the group was on their way with Lyle's fist weapons sharpened, Tina wearing the daggers, and Justin in possession of a new boot knife. By the time they reached the leatherworker the shopkeeper had recommended, word had already reached her. She greeted them like old friends and settled into negotiations for a full set of leathers.

"Alas, I have the most perfect set of armor," she told Tina, "but it will not be completed for two more days."

"When is the next tournament match?" Justin asked.

"Tomorrow," the woman said. "Only one team is willing to try to beat the Twins. It'll be a poor showing—the Master of Ceremonies is desperate to get more entrants, but there's only so much he can do. There's talk of an ancient treasure being unveiled and still people won't sign up."

"So a team could sign up now?" he asked urgently.

"Oh, of course." She lit up. "If the Twins win unopposed tomorrow, that's the end of the tournament. But if there are more than two teams, the top two will advance." She looked at Tina. "I have to say, it would be quite a coup to have a tournament team wearing my gear. And if you are in the top two tomorrow, I'll have time to finish the better set."

"Excellent." Justin looked at Lyle, who cracked his fingers and gave a wolfish grin. "I'll let you hammer out a price with my associate."

"Since this city was built by dwarven hands," the dwarf thundered as his companions escaped with a chortle.

"Do you think I can really get good enough to—" Tina started. She stopped when he cleared his throat meaningfully.

Two people waited for them outside the shop. They were almost identical in size and tall, and lean-muscled, although he could faintly tell that one was a woman and one was a man. Both wore their blond hair pulled back in a tight braid and wore metal masks over their face.

"Well, look who it is," the man said.

"The vagrant in burlap who says she's going to challenge us," the woman finished. She scrutinized Tina and turned to Justin. "And an adventurer with no accomplishments to his name, I'll bet."

"I defeated the wizard Sephith," Justin said and made a show of studying his nails. "But I'm sure that doesn't compare with play-fighting in an arena."

A deathly cold silence followed his words, and the crowd that had gathered to watch the confrontation held its collective breath.

"You want to challenge us?" she demanded. "Fine. Do it. It's your funeral. Wear better armor tomorrow," the woman said with another derisive look at Tina. "Make it a proper fight before you die, at least."

They strode away and the murmurs in the crowd began.

"Justin," Tina said, her voice entirely too level. "What in God's name have you signed me up for?"

"Let me tell you something about this place," he said. He gave her a grin and pitched his voice for her ears alone. "I've found that the best thing to do is team up with a dwarf who gives you no chance but to charge into battle before thinking too hard about the odds."

CHAPTER EIGHT

Tad Williams grimaced before he straightened his shoulders, plastered a smile on his face, and strode into the fundraiser. The group of people in this room was everything he had wanted to avoid when he decided to come to Washington. They were decked out in expensive clothes and talked seriously about how much they could afford to give to cancer relief efforts —as if they didn't have thousands of dollars on their fingers, necks, and wrists.

His presence wasn't noticed immediately, which gave him time to drift and listen to the conversations.

However, he had strict instructions from his aides to mingle.

It in turn necessitated small talk. He wanted to beat his head against a wall at the thought.

"Excuse me, are you Senator Williams?" A woman spoke from a nearby group.

"Ah, yes." He looked at her and made sure his fake smile was on. Hopefully, he didn't look like a psychopath. "I don't believe we've met."

"I'm Samantha Howley-Smith." She held a hand out for a

handshake that barely deserved the name. "I must say, it's wonderful to see you here trying to help other children."

There was no malice in her voice, only deep curiosity. His aides had drilled him on exactly what to say and how, which had seemed wise at the time. Now, however, he could see the evening stretching out like one long play and he was already weary of it.

"Families who are struggling with an illness have enough to worry about," he told Samantha seriously. "They deserve our support."

The words sickened him—not the meaning behind them, but the act—and it was even worse when everyone else nodded as if he'd said something truly profound.

"Don't bring Justin up," Kevin had instructed him. "Let them bring him up. To your face, they won't repeat the bad rumors— you can take the good spin and run with it."

"I don't want to be too familiar," the woman said now as if this weren't the entire reason she'd called him over, "but I've heard your son is also…ill. I hope he's recovering well."

He pretended not to notice the way everyone in the circle and several nearby groups had fallen silent and craned to listen.

"That is so kind of you to say," he replied and met her eyes with a smile as if he didn't want to throw his glass of wine and run screaming from the room. "With so many large issues facing us here, I didn't expect anyone to remember Justin's accident. And thank you for your kind wishes. The doctors can't give us any guarantees, of course, but his condition is stable." He nodded to her as if he couldn't tell that she was practically drooling for more details. "Now, tell me. How has childhood cancer affected you?"

From their stricken looks, no one wanted to let the conversation drift to the reason for the event.

A man cleared his throat meaningfully. "Ah, Senator—I, um…I hear your son has moved facilities. I have several constituents who have asked about securing treatment for their relatives, and I would love to know your recommendations."

It was clearly a bald-faced lie, but Tad took it and ran with it. "I don't want to derail the night, but I do want to thank you for your vote the other day on the classification changes bill. I take it your constituents called in with the same comments mine did." He smiled at the man. "Between the costs and the classification changes, I am so glad we were able to get our constituents better access to care. As for Justin, I'm afraid I can't share too many details."

Anna Price had given very clear-cut constraints on what could and could not be said about the experiment, clearly wary of over-promising on such a complex issue. Accordingly, he now said simply, "We were lucky enough to find an opening in a clinical trial. It provides all the standard care for trauma patients but with a new therapy that's been in the works for several years now. The company hopes to release preliminary results as soon as possible, but on a personal note, I can't tell you how grateful we are for Justin's medical team. They are some of the most dedicated people I've ever met. As soon as I have any details I can share, I will of course pass them to your office, Senator."

It was a long, fancy way of saying not much at all, which would make it an excellent political speech, he decided.

"If you'll excuse me," he told them. "I see the director over there and there is a matter I must discuss with him. Ms. Howley-Smith, a pleasure to meet you. Senator." He extracted himself with as much grace as he could manage and headed toward the director. Since he was there, he might as well learn about any challenges the organization faced. For all he knew, there were unique issues faced by pediatric cancer patients when it came to billing, and—Lord knew—he had experience in that area.

He didn't reach the man, however, as he bumped into someone—or, rather, someone bumped into him.

Someone he knew, unfortunately, and it took every effort to school his features into urbane recognition.

"Mr. Metcalfe," Tad said. He tried to echo the pleasant tone Mary had perfected in her youth while speaking to people she despised. "Fancy seeing you here."

"And you," the man said in the same tone. "A high-profile fundraiser isn't where I expected to see a famously anti-corruption junior senator."

"And yet," he replied and managed to hold his features in a smile in case anyone was watching, "I have the sense that you did expect to see me here—and that you contrived to bump into me."

The lobbyist looked around. He held his wine glass with practiced ease. It was only half-full but he clearly hadn't drunk from it at all. This event was all business for him. "Childhood cancer touches everyone," he said musingly. "Everyone knows of a family who lost someone, don't they? And a child, too…a completely innocent victim."

Tad felt his blood pressure begin to rise. He took a sip of wine and noticed the glass shaking in his hand. The liquid burned all the way down his throat.

Metcalfe didn't go in the direction he feared, however. He chose to slip the knife in between different ribs. "I suppose that's why you're here, isn't it? Such a nice, bipartisan issue. Give a few thousand to a children's charity, offer a few sound bites, and try to boost those poll numbers. Those abysmal poll numbers." He swirled his wine although he still didn't take a sip. "There have been calls for your resignation, you know."

"I'd take those more seriously if I didn't know where they came from," he pointed out. "At some point, you'll have to face the fact that you went way out of your way to stir trouble up where there was none—and you hardly got a good return on your investment. I'm only one senator, Mr. Metcalfe."

"Has it occurred to you that your refusal to support my employer's bill might hurt your constituents, senator?" The man gave him a smile that didn't quite reach his eyes. "You never asked what the measure was, did you? Instead, you discounted it out of hand." He looked pained. "We both said some unfortunate things. You thought I was pressuring you to do something ill-advised—a worthy worry—and I was offended by your assessment of my character. I do hate apologizing…but, please, accept mine."

"You want to apologize?" he asked him. "Go out there to where all the journalists are waiting and tell them what you've done." He didn't know where these words came from. It was the wine, probably, and his aides would not approve. "I don't want an apology, Metcalfe. I want you to undo the harm you've done and it'll never be undone if people don't know what's happened in the shadows. You're one of the best people to help because you know what's been happening." He pointed at the door. "Go. Go tell them all."

Metcalfe had gone oddly pale. He swallowed at the look in Tad's eyes.

In a moment, his face cleared. It was disturbing how calm he suddenly looked. His worry had been wiped away.

"Senator," he said, and his voice was warm and comforting. He leaned in with a smile that lit up his face. He was so inviting that he leaned in as well. He could see a new path before them in which the man could be an ally. He was smiling too when the lobbyist said, "It can still get so much worse for you. Remember that."

He left and Tad stared after him.

"Senator Williams." The director of the charity clapped him on the back. "It's good to see you. Your office confirmed your attendance at the last minute but we are so happy to have you here—are you all right, sir?"

"I, ah…" Tad shook his head. "I'm afraid I haven't slept enough lately. I'm sure you've seen many junior senators with the same look."

How he stumbled through the conversation, he didn't know, but the director seemed pleased by the donations and by his questions. When he excused himself to go to the bathroom, his head was buzzing from wine and from the sheer shock of Metcalfe's words.

It can still get so much worse for you. What kind of sociopath said something like that?

The kind who doctored photos to make it look like there was an affair, he reminded himself. The kind who stirred up protesters and journalists to call him a child murderer. He shouldn't be surprised at this point. He'd seen Metcalfe show his hand enough times.

He really should go out there again and schmooze more. Thus far, he was doing well. He'd heard a few murmurs echoing the things he told the first group he spoke to, and the director had been seen accepting a check from him. Now was his moment to resume his efforts.

The problem was that he didn't want to. He simply didn't. Fighting whispers with other whispers wasn't how he wanted to do this.

On the other hand, if Mary could try to help Justin by playing a video game—he still could not believe that video—he could make small talk for another couple of hours. He dried his hands and returned to the crowd. It helped to remind himself that he had nothing to be ashamed of. He had done the best he could for Justin and hopefully, the data would help to expand the testing. All he had to do was exude that honesty.

Grimly determined, he spent the night talking, laughing, and trying not to look at the corner, where Dru Metcalfe leaned against the wall and studied him.

Zaara was excited to learn to shadow-walk, and over the moon excited that she might become a sorceress's apprentice. She even looked forward to sneaking into the king's treasure rooms. After all, how often did you get to see something like that? Life had opened up all kinds of new possibilities.

Her ebullient mood lasted until Kural informed her she would have to wear a dress to shadow-walk in the palace. He called them robes, but she wasn't fooled. It involved considerable fabric around her legs and made it difficult to get around. How were you supposed to ride a horse, for instance?

"You won't ride a horse while shadow-walking in the palace," he said and sounded deeply amused. "I promise you that if you find any horses, you will be in the wrong place."

"I don't like dresses," she retorted indignantly. She picked at the bodice of her gown—something old and musty she'd found in a chest in her room—and shifted uncomfortably. "This fits all weird."

"And it will only barely pass for ceremonial robes, so be careful," the wizard admonished her. "The king is very strict when it comes to manners. He employs some humans, but he's not happy about it."

"The king really is an Elf?" she asked, diverted by this interesting tidbit.

"Not...exactly." Kural shook his head. "I can't explain more right now. Follow the instructions I gave you, try to stay out of sight, and see if you can find that key. I'm hoping it won't be too much of a trial."

She grumbled a goodbye and slid the scrying ball into its pouch at her waist. With that secured, she stepped into the circle she'd drawn on the floor of her room, closed her eyes, and tried to drop into the trance her mentor had taught her.

It didn't work the first few times and she opened her eyes to the same white plaster walls and the fields outside her window.

The carts rumbled on the main street and the villagers called to one another over the burble of the fountain in the square.

Determined, she closed her eyes tightly again and focused. All the sounds faded and she opened her eyes to darkness. She was in a cold place with stone beneath her bare feet and took a cautious step, then another and another. With one more, she would know if she'd been successful. Holding her breath, she stepped forward and thankfully, didn't collide with the wall of her room.

She had stepped beyond her body. The thought was terrifying enough to spin her back abruptly. Her gasp sounded breathless as she wobbled, tried to recover, and tipped onto her bed with a thump. She stood quickly and sighed, told herself sternly that she was absolutely fine, and returned to the circle.

This time, she walked forward with a purpose as soon as her eyes opened in the darkness. It wasn't very long before the faint, greyish light took on a tinge of gold. A lantern, perhaps? She kept walking, thinking how strange it was to not hear her footsteps on the ground even though she could feel the chill of it.

The glow wasn't from a lantern. She must be close to the outer walls of the palace, with sunlight filtering through the carved stone walls. The stone had gone from greyish-white to golden and she traced her fingers over it. Insea was said to look like any town, only with the buildings all made from one piece of stone, but this hallway didn't look normal at all. It was almost like a tunnel. The walls were eerily smooth and the floor slightly curved everywhere.

"It won't be far to the treasure rooms," Kural had told her. "You'll know them by the sigils over the doors—a scale picked out in red magic. Most cannot see it at all."

Zaara had to focus to see the glimmers of magic in the rock, and when she did, it was almost dizzying. Insea, it turned out, was not only rock but also magic. She should have expected as much. Whether it was millions of tiny pieces of rock made into one, or one piece that had been carved by spells, she could not say. All she knew was that it was shot through with both veins, as any might be, and so many spells and sigils that her eyes almost crossed.

Luckily, the red of the scales stood out from the gold-and-white of the other spells. She hurried through the first doorway she found with the scales and stepped into utter blackness.

It was quite extraordinary. There was no door and yet when she entered, the light was utterly gone. She froze but forced herself to keep walking after a moment. It helped to remind herself that she was not a coward or a thief, and she wasn't technically there. Whatever traps there were, they surely could not hurt her.

The dark was even rather comforting. It was complete but not malicious. When she stepped out of it, she was disappointed, but only for a moment. She looked around at the landscape in amazement. Her path had taken her to the top of a mountain where wind whistled around her and rough stone chilled her feet.

A few more steps took her into a field of wildflowers, their scent intoxicating, and into a forest with moss and birds singing.

It took her too long to realize that this was the treasure and not a trap. There must be thousands of worlds there—worlds she could only pass through but the owner of this room could travel to in the blink of an eye. The king could go to any place he wanted from this room, she would bet. With a small, contented sigh, she wandered through the wildflowers, the mountains, and the darkness. When she stepped into the corridor once again, she was sad to leave.

The next room held elven artifacts that took her breath away with their beauty. She examined statues and paintings, fragments of old mosaics, musical instruments that were carved from the same pale stone as the castle, and even old dresses that looked so fragile, they might fall apart if she touched them. Necklaces and rings were laid out carefully, a profusion of gold and gems and pearls.

No key was in evidence, however.

The corridor wound sideways and she followed it as she trailed her fingers on the wall but darted into the third room when she heard someone coming. Even knowing that no one could hear her, she still held her breath while the patrol walked past. The guards did not speak and they did not look into the treasure rooms. They must patrol this route so often that they were bored with what they saw inside.

Zaara could not imagine that. She turned to look at the room and gave a huge smile. This was it, she realized. This was where the Dwarven artifacts were, and the room stretched on for ages. If the key was anywhere in this world, it was surely there.

Of course, the area was massive.

She noticed a similar way of organizing artifacts, however, and was able to narrow her search quickly. Decorated saddles were intriguing, although from the size of them, they must be for something the size of a hippopotamus. Ceremonial clothes, many of them decorated with pieces of ore and rough gems caught her attention. The other side of each one was a mirror of the design but metalwork and faceted gems winked in the light.

Zaara trailed past statues, small carved balls of stone, and pieces of furniture. Numerous paintings were displayed, but she found them disturbing. All manner of clocks created a substantial collection—not surprising, she decided, if the dwarves had settled underground. Of course they would need a novel way to tell time.

Although everything was fascinating, she didn't lose focus on her purpose. Still, she had walked almost all the way down the room before she saw what she was looking for. It lay on a pillow, a three-sided key with one prong extended. She could see where it would slot in with the other two keys, although she was fascinated to see the lock it might open.

It was there. Her relief came with a sense of sadness.

She sank to her knees and studied it. Her next task was to get this to Justin and then, he would leave.

It seemed right but was still painful. When she thought of Lyle, she knew she could send a runner to promise him a pint of ale and he'd wander to Riverbend. Kural was two days' journey away, but she could see him whenever she chose to. Everyone else she had ever known lived in Riverbend and within a few hundred yards of one another.

Justin was the first friend she'd ever had who would be entirely gone to her.

But she wouldn't be selfish. She understood his desire to go home. He had a family there who were worried about him too. Finally, she stood and turned to leave but startled when she noticed a figure standing behind her.

Zaara uttered a shriek that, thankfully, could not be heard by anyone.

Theoretically.

"I didn't mean to startle you," the woman said before she folded her hood down. "You simply seemed to be deep in thought and I did not want to disturb you."

"Ah…" For a moment, she couldn't think of anything to say but the enormity of this caught up with her. "You're Justin's mother."

"Yes," Mary said.

"You're here for the key," she guessed. She stepped aside and tried to smile. "You'll be glad to have him back in your world, won't you?"

"I will." The woman had stopped with those words and she seemed deeply sad. "We miss him, Justin's father and I. And other people. But that is not why I am here, Zaara. Justin's path home is his own. I have a different purpose."

"Oh?" She looked at the key, then at Mary. "Wait, how can you hear me? I'm not here."

The woman seemed to find this deeply amusing. "Neither am I. Don't worry. No one can hear us here. Perhaps Kural mentioned me to you—a sorceress seeking an apprentice?"

"You're..." Zaara's eyes widened. She recalled the bolt of energy Mary had launched from her hands during their escape from the bandit hideout. It was power like she'd never seen. "You're the sorceress who wants to train someone?"

"Yes." She smiled. "I have been told of your desire to protect your home. It is a noble goal and one I am sure you can accomplish, given how I saw you face danger to fight at my son's side. If you will let me, I will train you. What do you say?"

"Yes," she whispered. "Wait, but—if Justin goes home and you're still here..."

"He is trapped in this world," Mary explained. Her voice broke slightly. "I can come in and out at will."

"So he might come back too, someday."

"Someday." The woman seemed intrigued by the idea. "Yes, I suppose he might. First things first, however. You have a great deal to learn."

"Fascinating," DuBois murmured. Two empty bags of popcorn lay on the desk beside him.

"What is it?" Jacob scooched his desk chair over.

"The AI is...I don't know how to put it."

The young engineer gave him a wary look. "Tell me you're not about to say the AI is becoming sentient and about to take over the world."

"Not the second part," DuBois said. "I'm actually not sure if it's aware. I don't know how we'd be sure. I only know that in order to make the connections that lead characters to one another, it fills in the gaps between actions. It doesn't write the outlines of a story, it...dreams them."

Jacob swallowed and looked at the screen. "This isn't so good. We set this game up on the bare bones of a story that was made to be fun and engaging, not the basis of an entirely new form of intelligence."

"Like I said," the doctor cautioned, "I don't know that it's awake. I'm only saying it's…dreaming."

"Don't tell Price," he said hastily, then paused to consider. "Well…will it hurt Justin?"

"No. I've seen no indications that it would harm anyone."

"Then don't tell Price. Not yet. She'd nuke it or…use it for something." He shivered. "Let's keep this to ourselves for a while, okay?"

"Okay," DuBois said, bemused, He opened another bag of popcorn and began to munch on it. "Fascinating," he murmured again.

Mary's eyes opened to a clean white ceiling and the lid of the pod open beside her. Nick waved at her and continued to remove the electrodes.

"You're smiling," he observed. "It looks like you're still enjoying the game."

"Oh, so much." She took his hand to sit. Her muscles were a little stiff after the hours inside the machine and she stretched subtly as she held her hands and feet out for him to remove the various elements of the haptic set. An assistant shadowed him and watched with rapt attention while he placed each item of the set in its designated place. Mary smiled at the assistant, who blushed bright red and made a show of taking the equipment to be cleaned.

"They're good people," he told her in an undertone. "I don't think they, ah…know all the other stuff Diatek does."

She swung her legs over the edge of the pod and watched his

face as he cleared the monitors. "I appreciate you all working with Diatek. I know you have concerns about them."

Nick sighed as he worked. He handed her a bottle of water without looking up. Finally, after she had finished it and he had done all his checks, he sighed again. "I don't get it," he admitted. "She never says what Diatek does, but it's clear it's not…warm, fuzzy, Care Bear stuff. She got into this to help families, but she also does things that would give most people nightmares? I don't get it."

Mary opened her mouth but closed it again when he waved a hand.

"I know, I know, greater good. Don't worry, I won't say anything stupid. And I've heard all the arguments. But I don't see how you can be so sure you're doing the right thing when you help some people and hurt others. And don't ask if I have an answer to how doing the soft, fuzzy thing can sometimes hurt more people, because I don't." He threw his hands up.

She laughed at that. "You're very much like Tad that way."

He looked up at her in surprise. "So…"

"So?"

"So, you don't think I'm being stupid?"

"Stupid? No." She pushed herself out of the pod and winced when her feet touched the floor. "I tell you, these pods are not made for old bodies. No, don't tie yourself in knots telling me I don't look old, you'll only hurt your brain." She patted his arm. "To go back to what you mentioned, I don't think anyone has ever answered that one definitively. The only fact to remember is that for most actions, there are those who benefit, and those who are hurt. Make sure you try to help those you've hurt."

"But when you help them, you hurt someone else," he said and pressed his fingers into his temples.

"It helps if you don't think of life as a problem to be solved once," Mary said, amused. "The world is constantly in flux. There will never be one perfect solution, Nick. You do the best you can and sometimes, it's difficult. If you believe people are hurt by your alliance with Diatek, you can take steps to change the world so those people are helped." She patted his arm in a motherly gesture. "But you don't have to find all the answers tonight. If you'll forgive me being a mother for a moment, but I think you should probably have dinner and rest for a while."

Nick laughed. "It's good to have an office mom, actually." He looked stricken. "I hope you don't mind me calling you that."

"As long as I still get to play the game, I'll be fine," Mary assured him. "Now, I'd like some dinner, even if all of you won't go."

"It's a good time to get some," Jacob agreed as he approached the pod with Amber. "Okay, everyone but the evening shift, it's time to go home and get some rest. Evening shift, how are you for food?"

Several assistants were rostered but had never yet been alone with Justin and gave nervous thumbs-up while they all avoided looking at Mary. Having seen their dedication and care—not to mention having met several of the nurses and on-call doctors at this point—she had no concerns about their presence. In fact, she was comforted by their jitters as it meant they were taking this seriously.

She and the others left down the main hallway, joking about the game. She had developed quite a friendship with Zaara. "If friendship is the right word," she said with a laugh. "Since she isn't…real."

For a split-second, she thought she caught a glance between Jacob and DuBois, but it was gone quickly and the young man said smoothly, "As you noted with Justin, part of the beauty of games like this is that the emotions they provoke are real, even if the situations aren't."

Mary nodded. She had always rolled her eyes when she saw news reports of people getting addicted to games, but she thought she could understand now. In the world of the game, she was able to see the impacts of what she did. She was able to try being someone else without having to run away to join the circus, as her grandmother would have said.

They had reached the lobby when the shouting became audible.

"Oh, fuck," Amber said. She pointed outside.

Signs were being waved and people yelled insults at the building. Her heart sank. "How did they find out where we were?" She looked over her shoulder. "Did Tina tell them?"

"No," a new voice said. Anna Price strode across the lobby. She looked as elegant as she had that morning with not a hair out of place or even a slight wrinkle in her suit. "Ms. Castro was already in the pod by the time the post was made online about the location of the laboratory. Whoever did this likely trailed one of you here." She held a hand up. "Please do not apologize. I made the conscious choice to not restrict all of you to the building." Her smile was surprisingly calm. "Now. my car is waiting and all of us can leave together. Remember, the protesters will only shout at you. Look at the car and do not look at them. Come along."

"I'm not sure I'm ready for this," Mary said quietly.

"If you stop to think about it, you won't be," the other woman advised. She placed her hand in the small of her back and ushered her forward without ceremony. "Think of something else. Distract yourself. But keep walking."

Whatever Mary had expected, the protest was worse. The doors opened into a roar of noise. A quick scan—she shouldn't look, but she couldn't help it—showed twenty or more protesters, all shouting at her. Accusations hit her from all directions, vile things she tried not to hear but that slid under her guard anyway.

She didn't remember folding into the car, only the feeling of it lurching into motion. Shocked, she laid her head against the headrest and tried not to let tears escape from the corners of her eyes.

"They don't know what's going on," Jacob said. When she raised her head, she could see him fighting for calm. "That much is clear. I don't know what they were told—"

"That Senator Williams had allowed his son to be used for a military experiment," Anna Price said simply. "It was strongly suggested that Diatek is using Justin to pilot drones without releasing him from his coma." She shook her head slightly. "The mechanics weren't explained, of course—but that's the best way to spread a rumor. Point someone in a vague direction and let them dream up horrific things to fill in the blanks. People are always more attached to the story when they dream it up themselves."

"I can't stand this," Mary whispered. "People we know must be wondering if it's true—"

"We'll need to make a statement," the CEO said absently. An assistant who had entered the car with them began to take notes furiously. "I thought we could ride this out, but not if we're playing against lobbyists. They won't let it fade away."

The passengers fell into miserable silence before Jacob said, "You know what? Screw this. If they knew the facts and it was their family, they'd do the same thing. Mary, I've never said this, but I envy you—I wish every day that I had been able to see my grandmother recover. When this is over, people will know the truth. All that's going on right now is mud-slinging."

Price nodded at him with a smile. "Exactly correct, Mr. Zachary. And Mrs. Williams, rest assured I will not let your husband's career suffer from that mud-slinging. I've built up a reserve of favors to call in for situations exactly like this. Let me use them now."

CHAPTER NINE

By silent agreement, Justin and Tina didn't talk about the accident or the outside world. Thankfully, he had innumerable stories from his brief stint in the game and the conversation flowed easily. After finding accommodation for the night, they sat outside on one of the patios and watched people wander past in the streets as they chatted.

"That's a lie," she challenged and laughed. "There's no way you stabbed yourself in the chest. Your sword is too long for that."

"No, not *my* chest, my clone's chest." He grinned. "Although…I am open to any accusations of my sword being too long."

She snorted into her beer.

"Don't you laugh. You don't know. It might be."

"Uh-huh. Wouldn't you prefer a sword that's not too short, not too long, but exactly right?"

"A Goldilocks sword?" he asked and snickered.

"That's disgusting, man. She was a little girl."

"For fuck's sake—"

"Oh, did you plan to use it on the three bears?"

He dropped his head onto the table with a thud. "I give up," he said over the sound of her laughter. "No swords. No bears. And definitely no porridge."

"Yeah, that's a way to get a nasty burn. But don't let me tell you how to live your life." She tapped him on the shoulder. "By the way, is that *our* lunatic dwarf running through the crowd?"

Justin raised his head to look. "Yes. Yes, it is. Good evening, Stout. Let me buy you a beer."

"Thanks." Lyle panted and dropped into the empty seat at the table. "I could use one…after that run. Oh. Three days without a fight and I'm already a goner. I had to tell ye, though."

"Tell us what?" He signaled to the bartender for a beer.

"Skirmishes," the dwarf blustered, still panting. "It's a new thing. The Master of Ceremonies… announced it… Oh, I shouldn't run like that."

"Didn't you defeat a demon army?" Tina asked him quizzically.

"Yes." He glared at her. "Which means I'd appreciate more benefit of the doubt from you, young lady. Justin tells me ye're some kind of legendary warrior but I've not seen it yet, have I?"

"Yes. He did say that." She gave Justin a hard look as she sipped her beer. "I can only endeavor to do justice to the stories he's told."

He cleared his throat and became very interested in his beer. "So," he said brightly. "Tell us about the skirmishes."

Thankfully, Lyle was diverted. "Ah. Yes. It seems the Master of Ceremonies hasn't been able to get anyone else to challenge the Twins, has he? So he decided to pause the clock before the final round. We'll have three days of open skirmishes with no standing in the final tournament. There'll be prizes for the skirmishes—not so big but nothin' t'sneeze at, it sounds like."

"Hmm." Justin frowned. "I suppose it's a good idea. People fight, they get more confident…they decide maybe they do have a shot against the Twins…"

"And the grand tournament isn't simply a sad spectacle with a foregone conclusion," Tina finished. "Smart guy. You'd think he would simply say the previous winner couldn't compete in the next tournament or something, though."

He nodded. "On the other hand, this does give us quite an interesting opportunity. The Twins are shutting the tournament down, but the ones who finally beat them…well, they'd be legends, wouldn't they?"

"You're already a legend," she pointed out.

"Not here," Lyle said. "In New Eastbrook—"

"East Newbrook," Justin corrected.

"Whatever, it's at the ass-end of nowhere." The dwarf took his mug of beer with a muttered thanks. "That's my point. No one cares. Killed a wizard? A hundred people here say they've killed wizards."

"But we actually did," he pointed out.

"They don't know that, do they?"

He gave Tina a pleading look.

"Pics or it didn't happen," she explained in an undertone. "It's the same everywhere, Williams. The thing is, they don't have cameras here so you're shit outta luck."

Justin sighed. "Okay. Well, since no one knows any of us and Tina could use some…uh…chances to adapt to our team and communication style, why don't we enter in the skirmishes?"

"Exactly my thought," Lyle agreed. "That's why I signed us up for tomorrow morning."

"You what?" she asked.

"We should get some rest," the young man said loudly. "After all, we have to get up bright and early and make our reputations, right?"

"Justin, so help me—"

He pushed smoothly to his feet and pulled her chair out so she had to stand hurriedly. "You know you'll never feel ready," he said to her with a bright grin. "So I say we dive into the deep end."

"You listen here, you shitbag," Tina whispered sharply. She

clearly tried not to laugh, but she also managed a good deadpan glare. "I went out on a date with a man who didn't come out of his room all that often, and he's the one I came here to save—not a psycho who decides to enter gladiatorial contests on a whim. Too soon?"

Justin was laughing too hard to answer. He waved his hand to the inn and tried to recover his composure. "Duly noted, Madame Rogue. Let's all go to our rooms and you can spend the night dreaming up properly pointed nicknames for me."

"Oh, I am so ready for this." She cracked her knuckles. "Hey, knuckles crack, here! I appreciate that attention to detail."

A scant few hours later, Tina bounced anxiously in place while nerves seared through her until she couldn't tell if she would levitate or fall. The waiting area for the arena was made of the same ever-present rock, now a golden color that seemed to hold the sunlight from far above. She and the others stood on a platform of stone, which had—as far as she could tell—no pulleys or levers to make it move anywhere.

"Citizens and travelers!" The voice resounded above them in the arena, magically amplified. "For the first skirmish, I bring you something truly special—two of our finest teams from Season Three of the tournament and Insea's most intriguing newcomers. First, I bring you the team that landed the most impressive strike of Season Three, the silent assassins, the sure-footed dancers themselves—*the Yanevas!*"

The stadium erupted into wild cheers and the platform beneath her feet began to move smoothly upward. Her throat lurched.

"I wonder what a Yaneva is," Justin muttered.

"Only in Insea would they think it's good," Lyle told him. "They…let's simply say they traded on certain talents."

His companions stared expectantly at him.

"O' course, Insea remembers them as a fancy, elite infantry," the dwarf continued and gestured with his hands.

"Wait, I have so many questions," Justin said, but the Master of Ceremonies' voice echoed again, almost deafening now that the group was closer to the arena.

"If you've wondered who could possibly challenge the first team, wonder no more. We have secured a repeat performance from…*Quartzfire!*"

Lyle nodded in deep approval of this name and again, his friends exchanged baffled glances.

"Yes!" the MC announced over the sound of cheering, "the most favored team of Season Three, very cruelly whisked away from Insea to avoid spoilsports such as the tax collectors"—laughter erupted in the stadium—"has returned. They assure us they have done so legally, although we have been given very questionable names, in order to give us the showdown we all wanted so many weeks ago. Please welcome our dwarven friends, *Quartzfire!*"

The laughter continued and this time, Lyle provided an explanation. "No dwarf would call themselves that. They must be humans calling themselves dwarves to dodge taxes. It's not all that uncommon for prize-fighters and it's how we get most of our non-dwarven citizens."

"Huh." Tina looked at Justin and a smile tugged at her lips. "I guess no matter where you go, people are all the same."

He grinned in response but before he could speak, the awning over their platform slid back and sunlight poured in. The group peered upward, startled.

"Who would be a fitting match for these two champions?" the Master of Ceremonies continued. "Surely the only fitting complement to two such favorites would be an entirely new team, one poised to steal the hearts of Insea's citizens. Heroes from a far-away land, these brave fighters have defeated opponents we could only dream of. I bring you…*Sephith's Bane!*"

"Good name," Justin told Lyle as the platform slid up to show the team to the stadium. The two of them waved and Tina followed suit. "Wow, it's, uh…it's quite something to see this many people looking at me."

"Ye've fought demons," the dwarf said. "An' this intimidates ye?"

"I haven't fought demons," Tina whispered.

"Sure you have," Justin told her. "The Elder Castros."

She snorted with laughter at the mention of her parents. "Truly, soul-sucking bastards."

"What do they do with the souls?" Lyle asked, intrigued.

"You wouldn't believe me if I told you," she whispered dramatically and fixed him with a somber look. She ignored Justin's unsuccessful attempt to keep from laughing. "I am the third in my line and only I have succeeded where the others failed. Two brave heroes fell before me and became their thralls."

"Oh, well done," Justin muttered. "But, uh…don't you two think we should look at the arena?"

"Right." They snapped to attention.

The battlefield looked like no landscape Tina had ever seen. She had expected there to be barriers of some kind, all on the golden rock. Instead, magic—it could only be magic—had conjured a strange, alien landscape. Tumbled boulders were piled between stands of trees with gray bark and brilliant leaves that rustled like crystals.

She scanned the area with a small frown. "What's that?" To one side of them, a few boulders away, was one that looked subtly different. "Is that one of the supply caches? It is!" Now that she studied it more closely, she could see the little door that would open and reveal the treasure inside.

"Good work!" Justin grinned at her. "Let's get some weapons." As one of the conditions of the skirmishes, contestants could bring their own armor, minus any enchantments, but all weapons would be found inside the arena. One of the trials each team would face would be to find a cache, arm themselves, and base their fighting style on what they found.

A magical border glowed around them and the whole stadium counted down together. Despite her reservations, Tina's anticipation level increased. She'd always been the one who tried to get out of presenting and had even skipped school on days she was supposed to have recitals, much to her parents' annoyance.

This, however, was something entirely different. Her blood began to pump with unexpected vigor and she grinned as she settled into a runners' crouch.

When the horn sounded to start the match, she raced forward with her two teammates. She was light on her feet and always had been, and she was able to hurdle the boulder-strewn terrain with only one slip. Lyle caught her, she did the same for him, and they both consequently reached the cache a few steps behind Justin, who grinned smugly.

He pressed the glowing rune on the side of the false boulder, and it sprang open to display a selection of daggers.

All daggers.

"Well, good for me," Tina said, her smile broad. She also took a few vials of liquid. "What are these?"

"They give yer weapon flames—or wind powers, or water." The dwarf looked suspiciously at her. "Aren't ye a legendary warrior?"

"Where I come from," she said, "we don't use hacks like this." She picked up a blue vial. "I have to say, though, I'm interested to see what the power of water will do with daggers." She opened the vial and dipped one of the blades into it.

"Well..." Justin made sample passes with his chosen weapons. "It looks like I'll have to fight at close range. I tell you, I'll be pissed if the other teams have bows and arrows."

"Nah," she pointed out cheerfully. "If they do, you simply need to wait for them to run out of arrows."

"Very true." He held a hand out, concentrated for a moment, and blew out an annoyed breath. "No magic here. Phooey."

"Less yappin', more movin'," Lyle told them shortly. He had dipped his blades into a bottle of black liquid that Tina found disturbing. "Or haven't ye noticed that we're attractin' attention?" He nodded his head to the area of the arena behind them.

She turned to look and gulped reflexively. The other team now headed directly toward them.

In fact, she realized in sudden alarm, both of them did.

"Quick," she said to Justin. "Left or right?"

He studied their two sets of opponents quickly. "Right," he said definitively. "When we get close, follow Lyle. You'll know what I mean when it happens."

Tina nodded and the three of them leapt into action. The cache had vanished into thin air as soon as the treasures were removed, and they bounded away over rocks to meet their chosen opponents.

The three were all tall and lean, unused to the terrain but clearly warriors. Two of them could only have been brothers as they had the same eyes and tousled, dark-brown hair. The third had longer hair with a tinge of red tied in a braid, and he hung back behind the other two.

Tina decided to deal with him. He had the look of someone who waited for his buddies to start the barfight, then snuck up on you with a kidney punch once you were focused on someone else.

"Sephith's Bane is heading for combat with Quartzfire!" the Master of Ceremonies boomed. "The battle is joined immediately, a good showing from our newest team here at the Insea Arena."

She tuned the voice out and made herself focus only on their opponents. They scrutinized her openly, clearly interested to see what a short, fairly scrawny woman would bring to the match.

It'll be a surprise to you and me both, she thought and shook her head. They were close, only a few seconds away from one another, and her heart pounded. "Uh, Justin—"

Her sentence remained unfinished.

"Stoooooooooout!" Lyle yelled and increased his speed dramatically. He drew both daggers, which burst into black flames, and vaulted upward in a flash of silver and purplish-black.

He took both the brothers by surprise.

Idiots. They'd had three people advancing toward them for the express purpose of combat. What did they think would happen? Tina didn't stop to think, however. She dropped back, circled behind Justin, and noticed a path that dipped down and to the side. As her friend followed Lyle with a battle cry of his own, she lingered in her position for a moment.

As she suspected, the redhead had settled into a crouch and waited to see who would slip up and create an opening first. He was armed with a sword, which gave her pause, but there was nothing she could do about it.

She could fight him now on her terms, or she could fight later on his. And, of course, they had another team incoming.

He wasn't stupid and he hadn't reached the Finals of Season three by being unobservant. When he heard her circle behind him, his gaze zeroed in on her in a flash.

"What's up, fucker?" Tina asked. She was a little surprised at the words as it wasn't what she'd have said if she'd thought first, but they were what they were.

Amusingly, he didn't seem to know how to interpret the slang and his moment of confusion gave her time to attack. She drew her blades as she moved, threw them out to the sides to counterbalance herself, and found out abruptly exactly what it meant to have a water charm on a dagger.

The blades pulled away from her and followed the momentum of a wave before it swept back.

"Ohhhh," Tina whispered. "Oh, motherfucker, you are in so much trouble."

Without giving herself time to consider the possible outcome, she threw the blades straight up.

They yanked her along with a smooth force and allowed her to pick both feet up and punch them forward. The redhead, still trying to gauge her talents, began to raise the sword but the attempted defense was too late. She had already bowled him over and tumbled away by the time he held it in front of him. Of course, by then, he was flat on his back.

She was fairly sure she bounced to a stop. "Ow, ow, ow, fuck."

With no time to think about possible injuries, she rolled to her feet, imagined the tidepools and eddies at Bolinas Beach, and allowed her thoughts to guide her movements. She'd never fought with daggers but she'd surfed storm swells. As a result, she knew the pound and momentum of water and the sheer liquid force of it.

Once or twice, she came close to a lethal blow. Redhead McGankpants—as she had nicknamed him in her head—had a longer reach with his weapon and a wave, of course, didn't fear a sword. A blade like that would pass through water without damage in the way it wouldn't with a human head, for instance.

Things improved, however, when she let her blades be the wave. She and her adversary danced across the boulders, his gaze focused entirely on her and hers on him. Justin and Lyle could be seen moving out of the corner of her eyes, but she heard no shouts of alarm or warning.

This one was hers.

He drove forward in a sudden rush, his mouth compressed into a thin line. From what she could tell, he hated it more and more every time he stumbled or one of his blows failed to land.

Now, instead of slashing down or sideways, he went into a heavy lunge and stabbed directly at her.

Tina laughed. She brought her hands together and raised them so the blades crossed and caught his. The sword twisted and spun out of his hands, the two waves of her daggers collided and swirled, and she landed hard on his chest with her blades against either side of his neck.

Pure hatred burned in his eyes as he held his hands up in surrender. His form froze, encased in magic. He had surrendered and so was out.

Tina stood and took a few steps back. Her chest heaved. She didn't know quite what to do now and she was so tired she couldn't hear the stadium.

It took a few moments for her to realize the crowd had gone silent.

She looked around. Justin and Lyle were seated on boulders, kicking their legs. Around them, each of their opponents lay frozen. Some had clearly suffered wounds, although the magic seemed to protect them against death.

"The other team reached us while you were still fighting," Justin called, "so we took care of them."

"An' ye," Lyle added in appreciation, "put on quite a show, missy!"

With a long, slow breath, she looked at the waiting crowd. A grin crept across her face and she stabbed both daggers into the sky. The spectators erupted into applause.

"Sephith's Bane wins the match!" the Master of Ceremonies shouted. "With, I must say, the best one-on-one match we've seen in quite some time. Insea, give a cheer for the champions of Match One."

He hardly needed to tell them. The audience stamped and whistled as they cheered.

"There," Justin said and hurried forward to clap her on the back. "Tina Castro, legendary warrior."

Tina laughed. The adrenaline made her shaky, but she already wanted another hit. "When can we go again?"

"That's what I like to hear," Lyle said in satisfaction. "And the answer, I'll have you know, is after a beer."

"That's what I like to hear," she told him and clanged her blade against his. The three of them moved to the dais at the end of the arena. Nearby, medics rushed to attend to the various members of other teams.

"Are you okay?" Justin asked her. "You're limping.

She panted slightly. "Yeah. Yeah, I feel great. There's slight chafing, though."

"You said, I remind you, that you wanted to choose based on aesthetics," the AI told her.

"Yeah, yeah," she muttered. "I'll go find a healer. In a city full of warriors in leather, someone must have an anti-chafing balm."

Zaara lingered in the shadow of a column and watched the winning team approach the dais. She had maintained this trance for longer than she should have and could feel her energy flagging, but she had not been able to resist the desire to see her friends.

It hadn't taken long for Justin and Lyle to find someone who fit with their team, and she clearly already had an easy rapport with both of them—as well as a fighting style Zaara had never seen in her life. She'd cheered along with the spectators in the stadium, even though she knew the other would never hear her.

There was a strange poetry to the way she moved, something natural and powerful. She wondered what it was but accepted that, of course, she would never have a chance to ask.

The team walked to the platform, where the Master of Ceremonies stood in his deep-blue robes, his arms spread. Before him were two golden bowls, one piled with coins and the other with swirling blue power—an illusion, she could see. There was nothing truly there. She narrowed her eyes and leaned closer.

"A hearty hello to our first champions!" the official cried. "Sephith's Bane is the first to choose from our new prizes. Would you like to see them?"

The crowd roared. Huge images of the two bowls flashed above them.

"Should the team desire riches, they shall have them. In the first bowl, there is a hundred gold pieces for each member of the team!"

Zaara's jaw dropped. As a throwaway prize, it was ludicrously big. The grand prize, of course, was always worth thousands—but this was only a skirmish. What else could match that gift?

"In the second bowl, however…" The Master of Ceremonies beamed broadly. "Is perhaps a greater treasure—an advantage for the winners' next match. Although neither they nor their opponents shall know what that advantage will be, I assure you it is worth having."

Zaara leaned back with an intrigued quirk to one eyebrow. An advantage. That was clever. This was an intriguing set of skirmishes. She knew which Justin would have chosen once and she now waited to see what he would do.

He didn't disappoint her. A close-headed conference with his compatriots resulted in nods, and he turned to the official with a smile.

"We choose the advantage," he called and raised a fist into the air. His voice was amplified as well. "Although the best advantage would be to have this crowd cheer us on again."

"Kiss-ass," she muttered but smiled broadly. He seemed to realize how much a crowd's favor could mean. Having ten thousand people screaming your name tended to bring confidence that nothing else could match—and certain high-profile patrons might come out of the woodwork for favorites.

Her attention, however, was caught by the Master of Ceremonies. To her surprise, when he turned away from the team, she realized how false his smile was. He was sweating and rivulets trickled into the collar of his robes, and he looked pale.

To her keen study, he didn't look like someone who basked in the glow of a successful plan but like someone who was still on the edge of failure.

The stadium began to flicker in her vision, and Zaara gritted her teeth as she brought all her energy to bear on the trance. If there was danger, she had to know about it. Justin and Lyle, as well as their new friend, might be at risk somehow.

While the crowd was focused on the winning team—who now did a victory lap around the edge of the arena—she ran through the maze of staircases and corridors and tried to find the Master of Ceremonies. She almost lost him, especially with her vision flickering, but eventually she caught sight of his robes swishing out of sight. Hastily, she checked for anyone watching and raced after him.

He didn't go far, thankfully, but into a room full of couches and refreshments nearby. That kind of careless luxury still boggled her mind, even after seeing Sephith's tower and the king's treasure rooms. The couches had gilt trim, the wine that stood freely available was better than any she'd have in her lifetime, and sugared pastries were going stale.

Her mouth watered. Next time, she would have Kural teach her how to teleport and she knew exactly where she'd come first.

On the plus side, focusing on those pastries had kept her trance strong.

The Master of Ceremonies stripped his outer robe off and dropped onto one of the couches. A clerk in plain black came to pour him wine.

"It sounds like an incredible success," the attendant said with a smile.

The official did not return the smile. He drank all the wine in a few long swallows and held out his glass again. "They like it, but what if the other teams don't stay?"

"Quartzfire and the Twins will make a good final match," the clerk said soothingly.

"Numbers have fallen." He put his head in his hands. "Adventurers are leaving. A spectacle means nothing if we aren't preparing."

That must be it, Zaara realized. They needed people there who were learning to fight. But why?

Her vision began to fade. She tried to hold it but exhaustion crept in and before she could counter it, the world tilted crazily and transformed into her bedroom. While she managed to get the scrying orb out of her pocket and onto her desk, she couldn't finish the spell to contact Kural before she slid onto the floor.

"Fuck," she said succinctly. "Well…as long as I'm lying down…"

She woke sometime later to her mentor's voice emanating from the orb. "Zaara?"

"I'm here," she said from the floor with as much dignity as she could muster. "I'm lying down."

"Not on your bed."

"No." She did not feel the need to explain at this juncture.

"Uh…huh." He cleared his throat. "So, did you find it?"

"Yes." Zaara wanted to sit but was unable to. A little irritated, she settled for waving a thumbs-up in what she hoped was his line of sight. "It's there—and I found something out about the Master of Ceremonies."

"You stayed for longer than you should have, didn't you?" Kural sounded amused. "And that's why you're so exhausted."

"Oh, like you never overextended yourself as an apprentice." She knew him. Even as a traveling magician, he'd been inclined to being reckless and constantly experimented with things.

"All the time." He laughed. "It's how we weed out the dedicated. People who always stay within guidelines and never overexert themselves usually don't have enough interest to complete the training."

"Really?" It was intriguing. "That's good to know. Anyway, the Master of Ceremonies is quite scared. One team has been winning consistently and now, other teams don't want to participate. He's started skirmish events as a way to encourage more people to compete again. I heard him say something about how it didn't matter how much of a spectacle it was if they weren't preparing, but he didn't say for what."

"Presumably, the person he spoke to already knew." Kural was silent, and she was fairly sure he chewed on his lip. "That's interesting. It gives me something to work with as well. I will persuade the Master of Ceremonies to offer the key as one of the potential prizes. Meanwhile, you take care to recover. If you can find any citrus fruit, that will help. Limes are best."

"I've only had an orange once," Zaara croaked. "They don't grow here, you know."

"Hmm. I'll see what I can do. With regard to the sorceress, I haven't heard from her—"

"She came to see me," she said and waved her arm again in the direction of the scrying orb. "I met her. It's Justin's mother!"

"The death sorceress?" He sounded highly skeptical.

"Yes. I've seen her use her power before. It was at the bandit hideout."

"That was her I felt two weeks ago?" He sounded incredulous. "Very well, then. If she found you, well enough. I'll let you rest, but before you do…hang on a moment…"

Several limes dropped out of midair and onto her stomach.

"Oof!"

"Sorry, sorry. I had to guess where you were. Eat all of those before you go to sleep. They're bitter but it will be worth it. Then get some sleep. Our next lesson will be in how to grow a lime tree in your room because I sense you'll need one."

CHAPTER TEN

The winners of the match, it turned out, were given seating in a special reserved area of the stadium near the Master of Ceremonies. Refreshments were served, including overly sweet pastries that reminded Justin of baklava and some of the best wine he'd ever had.

Lyle, disgusted, went off to find beer while the other two stayed behind to watch the next match.

"So, who did we beat?" she asked as she licked sugar off her fingers.

"The one you fought was a member of Quartzfire," he told her. "He's a one-on-one champion…kind of. You saw how he tried to hang back while the other two charged so he could pick people off one by one."

"If he relies entirely on the element of surprise, he can't be shocked when it backfires," she said with a shrug.

"Well, he's good," Justin replied. "I listened to some of the servants talking, see. The thing is, he's never come up against someone who fought like you did."

"That was, er…" Tina looked embarrassed. "I probably didn't do things right."

"I couldn't watch the whole time," he said thoughtfully, "but it looked like you used your advantages and learned from your mistakes. Isn't that doing things right?"

"Justin." She sounded genuinely frustrated now. "You know what I'm trying to say. We have to win the tournament—the whole tournament—to get you the key so you can wake up. And it hangs on whether or not I can fight well enough to beat the champions who have won consecutively for six seasons straight. How will we do that?"

He decided not to tell her that he hadn't realized what she'd tried to say.

Now that he understood, he had to admit it was a valid point. He had defeated Sephith with Lyle and Zaara, but both had been trained in fighting for years. His advantage had been that he'd played video games for as long as he could remember, and it had helped that Sephith clearly wasn't prepared for three people to attack him at once.

"I'm not worried," he said. "I'm serious. One of the things I liked about you when we first met was that you were brave about trying things. You apply that to your fighting and you're scrappy—you don't let a little pain hold you back."

"What if…" Tina closed her eyes. "What if we fail and—"

"Tina, it's a game. If we fail and we don't get the key I'm looking for this way, the people running the game will find another way to get it to me."

"Oh." She looked faintly embarrassed now. "Right. I…forgot. It's hard to remember you're in a game when everything around you is so realistic." Her gaze strayed over his shoulder.

"What is it?" Justin turned to look and saw a woman in the stands look away from them hastily.

"She's watched us for a while," she told him.

"We just won the first skirmish against two champion teams," he pointed out.

"Ohhhh. I'm not all on my game today mentally, am I?"

"You also drank two glasses of wine." He grinned at her. "However, the next match is about to start so I need you to—*oh.*" In the air above the stadium, the three team names had come up and one of them was the Twins. He elbowed her in the side and made her snort wine up her nose. "Focus, Castro. We're about to see the Twins in action. This is where we plan our strategy against them."

"Mmf." Tina blew her nose into a handkerchief and looked at the cloth in disgust. "Don't snort wine and baklava up your nose at the same time. That is nasty. Okay, I'll try to focus."

The center of the arena faded into black fog, only to clear a moment later to reveal a desert scene of rolling dunes. Boulders and trees studded the area, and a magical glow surrounded nine caches before it vanished. The one nearest to each team was largest and the next two were smaller.

"Were there three per team?" she asked. "I guess we'll know for next time."

Justin nodded. The Master of Ceremonies announced the three teams to the sound of cheers and boos. The Twins, unsurprisingly, elicited the most emotion from the crowd. They had a large share of passionate fans and as many who—either as failed contestants or their disappointed fans—seemed to hate them.

The official saved them for last, of course, and they came up closest to the winners' viewing section. Justin and Tina leaned forward for a better look, and out of the corner of his eye, he caught the woman watching them again. She was older than he'd first thought with gray hair, and she gave him a smile this time. He smiled in response and waved, hoping he looked enough like a gracious winner.

She didn't seem overawed, he realized.

The match started, however, and he had to direct his attention to the arena. The twins had clearly chosen their battle plan before they came up because they surged in the same direction without consulting one another and bounded over the dunes.

The sand was difficult to run on but it didn't slow their headlong rush much.

What was interesting, however, was that they avoided the first cache in their singlemindedness. They sprinted to the second, yanked it open, and held a brief exchange to decide who got what. A bow and arrows and two potions, together with their deliberations, were displayed on large screens above the stadium. Justin didn't recall those from his match and guessed that they weren't visible to the contestants.

The woman—Callie, he recalled, having heard their names somewhere along the way— took the bow and arrows, along with a water potion, and her teammate Dexi chose the same black-purple potion Lyle had used and spread it directly onto his hands. He seemed to be in pain, but it didn't do any immediate or visible damage.

"Bets they're not as well armed as the other teams?" Tina asked.

"Absolutely," he said in an undertone. He leaned back as the Twins began to run again. They circled toward the middle, a dangerous strategy but one that might win them the element of surprise.

"It's reckless," she pointed out with a note of confusion.

"Not entirely." He had listened to many stories from his grandfathers, both of whom had served in the armed forces. "It's better to make a decision and stay in motion early, even without all the information, than it is to be frozen while you wait for the rest of the information to come in."

"Really?" After a moment, she nodded. "Okay, yeah. I suppose that's what I did in our match, didn't I?"

"Exactly. If you'd waited, we would have fought two teams at once while Quartzfire's assassin picked us off one by one." He gave her a fist bump. "So, thanks."

She returned the gesture. "Thank you. Don't forget you guys

took on the other team all on your own. Oh, look—they're getting close."

The Twins had made a plan that was as sneaky as it was quick. They had circled in a particular way and very obviously chose to approach behind another team. Now, they attacked with absolute ruthlessness. Dexi circled again while Callie fired her bow to drive the other two toward him. His strikes were brutally quick. He struck one contestant across the face with such force that the magical barrier came up at once.

The second panicked and fell prey to another arrow.

Dexi and Callie immediately pushed into motion. What they hadn't seen, however, was that the third team had found and looted two Grade A caches by this point.

"Ohhh, I wanna see them lose," Tina said.

"Hell yeah," Justin agreed.

They were on the edge of their seat and mutual anticipation hung in the air between them.

Unfortunately, they were disappointed. Callie and Dexi separated quickly and she circled left while he moved right. They advanced in a pincer movement and began to close. When she first sighted the other team, she gave a piercing whistle like a hawk's call and began to fire.

Cannily, she altered her positions slightly between each arrow to make it look like both of the Twins were behind the dune.

The other team pushed in too deep and hadn't realized what was happening. Their strategy—a modified leapfrog—used the rush technique to push closer and closer to her. They thought that if they only got into range, the Twins would be powerless against them.

Two of the three were felled by Dexi before they even saw him. The third must have caught something out of the corner of his eye because he turned with a gasp and a snarl. Armed with a sword, he charged his attacker but fell to an arrow.

Half the stadium sank into sulky silence while the other half erupted into cheers.

"Damn." Tina shook her head and gave a golf clap. "I don't want to admit it, but they outplayed them." She raised an eyebrow at her teammate. "And yet…"

"They make snap decisions and commit entirely," Justin said and immediately caught her train of thought. "They miss caches and are aggressive. A team that lays traps for them might make them sign their own death warrants—figuratively, of course."

"That's unfortunate," she said. "They're such jerks." She saw his look and waved her hands dismissively. "Don't you look at me like that. They aren't real. It's okay to wish they would go away."

"I suppose there's that." He grinned. "Hey, should we get a meal? I, for one, don't still want to be here when the Twins come for their refreshments."

"Good call." She stood and stretched. "Let's find Lyle and see what he thinks. Okay, I know what he thinks—he'll simply charge straight in. But we might as well talk about doing something different."

He laughed and followed her. In all honesty, he hadn't expected his two friends to get along so well but he was glad they did. He still missed Zaara, though. Sometimes, he thought of the jokes she would make or the disgusted way she would have looked at the Twins.

It was different to have Tina there but in a way he couldn't describe. He shook his head and followed as he darted a glance to where the woman who had watched them had been seated. She was gone now.

Justin frowned and followed Tina into the darkness of the stadium tunnels.

The pod cover was removed and Anna Price opened her eyes as Jacob and Dr. DuBois removed her sensor pads. They helped her sit and the young engineer waited, clearly nervous about her assessment.

"It was surprisingly immersive," she told him. "I have to say, I enjoyed myself immensely. It was rather like I imagine the colosseum of Rome—well, in some ways."

"It still annoys me that we couldn't sell them," he told her. "As a game, I mean, because it is fun, isn't it? It's super fun. And there's so much more to the world."

"Now, tell me how the procedural generation works," Price told him. She stood and slipped her shoes on. "Wherever players are present, the game prioritizes procedural generation and banks some of it for recall and so on, yes?"

"Yes." To her surprise, he now looked nervous. "There have to be priorities, you see. Otherwise, it would be too much processing power."

This was an incredibly mundane point and one he should have expected her to understand from her previous comment. That, combined with his nerves, meant he was hiding something.

Anna considered this for a split-second. She was used to people hiding things from her. The end purpose of many of her company's contracts was not always clear, which led to obtuse requests from Defense Department officials. She was accustomed to arguing for more information, which she often needed in order to create the deliverables.

What, however, would Jacob be hiding?

She had an advantage over him and decided to use it. Rather than continue, she smiled as though she had not seen the look on his face. "Well, you're doing incredible work and I have to say, DuBois's hunch about Justin's friend seems to be accurate. They're clearly bonding. Now, as much as I've enjoyed this, I do have to return to my office. Thank you all for indulging me."

The look of relief on the young engineer's face was all the confirmation she needed.

He was definitely hiding something. The question, however, was what he could be hiding when the experiment was indisputably going well.

Price intended to find out.

The bells in Insea's gorgeous goldstone spire tolled midnight.

Unnoticed, Kural shadow-walked through the abandoned arena. The inner corridors and contestants' chambers were locked and guarded, but the rest of it was open to the public. A few citizens slept on the long, stone benches and others sat in huddles and conversed. Dissidents, perhaps? Amateur philosophers?

The wizard felt a pang. It had been a long time since he was a young apprentice. He had been in Junor, of course, beyond the strait, but cities tended to have the same rhythms to them. The world had seemed so open to him when he was young.

He didn't worry that Zaara would fail as a wizard, not at all. She had the talent and determination in spades. He suspected, also, that it would suit her better to stay in one place and cultivate it rather than adventure the world over. She had never been suited to life as a wanderer and had simply been stifled by her parents' expectations.

But being a wizard was a bargain no one anticipated when they made it. To live in the world so long was to grow apart from it. Once you saw the same patterns play out time and again, you began to view them all differently. A human mind behaved differently at four hundred years old than it did at twenty—or even eighty, for that matter.

For one thing, he had not expected how tired he would sometimes be of himself.

Ah, well. He quickened his pace as he reached the far side of the arena from the Master of Ceremonies' post.

The door was in Insea somewhere, and the more he read, the more sure he was that it was there in the arena, itself. He couldn't explain the certainty, though. Doors between worlds tended to be remote and well-guarded. It was bizarre that one would be there in the most well-traveled venue in the city.

With his luck, it would be in the middle of one of the tiers and marked with a hidden rune. Kural rolled his eyes. He had been all around the outside of the arena and had found nothing. Then, he had checked the entire structure for the telltale signs of hidden dwarven doors and again, had found nothing. By rights, he should have given up and gone home.

However, after four hundred years, one began to learn to follow hunches—and one's hunches got stronger and better.

He darted an annoyed look at the podium and stopped, suddenly thoughtful. It extended into the arena somewhat, and the front of it was carved in a beautiful elven pattern. It was remarkable, the wizard thought as his heart rate quickened, how much that large, rectangular panel looked like an out-of-scale door.

For a brief moment, he considered hurdling the railing to sprint across the arena. No one would stop him but he would be incredibly noteworthy—as would be the fact that his footsteps didn't make little puffs of dust. He rounded the walkway at a brisk pace instead and took the time to try to recall elven symbology.

Elves were relentless when it came to organization, which could be hellish when trying to get them to do anything spontaneous but was helpful for archeologists. If the front of the podium were the door, he would see trees on either side and the rune *trulya*, which brought protection to wayfarers.

Kural moved closer and waited for the clouds above to drift and let the moon shine through.

His instincts seemed accurate. Silver light streamed down and illuminated something.

He wasn't sure what, though, and leaned forward. Those were dwarven runes, were they not? After a hasty study of the area, he hopped the fence when no one was looking and crept closer.

Yes. The runes spoke of the edge of the mountain and the edge of the forest, the gate between the sea and the land, the desert and the oasis. They were structured to evoke trees—in a very angular, dwarven way, of course. And at the center, girded by a circle around a triangular keyhole, was the dwarven prayer for the wayfarer.

The wizard exhaled slowly with a smile. The door was there.

And he now knew how he would persuade the Master of Ceremonies.

CHAPTER ELEVEN

Amber was the first one into the office the next morning. When the door opened shortly after, she looked up to call a greeting which died on her lips when she saw who it was.

"Good morning," Anna Price said pleasantly as if she hadn't committed a faux pas. "I'm glad I caught you."

"Oh?" She took a bite of toast with the distinct feeling of someone trying to enjoy a last meal and glanced at her desk. With nothing to use as an excuse to avoid the encounter, she stood and forced a smile. "What can I do for you, Ms. Price?"

"First of all, sit and finish your breakfast." The woman grasped Jacob's office chair and wheeled it to the desk. "We'll have to talk about expectations, by the way. I'm a notorious workaholic, but I keep very strict guidelines for my employees—nothing over forty-five hours per week in the office."

"I've, uh…" Amber tried to calculate in her head.

"Last week, you spent a little over seventy hours in the office," her boss told her. "I always like to work with exact numbers. I understand there's a certain energy when a project is beginning and that you all needed to bootstrap the operation when you were on your own, but I prefer my employees—especially those in creative areas— to avoid burning out."

"Uh-huh." She could sense a trap closing.

"However, right now, I wanted to go over some of the financials."

"Oh." Thankful for something practical to do, she began to bring the spreadsheets up, then stopped. "Is there a specific problem you want to address?"

Price merely raised an eyebrow.

She sighed. "Look, I'm not an accountant. I did read up on standard practices and I left a ton of notes, but I'll be honest, I wouldn't be surprised if I classified something incorrectly. Whatever your accounting team has asked about, I'd be happy to explain and buy them a pizza."

"A…pizza?" The woman looked confused for the first time since she had met her.

"Oh, sorry." Amber wanted to sink through the floor. "It's stupid. Whenever one of us on the team broke something or whatever, we'd bring in pizza as an apology. I probably don't need to do that here."

"Ah." Her boss leaned back in her chair with an amused smile. "No, but I'm sure they'll appreciate the gesture. I know our software team does the same with donuts, so I wouldn't be surprised to find out accounting has a similar practice. Why don't you take me through what you handed over? I wouldn't normally be able to digest everything but your company is smaller than most of the ones I acquire."

The truth was, although she still felt it was right to have Jacob make the final decision about the acquisition—he was the one facing jail time, after all—she was a little uncomfortable. She swallowed in an effort to move past that and regain a businesslike demeanor.

Thankfully, she was able to put that aside as she took Price through the financials and pointed out initial investments and

Kickstarter funds, outstanding rewards and loans, and the list of equipment with dates of acquisition.

"Well," Price said when she had finished. "I have to say, the accountants might make some tweaks but I found that to be very straightforward."

"That's what I was afraid of," Amber said glumly. "If a non-accountant can understand, it's not good accounting."

The woman was startled into a laugh. She took a sip from a mug that had the Diatek logo emblazoned on the side. "Nick mentioned you had a good sense of humor. It's good to see it." She put the cup down and asked delicately, "Would it be accurate to say that I make you uncomfortable?"

She flushed. *Yes,* she wanted to say. *You're everything I want to be when I grow up.* Price was effortlessly elegant and clearly more invested in her work than her appearance, but still knocked both out of the park. She seemed to know exactly where she wanted her effort to go at any given point in time and never worked with competing priorities.

When she explained that, her boss responded with a rueful smile and for the first time, revealed a hint of how she had been as a younger woman.

"I would much rather," she said honestly, "wear my second-hand t-shirts and try to remember whether or not I brought my lunch. Often, the greatest accomplishments in life come from the greatest pain. I know how many families my work will save but selfishly, I would far prefer never to have undertaken it."

Amber swallowed hard.

"I can't tell you that I've picked the best path," Price told her honestly. "There are many uses I can think of for the amount of money I've made. I don't know that this is the one that will do the most good. I think that's the secret to success, Amber. You'll never know if you did the right thing, but if you aim in roughly the right direction and go with your talents, I like to think you can honestly let go of any guilt."

She nodded. "I…didn't mean to pry."

"I know," the woman said lightly. She looked at her in a quietly searching way. "Do you have any worries still?"

Amber considered the question. "Well, this feels a little frivolous, but—I was proud of what we'd accomplished even before we found this use for it. Part of me is worried that if Justin doesn't recover, you'll drop us and that either way, the senator will forget about us."

"Ah," Anna said. She sighed. "I know that feeling. Amber, I will make you a promise. If ever our interests diverge and I cut PIVOT loose, I will leave the company in better shape than when I found it."

"That's a fairly low bar," she pointed out.

Price laughed. "No one will be in legal trouble and you will be in the black."

"That's more reassuring. We weren't doing too well."

The admission met with a calm smile. "If you'll excuse me, I really should speak to Dr. DuBois. But, Amber, I appreciate your time—and your candor."

"Of course," she said automatically. She nodded and turned to her breakfast, which was why she missed the look on her boss' face.

It was one of confusion.

Amber had been Anna Price's first guess for a weak link. It wasn't that the woman was incompetent—in fact, it was the opposite. Her relentless focus on facts made her far more anxious than her two partners, especially where things such as funding or legalities were concerned.

After speaking to her, she was sure that whatever problem Jacob was hiding, she didn't know about it.

That, in itself, was odd. The PIVOT team seemed close-knit.

At least, she thought, there wasn't a lurking legal or financial issue waiting to overwhelm the company.

Her lack of success thus far merely made her more wary when she approached DuBois.

At her insistence, he no longer ate popcorn in the laboratory. Instead, he propped the bags on his desk and looked longingly at them from time to time. When he saw her approaching, he beckoned her over excitedly.

"The data we've received from non-comatose patients is really expanding our parameters," he told her. "I've studied comatose brains for decades, of course, but this is the first time I've had the chance to test the differences between comatose and conscious brains undergoing the same stimulus."

He also, she noted, did not behave as if something was wrong. The doctor had been her other choice of a weak link, simply because he tended to be incredibly straightforward. If something was wrong, he was likely to tell her about it without realizing it.

She pored over the data for a few moments. He was correct that it was extraordinary. She could see the data from Justin's viewing of the arena trial matched hers and Tina's.

"It was good to see him in the game," she told him. "I didn't speak to him but he had a fine conversation with Tina. He seems to have made great strides. I admit, I was cautious."

"It's good to be cautious with this," DuBois agreed. "Recovery from head trauma can be so varied. It will be difficult to see the long-term patterns until we have more data. I don't think it's overstating the case to say that we lucked out with Justin. His brain was well-adapted to games already and he was therefore able to come on board very quickly."

There was no hint of evasiveness in him, goddammit. Price seriously considered, for a moment, locking Jacob in a room until he admitted what was going on.

She would rather find out about it on her own, however. Thoughtful, she tapped her fingers against her arm.

"Have you run into any limitations of the game format?" How many ways could she come up with to ask about this? Would they always say everything was fine?

"No," the doctor said promptly. "Well…Mrs. Williams going in wasn't as successful as we thought, but as you noted, Tina is doing well. Finding the general principle of when there should be external communication and when there shouldn't be will likely be quite difficult."

"Mmm." Jacob came into the lab and she glanced at him. He gave her a tight smile and went to wash his hands and put a lab coat on. *In a few minutes,* she thought, *you and I will have a chat, Mr. Zachary.*

"I didn't expect the game to be immersive enough," DuBois said. "My original concept was a few simple puzzles but I was lost on how to deliver them. I hadn't thought of it then, but the brain does not like to accept places that do not follow the rules of physics, for instance. I worried that the world would be so far from reality that it would be impossible. But the AI has…" He broke off suddenly. "Well, as you can see, the world is developing nicely."

Price had been focused on the papers in front of her when she heard the break in his voice and looked at him quickly. "Jacob mentioned that the world is procedurally generated."

"Yes," he said but looked uncertain now. "But…uh, that's not exactly my area of expertise."

The AI. There was no way he wasn't even a little curious about the AI. Whenever he spoke about anything, he either gave facts or directed his audience to someone else with the facts. Now, he was deflecting.

"It's not my area, either," she said with a smile. "I'm glad your data collection is going well. Come find me if you need anything else."

She approached Jacob with the feeling of stalking prey. "Mr. Zachary—a moment?"

"Yes?" He turned to face her. His shoulders were stiff, but she could see them creeping upward to his neck.

"I wondered if I could speak to you about naming this laboratory," Price told him. "It was never officially named, you see, and I remembered you mentioning some of your personal impetus for this project. I wondered if we could name it the Elizabeth Keegan Medical Facility in memory of your grandmother."

His jaw dropped. "Ms. Price—ma'am—I…yes, that would be appreciated. It would be an honor. My parents would be thrilled to hear it."

Whatever else he was lying about, this was not part of it. She gave him a small smile. "I'll see it done. Now, remind me—if I were to go into the game again, should I do so in close proximity to Justin or should I choose somewhere else? What would cause the least excess server load for the algorithms? I don't want to overwhelm the AI and give it too much to…dream up."

The flash of panic in his eyes was unmistakable and something clenched in the pit of her stomach that could be either opportunity or misgiving. Her mind raced ahead as he stammered a reply, and she extricated herself from the lab soon after.

In her office, she sat and stared blankly out the window. She saw none of the other buildings or the reflections on the glass.

A sentient AI. She wanted to laugh but she also wanted to cry.

If she were looking for something to cement her legacy—something that would bring untold billions to Diatek and fund as much research as she could ever need—this was it.

But she had one client, and as much as she spoke to Amber and Nick about making her peace with what she did, she wasn't ready to see how a military organization would use AI. She clenched her hands and looked at the desk. It was possible they had already made the same leap, wasn't it?

Unfortunately, she knew it wasn't. They'd sniffed around for years and offered century-long contracts for any company that could give them AI.

Price wasn't exactly superstitious. She also wasn't prone to melodrama and honestly, had no time for it. But one thing she knew for certain was that sentient programs raised all kinds of ethical questions that were, quite frankly, beyond her—together with many possibilities that didn't exactly end well for humanity.

She doubted Jacob had anything more than a hunch at this point. If he were truly worried, he would have found an excuse to take Justin out of the system. She trusted the PIVOT team implicitly when it came to their patient's safety.

Which meant she had time to think. Price nodded and proceeded to do the one thing that had become a critical priority. She had to make it absolutely impossible for any of PIVOT's servers to contact any of the others Diatek owned.

CHAPTER TWELVE

When Tad sent a message to Senator Snelling's office, he didn't expect the man to agree to meet with him.

He definitely didn't expect him to suggest a small, run-down diner as the venue either. When he arrived, bemused, Snelling was in the process of demolishing an improbably large plate of pancakes with gusto.

"I hope you don't mind," the senator told him. "I went running before this and…" He waved to the steaming mug of coffee on the table. "I didn't want to order you anything else but I know I've seen you drinking coffee before."

"I didn't know, uh…"

"That I go running?" the man asked with a gesture at his potbelly. He laughed at his companion's expression. "Oh, come on. It's funny. I show up at the races and I weigh more than any three of the top ten put together. I can't give up pancakes, though."

"My kind of guy," he said before he could stop himself.

"Careful. We agreed on that one bill, now it's pancakes as well —where will it stop?" The man took a bite of bacon.

Tad ordered when the waitress stopped at the table and took

another sip of his coffee. "Well, it's funny you should mention that…"

"Oh?" Snelling leaned back in his seat. "I have to say, I never thought you had much of an interest in child cancer."

"What? Oh." He shook his head. "Ah…" He remembered in time that it was supposed to be a good public-relations move and decided not to proclaim loudly that he didn't care about it. After all, no parent could say the thought of child cancer didn't bring them out in a cold sweat. "My cousin's son had a scare a few years back. I saw the event was scheduled and dropped by. This isn't about that."

His companion blinked at him. "This should be good."

"Well…" He smiled at him. "You see, there's a little bill coming up to do with working research costs on different projects into treatment costs."

The man's face went stony. "And?" he asked dangerously.

"And," he continued pleasantly, "I'm almost certain it's a bill a certain CEO is trying to blackmail me into voting for."

Snelling put his fork down. "Wait…"

"Didn't you ever wonder how the news about Justin leaked?" Tad asked him.

"Oh, my God." Snelling looked thoughtful. "So, your vote on the last measure—they were angry with you about that?"

"It's a slightly longer story than that, but broadly speaking, yes. Let's simply say that Justin's accident gave them a lovely opening to exploit." He took a deep breath. "And, if we're honest…I've considered caving. More than I care to admit."

"What, you can't walk past people screaming that you're a horrible father and a child abuser without getting shaken?" The man rolled his eyes and shook his head. "Some of the things people think about us. It's difficult. It really is."

"I'm lucky Mary is as even-keeled as she is," he said and chose to omit her more bloodthirsty vows of revenge against Metcalfe.

"Their first attempt was doctored photos to show me having an affair."

"They get most people," the other man said thoughtfully. "You know, I've had to bump a few lobbyist meetings in the past two months and I think I might quietly cancel those."

"It's a good idea," Tad told him, his tone acerbic. "Anyway, here's the thing. They want me to vote for this bill and I don't want to vote for it, but I'll be damned if I let them set the terms. If I lose, it'll be on a better bill than that."

Snelling's eyes lit up. "You want to write your own bill."

"I have." Tad took the sample out of his folio and passed it to the other senator.

The man took it but didn't start reading. He raised an eyebrow. "So…if you've already written it, you don't need a collaborator."

"I need votes," he said bluntly. "And I don't have them in my party."

"Ahhhh." Snelling studied him. "So you're coming across the aisle, and offering…"

"The chance to vote for a bill you believe in," he said flatly. "No more, no less."

His companion shook his head. "Nope. I want a little more from you." He put the bill down and tapped it. "I promise you that I will read this and I will either agree with it and want to vote for it, or I will tell you what I do not like and what would get my vote. In return, I want you to do the same for any bills I put forward."

Tad, who had been about to explode in fury, uttered a rueful laugh. "Man, you had me going for a second there. Okay, I'll up the ante again."

The other senator laughed. "Bring it on."

"Every year, we meet up to renew that pledge," he said, "and have a beer—my choice of beer, Snelling—and tell each other what we really think of the other's voting history."

Snelling burst out laughing and nodded. "All right. If I agree with this, do you want me to pass it on?"

"Go for it."

"And keep it quiet?"

Tad sighed. "I…don't know. You know what? No. I'm not good at all that cloak and dagger shit. I talked to my party and they wouldn't sign on. If they want to get pissed now that I'm reaching across the aisle, well…how much worse can it get? I'm already informed I've torpedoed my chances of being re-elected."

"Here's a little piece of advice. Party whips always say that when you step out of line." His companion shrugged and remained silent until the waitress had set Tad's food down and left before he added, "But if this is anything like your thoughts on the last bill, you might have more support than you think. Virtually everyone knows someone who's had trouble paying for treatment. Most senators have people calling their office about it. Don't be surprised if you really do have the votes in your party. Now." He waved his fork. "Eat those pancakes before I do."

CHAPTER THIRTEEN

Justin shook his limbs out and tried to focus. With the countdown dinging above them in the arena, it was hard to focus on anything at all, but he constantly ran over the team's plan in his head. It had taken several beers and an exceedingly late night to fine-tune it, but in the two days since, they hadn't found any unexpected weaknesses.

Task one was to find the closest cache and defensible position.

Task two would split them up temporarily. Justin and Tina would hightail it to the cache, get the gear and weapons, and return to their "base" to join Lyle. If they saw a second cache, Justin would hurry to retrieve whatever it contained and Tina would continue to Lyle.

Task three would be when they made a more specific plan for their defense while they waited to see what the other teams did.

Over the past day and a half, Justin and the dwarf had tested Tina with various weapons. The young man had told Lyle the lie that he merely wanted to see the technique of the world's "champion." She'd acquitted herself so well during the first match that he saw no reason to come clean about her lack of training and history.

To his surprise, she did best not with daggers or fists—which he had assumed would be her forte—but with battle-axes. The same intuitive grasp of fluid dynamics that had made her fighting style so powerful worked even better with a large, heavy weapon.

Having her in leather armor wasn't the best complement to a battle-ax, but her character still didn't have the strength to cope with both plate armor and an ax. They had paid what they had to for the leatherworker's finest armor upgrades, and he had to admit that she looked good.

He kept trying not to stare, partially so as to not be rude and partially because he was genuinely afraid that she would kill him. During their date, he had seen that she was short and fairly lean, but she had covered much of her body with layers. The armor left far less to the imagination and highlighted…well, too many things he needed to not think about right now. His only priority at that moment was to focus on the match.

The Master of Ceremonies sang their praises as the lift began to rise smoothly. Light swelled and broke over them to the sounds of applause. There weren't many boos yet that he could hear—they hadn't had the time to attract many people who hated them.

"In the last match, two of our three teams took the cash prize," the Master of Ceremonies declared. "Sephith's Bane, however, opted for the advantage in this match. Do you want to hear what it is?"

"I want to see outside this magic cage," Tina muttered. They had come above ground level and could see the vague outlines of varied terrain around them, but nothing more.

He laughed as the crowd shouted approval.

"Sephith's Bane has been given…" The man paused for effect and the stadium went quiet. "A one-minute head-start."

The crowd yelled their approbation as the magical walls came down. Justin tried to tune them out as he turned quickly to scan the area.

It was a fantasy village of some kind set on rolling terrain with small fields and gardens and two houses. He noticed one two-story house nearby and a cache surprisingly close to it.

"House," he called.

"Agreed," Lyle responded a moment later.

"Likewise," Tina said. "Two caches, one to the left of the house, the other this way."

"That one first," Justin said. "Lyle, see you there."

He and Tina leapt off the platform and sprinted down the nearby hill.

The terrain, this time, wasn't quite as treacherous under their feet. It was even, he thought in amusement, somewhat pleasant to be there. He recalled any number of idyllic, pastoral scenes in the video games of his youth. During one particularly bad year, he had liked to sit on a rock in his favorite video game forest and fish as the sky faded from day to night and back again.

The smaller cache revealed a short sword and two fist weapons, as well as a purple health-and-magic potion, and one that read *stone skin* on the side in spiky script. He grimaced. While he liked the idea in video games where he could feel the effects, he wasn't sure he wanted to feel stony skin.

There was no time to lose. A minute was a good head start but it wasn't nearly enough time to get complacent. He raced back with Tina and was pleased to see that she scanned their surroundings as they ran.

"If we find a bow, we could station someone in that tree," she called to him. "It looks like it would be possible to get into it."

Justin nodded, although he wasn't sure any of them had the skills to use a bow properly—especially without falling out of the tree in the process.

"All three teams are in the arena!" the Master of Ceremonies bellowed.

"Fuuuuuuck." He wheezed as he and his teammate increased the pace. "I never liked track."

The larger cache was a better find. There was a battle-ax in this one, although there were no water potions. He wondered if that had been deliberate. With no time to waste, he snatched the two daggers and shoved them through his belt before he bundled the remainder of the potions in his shirt. The two of them raced to the house.

Lyle emerged from the shadows under the stairs as they came into the building. They laid the items out on the floor and began a quick division. Justin chose the short sword, Lyle took one dagger as a backup for his fists, and Tina held a light-green potion up.

"Poison," she read. "Damage over time. Should I use it or—"

"If you are struck full-on with a battle-ax, a damage over time debuff is kind of overkill," he pointed out.

"Good point." She rolled it at her companions.

He opted to give it to Lyle—if the dwarf needed to fall back to blades, it would give him a way to accelerate the fight before he could be further outflanked. For himself, he took the fire buff. Ever since his fight against the demon army, he'd enjoyed flaming blades.

"There are two rooms upstairs," the dwarf said. "I say one of us stays in the shadow of the stairs, and the other two go upstairs."

"Justin stays here," Tina said. "He's best equipped to take on a range of weaponry, right? He can call to tell us what's coming. I'll wait at the top of the stairs and eliminate as many as I can with a battle-ax—"

"What, and I get no one?" Lyle sounded deeply unimpressed.

"No," she said patiently. "You man the window, tell us who's coming, and back up the two of us as needed. You have a poison blade and can move between fights very effectively."

"Hmmm." He considered this and nodded. "Fine. But next time—"

"Yes, next time we'll let you charge in yelling Stoooooout," Justin promised. "Pinkie swear."

"Eh?"

"Never mind. It's not important." He flashed a grin at Tina. "Positions, everyone."

The three of them shared a fist-bump before Tina and Lyle ran up the stairs. It wasn't long until the dwarf gave a low whistle followed by two thumps of his foot against the floor. Justin faded into the shadows and began to wish he hadn't chosen the fire potion. The blade shone slightly and he wondered if someone would see it.

Their opponents circled the house once. He could hear their footsteps and see them pass the windows, but their shapes were faint through the thick, wavy glass and he was fairly sure they had no idea he was there. Upstairs, he heard a faint creak as Tina shifted slightly on the balls of her feet.

Only one came into the house, and he wished he knew whether or not they were alone or if the other one waited outside.

With a silent prayer that Tina would understand why he chose not to engage, he decided to remain in his hiding place. The person stopped inside the door and must have scanned the room before they strode forward to ascend the stairs. Their steps were sure and light-footed.

Whether she knew what he was going for or not, he didn't know. Either way, she rose to the occasion. Their opponent—a man, judging by the voice—screamed followed by a crash.

One strike was all it had taken. He smiled.

The second team member had, in fact, waited outside the door. Now, he barreled in, yelling his team member's name. His gaze was so focused on the top of the stairs that when Justin stepped out of the shadows, he had no way to stop in time.

The man was armed with daggers. Justin drove him back with a quick attack. He wished he had his sword, which had a longer range, but he still did better than he had with the daggers, and that was what counted.

Not only that, his opponent looked genuinely unnerved by the fact that he attacked with a flaming sword. He made a half-hearted attempt to fight, circled away, and tried to strike under his adversary's range of motion, but he received a boot in his face for the trouble.

Justin hadn't trained with Lyle for nothing.

As the man reeled back, he stamped hard, directly on his hand. He had a moment of guilt and wondered how injuries were healed there, but he was certain no one would let this man die. With a swift swipe, he opened a cut in the other man's neck and wasn't surprised, after his first match, to see the blue shield come up and immobilize the contestant.

Quickly, he slid into the shadows of his hiding place.

Out of the corner of his eye and through the wavy glass, he caught sight of movement. He gave a sharp whistle and only a few moments later, all three of the other team members reached the door. There was a tense, whispered discussion before they ran to the stairs as a group.

"Lyle!" Justin yelled. Tina would need backup, and there was precious little time for her to call for it.

The last team member up the stairs spun and when Justin stepped out of the shadows, she leapt the banister and attacked without hesitation.

From upstairs, shouts and pounding feet were very audible. It still sounded like there were four people moving around. He decided his warning had to be good enough and focused on his fight. There wasn't another option because his opponent had a battle-ax, and he had the feeling that he stared into a future where Tina had more practice and was on the opposing side.

It was terrifying. The woman had swung immediately into the offensive as she came up from her crouch. Her eyes were narrowed and she fought single-mindedly. The battle-ax must have been what she trained with because she used it as if it were a piece of her own body. Muscles rippled in her arms while she parried his attacks.

Whether she simply put on a good show or she was freakishly strong, Justin didn't know, but he did remember one other piece of his grandfather's advice. The best time to end a fight was immediately—better a quick fight than a pretty one.

He launched into a counterattack of his own. Strength and stamina aside, the sheer weight of the battle-ax made its swings slower than his sword. They weren't as slow as he would have liked but he had to work with what he had. He began to slash from one side, then the other, and from directly overhead, interspersed with direct thrusts of his short sword.

She was weaker on her right but with her right hand as her dominant one, she was better able to swing the ax to cover attacks on her left side. He leaned out of the way of a swing and danced back to give her an opening.

Unfortunately, she didn't take it and instead, began to circle, panting now. Was she beginning to tire? That was interesting.

"You know, I have to say you're getting fairly good at this."

Justin was so shocked to hear words of praise from the AI that he froze and almost lost his head in an attack. "Did you do that on purpose?" he whispered.

"No, but that was hilarious."

He groaned, crouched quickly, and spun on one foot. The ax whipped overhead and his opponent, dragged off-balance by the swing, tripped over him.

Upstairs, Lyle uttered a sudden below of pain and Tina screamed—and Justin went into autopilot. He had to get there. Conscious only of his friends' predicament, he seized his opportunity and dove forward to tackle his adversary. She had tried to gain the momentum to lift the ax from the floor and he clamped one hand down over her wrist. He dragged the weapon out of her hand and hurled it against the far wall, and in the next minute, his knee pressed against her throat. Murder gleamed in her eyes, but she saw the sword within his reach and sighed. Her hands raised in surrender and she was encased in the blue magical shield.

Justin snatched both the sword and the battle-ax and sprinted up the stairs.

"Justin! Down!"

He reacted to Tina's voice on instinct and dropped to his stomach as arrows whizzed overhead. "What's going on?" he called.

"Remember that tree?" Her voice sounded choked. "The first team put their third person there. They shot Lyle in the back of the leg."

"What?" He craned his head so he could see her. The dwarf was, indeed, frozen on the floor. His hand was clamped over one leg and Justin could see how much blood had flowed out of the wound even before he was frozen. Tina, meanwhile, was pressed up against the wall under the window.

He army-crawled to where she was.

"What now?" she asked him. "We can't get near that tree and he won't come in here, not when he only has a bow."

As if in answer, huge numbers appeared in the sky—fifty-nine, fifty-eight, fifty-seven…

"A stand-off has been established," said the voice of the Master of Ceremonies. "With two members of Sephith's Bane remaining and one member of Ulgutta, Sephith's Bane will be declared the winner unless a fight is joined within the next minute."

With a shout of anger, their opponent dropped out of the tree and raced to the house. He didn't have much of a choice, although his odds weren't good.

"This one's mine," Tina said furiously. She darted a glance at Lyle, and he remembered the way she had screamed. Seeing the dwarf shot had hit her hard and she was out for blood.

In the laboratory, Mary settled onto one of the stools and watched the monitors. She still couldn't read the bulk of the output there but she could hear Justin and Tina's voices—and she knew the girl was taking this particular fight.

Along with the danger.

"She was a good choice," Amber said quietly.

She pressed her lips together and was surprised to feel a touch on her shoulder. When she looked up, she met Amber's gaze.

"I know it was hard," the young woman said so quietly that even she could barely hear her. "But you did the right thing."

Mary felt something release in her chest and she smiled. "Thank you."

Their opponent didn't have a chance. He knew it and they knew it, but he had nothing to lose and he barreled up the stairs with a berserker roar. Tina's ax thudded into the ground with splintering force directly in front of him.

He stopped so fast he tripped over it and she stepped out of the shadows with murder on her face.

"End it," Justin whispered under his breath. "Don't play with him and don't try to get revenge. End it."

She didn't hear him. Entirely focused, she advanced on their opponent, who scuttled away on his back. Justin, who melted into the shadows in the room, noticed him fumble under the back of his shirt for something—a knife?

Fuck.

"Yeah," Tina said. "Yeah, you have a knife. Do you think you're gonna shank me, fucker? Well, you won't. You'll stand up and fight me one on one like you're not a total coward. You got that?"

He stood, all six foot something of him, and Justin adjusted his hold on his sword. With one more step, he could end this. There was no way she could win a one on one fight with this man, not with daggers, and he would have to sit her down and talk to her about letting her emotions get in the way of what really mattered.

The man hadn't fully drawn his dagger out when she attacked. One fist drove into his sternum, and she slashed with one of Lyle's daggers with the other hand. Her opponent tumbled back with a scream, and she looked at her teammate.

"My grandfather taught me," she said, "to make a big, dramatic speech, have them get ready for the fight, and then take them out while they were doing that."

He burst out laughing. "I'll never doubt you again, I promise."

"Sephith's Bane has won the match!" the Master of Ceremonies shouted. Cheering came from the stands and the friends looked outside before they hurried to Lyle's side. Neither of them would leave before he was seen to.

The healers arrived soon. One had the lean, almost sinuous height that Justin could only guess came from elven blood. She readied a spell and touched a blue crystal orb to the dwarf's shield. He collapsed and she immediately began to attend to the wound. Justin thought he saw her give a look of deep distaste at the man on the ground.

"He was really scared," Tina said under her breath. "It bled so much even before the stasis field came up, Justin, and I think the guy planned it that way. Lyle might have died before they could shield him."

His blood ran cold. The two companions accompanied the healers into the open air and made a show of waving to their fans, but he could only think of the possibility of Lyle bleeding out—or Tina, or himself. He hadn't thought that was a possibility, but he began to wonder if he should have looked at the history of the tournament more carefully.

And he'd reached a point where he thought people couldn't stoop any lower.

On the dais, the Master of Ceremonies greeted them with an expansive smile. "You are fast becoming a crowd favorite," he said heartily, and the spectators cheered wildly. "Should I even ask which you prefer to take?"

He would have smiled in return but for the look on Lyle's face. He knelt next to the stretcher. "Hey," he said quietly. "You'll be okay, you know that, right?"

"I do." The dwarf's voice was faint. He was pale but Justin knew that was from nerves and not blood loss. He looked at the young man and there was a gravity in his face that Justin had never seen before. Even facing Sephith, even locked in jail, Lyle had been reckless and unimpressed by the threats before him.

This had struck him differently.

"I've been away too long," he said quietly. "I never said a proper goodbye to my family." His smile was forced. "I don' want to leave ye without a team—"

"Go," he said quietly. Something in him ached. The third key would send him home, he was sure of it now. The game was slowly taking away the people he had come to rely on and he would soon return to his own life.

Had it only been a few weeks in this world? It seemed like so much longer.

"Hey." Lyle caught his arm. "Take the advantage."

"No way," he said firmly. "If you're going home and I can't buy you an ale in person, I'll damned well send you with money so I can buy you some from a distance."

The dwarf managed a laugh as Justin stood. He caught Tina's nod as well as the suspicious glint of tears in her eyes. She looked away and pretended to study the crowd. He had the sense that she didn't like to cry in front of people.

"We take the payout," he told the Master of Ceremonies.

The man's smile fell slightly. "Don't tell me you'll bow out."

"Let him wonder," the AI said suddenly.

Justin only had a split-second to make his decision and with an internal sigh, he decided to go with the AI's suggestion. He shrugged. "We'll have to see."

He and Tina raised the bowl over their heads to the sound of cheers and left the Master of Ceremonies staring after them, stricken.

"So, why did I do that?" Justin asked the AI in an undertone.

"You'll have to wait and see, won't you?" The AI sounded as smug as usual. *"Maybe I made you do it for shits and giggles."*

He rolled his eyes.

CHAPTER FOURTEEN

Tina was waiting on the back patio of the inn when Justin came downstairs. Having nothing other than burlap and armor, she had borrowed something from the innkeeper's wife—a flowing linen robe she had belted incongruously with her dagger belt. She saw him looking and threw her hands up.

"I know I look ridiculous but I couldn't stand the armor for one more minute."

"You look…really good." He cleared his throat. With her hair still wet from the bath and curling as it dried, she looked surprisingly…elegant, which wasn't a word he ever thought he'd use for her.

He cleared his throat as he gestured to the table nearby. "Food? I don't know about you but I'm starving."

"Me, too." Tina went to sit and it took a little time to make sure the robe didn't gape in any unexpected ways. "The innkeeper said he'd be out with food soon. I hope you don't mind, I…uh, splurged a little."

"Well, we have a ton of money and it's not like we'll stick around very long." Justin grinned at her. "I say we go all out. Maybe this isn't the best place to do that—"

"I won't go anywhere else in this getup," she said at once.

"You know you look good, right? Not that I'm surprised. You always look good—I mean, you seemed surprised that…oh, I'm awful at this." He let his head thud onto the table.

She laughed. "Thank you. I know what you meant." A door opened nearby and she clapped enthusiastically. "Oh, thank you so much."

"Of course." The innkeeper approached, bearing a jug of wine and glasses as well as a loaf of freshly baked bread. "Sir, are you well?" He looked at where Justin still huddled with his head on the table.

"Yes, thank you." He raised his head, embarrassed all over again. "Could I ask you to take some refreshments to our friend in the corner room?"

"Rest assured, we were already doing so." The man nodded at Tina. "The lady requested that we give him the very finest food. Of course, he has since requested that we take it away and replace it with something heartier."

Tina hid her face with one hand and her shoulders shook in a silent laugh. "I should have expected that. Ale and…what, potatoes?"

"And sausages," the innkeeper agreed. "My wife is pleased. She takes great pride in her ale."

"Oh. Well, then." She smiled. "Thank you for this. I'm sure we'll enjoy whatever you have."

"We've taken the liberty of making a meal specially for you," he told the two of them. "And you'll have the patio to yourselves."

"There's no need for that," Justin protested.

"You're not used to being a tournament champion, are you?" The innkeeper gave him an amused look. "If I let anyone else out here, you wouldn't have a moment of peace all night."

He disappeared, but not before he waved a hand in a deft gesture. It ignited magical lanterns that hung overhead and down the walls and the friends were immediately bathed in a soft glow.

She gasped and the innkeeper gave him a meaningful look before he left.

Justin cleared his throat. He suddenly felt deeply self-conscious. Between the twilight sky, the gorgeous city, the wine, and the magical lights, this was a more romantic night than he had bargained on. He took a gulp of wine to steady himself and realized too late that he might have made a mistake.

Thankfully, he and Tina were both hungry enough that he could occupy himself for a moment with the bread. He dipped hunks of it in the oil that had been provided and savored the hint of salt and the warm, fluffy texture.

She licked her fingers with a happy sigh. "Do you think they have twenty more loaves?"

He laughed. "God, I hope so. You take the last piece. I'm sure they'll have more soon and I had an ale while talking to Lyle."

Tina gave him a sober look at that. "So, he's really going home, then?"

"He is." He focused on his glass of wine. "I never thought I'd see the day, to be honest. He doesn't strike me as someone who would do well with a staid life…but then again, he wasn't fighting for much of a purpose here. He merely wandered and drank himself silly most of the time. When I first met him, he was in jail for brawling and not paying his bar tab."

"He's a good man." She ran one finger contemplatively around the rim of her goblet. "Er…dwarf?"

"I have no idea what the right term is." Justin shrugged. "And, yes, he is."

"I wouldn't be surprised if all your good deeds have made him want to go home and help his family," Tina pointed out. "You've defeated evil wizards and demons and so on, right? Maybe he wants to do more of that. The dwarves must have some enemies."

"I don't know." He looked at her in surprise. "I suppose I never knew much about the wider world. In a video game—a normal one—there's always a pressing crisis like a huge war. I never heard about anything like that. It was only things like Sephith—little villains terrorizing one village at a time."

She nodded. "Well, we can ask him. He's not leaving tonight, is he?"

"No. He said he'll take a few days and he'll go with a caravan. I think I managed to persuade him not to go as a guard." He shook his head. "I had to tell him he deserved to be carried home like a prince instead of letting him think I was coddling him."

"But you were," she guessed and took a sip of wine.

Justin nodded somberly. "The healer said it will take time before he's back to full strength. She healed the wound but apparently, only the body can do some of it. I hadn't realized someone could get injured so badly in the tournament."

Tina fixed him with a curious look. "We keep rising through the ranks. Will we continue to compete?"

"I think we have to." He shook his head. "That's how we get the key." He sank into silence.

"Justin?" Her voice was low. "You'll be able to come back, you know."

He looked quickly at her.

"You have to be here right now because you're healing," she said, "but I'm here and I'm healthy. They can put you in the game. You can see Lyle again."

"I know it's ridiculous to care." He gave her an embarrassed look.

"I read my favorite books over and over again," she responded with a shrug. "And if I could actually talk to the characters? I'd never stop reading."

Justin smiled at her. "Thank you for coming here—and for understanding."

"I'm glad your mother forgave me enough to let me try," she said.

"Wait, what?" He looked sharply at her. Now he remembered the way his mother had looked when he asked about Tina. She had been angry. "Oh, no—my mother blames you, doesn't she? You know, if our parents hadn't insisted we go on that date—"

"It was my fault." She took his hand and looked seriously at him. "And I'm glad I can come here. I wanted to help, even though I didn't know it would be this much fun." She squeezed his fingers.

He returned the smile easily until he realized how perfect this moment felt, with their fingers touching and the wine making his head buzz, and the lights the perfect muted glow.

When the door opened, they both drew back as if they'd been burned. Justin could see her blush as the innkeeper and his wife entered with heavy trays of food. They were careful not to look at the young couple, but he could sense them trying to decide if they had interrupted anything.

The amount of food they provided was truly staggering. There was a shank of something that looked like lamb but must have come from something the size of an up-armored Humvee. It was coated in spices and salt, its skin crackly, and it smelled divine. Roasted vegetables lay around it. Platters of salad were provided as well, and rice with herbs, and more bread. Dumplings sizzled in a hot dish, covered with bubbling cheese, and another bowl contained something that might be pasta.

And there was so much more wine. The innkeeper and his wife topped off the goblets and withdrew like ghosts.

"Well, I don't think we'll fight in the tournament again," Tina said. "Unless there's a way we can win by lying on the ground and crying about how full our stomachs are."

"Are you suggesting…" He felt truly sad. "That we should try to moderate ourselves?"

"Fuck no," she retorted. "This is a made-up world. They'll find another way to get you that key. Eat up." She picked a potato up with her bare hands and popped it into her mouth, only to spit it out a moment later. "Fuck! Hot. This game is too realistic."

He laughed hysterically as he served himself from the platters.

While he wanted to take some of everything, it wouldn't fit on his plate. With a silent prayer that he wouldn't be full before he had tried them all, he began to eat.

Every bite was delicious but it was probably because he was literally living in a dream.

"I don't think I have words," he said after he'd swallowed one of the dumplings. "That cheese. What kind is it?"

"I don't know." Tina dipped one of the pieces of bread in it. "All I know is that it had better exist or I'm gonna kick some ass when I get out of here."

He nodded emphatically.

"You know, it's weird," she said.

"Hrm?" He looked up, his cheeks bulging with rice and meat.

"Well, I was going to say that we were finally having the romantic evening our parents had hoped for but then I saw you looking like a chipmunk." She clearly tried not to laugh.

"Nice one, Casanova. You're doing great."

"I will find the server you are stored in," he muttered to the AI, "and rip your heart out." To Tina, he raised an eyebrow. "Is the woman who came to the date in a borrowed bathrobe really getting on my case?"

"Oh, unfair!" She threw a piece of bread at him. "I don't have any other clothes."

"You could have—"

"Don't you dare finish that sentence," she warned and laughed. "Although…who knows where we'll be after all this wine?"

In the lab, Jacob looked around in a sudden moment of awkwardness. Mary was already at the door of the room. She looked at everyone, who stared at her.

"Uh…" She gave them a deer-in-the-headlights look. "Let me know when it's safe to come back."

He gave her a thumbs-up and tried not to laugh as she fairly sprinted out of the room.

The Master of Ceremonies had chambers in the Royal Palace, a fact Kural guessed correctly. This left, of course, the question of exactly where in the giant palace the chambers were. What followed his arrival was a truly boring series of excursions down similar-looking hallways until all the exquisite architecture blurred together in his head.

Thankfully, he had remembered to leave magical markers for himself so he knew which corridors he had already explored. If he hadn't done so, he would have been lost very quickly.

The palace was almost empty. The guards patrolled regularly —which wasn't a problem for the wizard, who presently floated above their heads as a dust mote—but he saw not a single noble and only a few clerks.

His curiosity grew as he searched. He had known, of course, that the king of Insea had not been seen in years. Everyone knew that. The city continued to run like clockwork, however, and there were never any invasions, so Kural had decided that whatever was going on, it wasn't a problem. He'd always had something else to occupy him, like his experiments.

Or his defeat and subsequent years spent trying not to get killed by Sephith.

Now, he wondered what was going on there. Even a sick king could be expected to be surrounded by fawning nobles and crowds of servants, but he didn't see any general direction in which the guards or servants moved.

He resolved to ask the Master of Ceremonies whenever he finally found the man. Although he would have to be careful, he might even be able to work that into the persuasion portion of their discussion.

It had been over an hour by the time he managed to find the correct set of chambers. They were palatial, although it did not appear that this was due to greed. The rooms were far from the height of luxury. A desk stood at one side of the main room and a set of low couches near the fireplace, and a full wall of windows overlooked them. Beyond, he could see a bedchamber with an eastern-style mattress laid directly on the floor.

The Master of Ceremonies worked alone at his desk with a humble meal of flatbread and yogurt next to him as well as a cup of strong tea. Kural took the opportunity to change from a dust mote into his full self and walked into the room. This took vastly more strength than shadow-walking, but he needed to be there in person if he wanted to persuade the Master of Ceremonies to part with a priceless artifact.

He rapped on the open door and waited for the man to look up. "Jaco?"

"Yes?" It had been years since they had seen each other, so it took a good few minutes for the Master of Ceremonies to realize who he was looking at. "Kural?" He stood and came around the edge of the desk, disbelief and wariness on his face. "The last I heard, you had been killed by Sephith."

"Defeated," he corrected. "And then in hiding. Sephith was killed a few weeks back, though, and so I have my powers again."

"I'd heard rumors of it, but…" The official gestured to his desk. "But I've been busy."

"Yes, I can see that." The wizard looked around the room. "I don't suppose I could trouble you with a certain detail."

"You might as well." Jaco smiled wearily at him. "I'm getting nowhere. I don't suppose you have any ideas on how to revive the tournament properly."

"You seem to be doing a fine job of it so far," he observed. He waited as the man rang a small bell and murmured something below his breath. A full tea set, complete with sweets, appeared on the table near the hearth and a fire sprang into being.

The two men sat and took refreshments for a moment.

"As it happens, however…" Kural rolled the glass of tea between his hands. "I do have a suggestion. But questions first, of course. It might inform the suggestion I make. I wasn't sure it would be you I found."

His host gave him a tired smile. Over a hundred years before, he and his visitor had been rivals, both competing for the favor of certain patrons. Kural had left to find his place as a wizard, and Jaco had taken a different route. Never a wizard himself, he possessed quite a talent for creating spectacles and entertainments. He'd always had the edge when it came to delighting rich nobles.

"I have it on good authority," the wizard said, "that this tournament is not merely an entertainment for the city." He watched the man closely and was rewarded by a flash of worry in his eyes. "Do you care to explain?" he asked silkily.

The official considered him narrowly. "And have you come steal my place?"

"Have you ever been to a party I've thrown?" he asked him archly.

"Yes, actually. You served crackers. Only crackers. There was no music."

"So you know I won't steal your job." He gestured at him. "I promise you, I have a goal that does not in any way conflict with yours."

"Ah, but you don't know what mine is." Jaco sighed. He was still wary but clearly desperate to unburden himself of his worries. "Oh, what the hell. Maybe you'll have some ideas."

The story he proceeded to tell was beyond his guest's wildest imaginings.

The King of Insea was not sick. Indeed, he had never existed in the way the people believed. He had never been elven at all but was a dragon, born millennia before even the elves walked the earth. It was his servants who had built Insea under his direction after he stumbled upon the beautiful deposit of rock that made the city. His power had allowed them to forge the finished product into one stone, which made it unbreakable.

The dragon had no interest in the wars of his people. He had escaped a battle between rival armies and had fled. Whether it was from another world or this one, Jaco did not know. He only knew that the dragon wanted to be left in peace—and that he was fascinated by the doings of lesser beasts. It was for this reason that he had convinced the elves to build Insea. The rock gave him strength and he lived within the city, endlessly intrigued by what went on, and kept it safe.

"Is he…in the palace?" Kural asked.

"I don't know." Jaco shook his head. "I've never seen him, not truly."

"So it could all be a ruse."

"It could." The man leaned back on the couch and considered the idea. "I've had time to wonder if that was the case. I can think of no other explanation, however. He has used servants, over the years, for public appearances, but now fears someone might learn the truth."

"If he's told you, and you've told me…" The wizard took a sip of his tea as he frowned in thought. "I won't spread the secret, but it won't stay hidden forever."

"I know that. So does he." Jaco swirled the tea in his glass. "That's why the tournament is in progress. Something is coming but we don't know what. It might be dragons or it might be another kind of invasion. I was called here when I reached the city and he asked me if I could put together a tournament—"

"That would create and draw a populace of talented warriors?" Kural finished for him.

"Yes," the man said softly. "And it was working until the Twins kept winning."

"Well. I have a suggestion that will help you, then." He smiled. "I happen to know that one of the teams includes a man who is searching for a very particular artifact—a dwarven key."

His host leaned forward. "I know the key you speak of, I think. And it is priceless, yes, but not to any collectors. It is valuable only to historians. Are you truly telling me a scholar has entered the tournament?"

"He's a member of the team that calls itself Sephith's Bane," he told him. "Ah, yes, now you see how I know him. I helped equip him to defeat Sephith, you see. As for why he needs the key… well, let me simply say he has the other two."

"That answers none of my questions," Jaco told him tartly. "Quite the opposite, in fact."

"Mmm. Ask your dragon where the door is that those keys open." Kural leaned forward. "I promise you—I *promise* you—if you give him the key when he wins, he will create a spectacle that will not soon be forgotten. It will revive interest in the tournament in a way you cannot imagine. And when that man travels between the worlds, he may well come back, bringing the healing that Insea needs."

His companion's jaw hung open and it was a few moments before he swallowed. "And if the Twins win?" he asked tartly.

"Then offer a different prize," the wizard said wearily. "Although I'd recommend you make sure they don't."

"I refuse to interfere," Jaco said stiffly.

"You're trying to drum up opponents," Kural pointed out.

"Strong opponents," the man told him. "It helps nothing if weaklings triumph. And if a single whisper gets out that the contest is weighted, that will undo everything I have worked so hard to create."

"Mmm." He shrugged. "Well then, I leave that up to you. Justin is resourceful and I'm confident that he can do what must be done. If he wins, however, offer him the key. Trust me."

"I'm not sure I do," his companion said wryly. "But if the king agrees, I'll do it. There's something bad coming, and if this man can bring us resources…"

The wizard nodded. "Call on me if you need me. I happen to know of two others as well—a sorceress of surpassing power and her apprentice. I shall make sure the apprentice is trained with all haste in case an invading army does come."

———

It wasn't long after the banter started that Justin stopped and his eyes widened.

"Everyone in the lab can…hear us, can't they?"

"Oh, my God." Tina put her hand over her mouth. She wanted to disappear. "Oh, my God, oh, my God… Yes. Yes, they can."

He tipped his head back and laughed. "We finally have a date and we have a whole army of chaperones." He looked curiously at her. "What is the lab like?"

Letters appeared on her screen: **TRY TO STEER THE CONVERSATION BACK TO THE GAME**

Huh. She shrugged and hoped she could pull this off without being too obvious. Even with no pressure, she wasn't a great liar. "It looks like a lab. You'll see it soon, right?"

"I suppose." He gave her a tight smile.

"Justin." She leaned forward. "You're close to the third key. What does that tell you?"

He stared at her.

"That you're making progress," she told him. "We you need to be careful. I know we're not supposed to let you get harmed, but I also know what people look like when they're really scared all the time and I know the doctors aren't."

The reassurance helped him to relax somewhat.

"Tell me about the game," she suggested. "Tell me all of the tiny things." She stood and held her hand out. "Come on, let's go upstairs—no, not for that. We'll people-watch out the window and have a nice glass of wine."

"Oh," Justin said. "Right." He retrieved the pitcher and glanced at the table. "All that eating, and we barely made a dent."

"Good." Tina grinned. "That means there'll be leftovers. Now, come on."

They slipped up the stairs and then, on a whim, up the next set. To their pleasure, they led to an attic with broad windows. As they ascended the final flight, Tina was fairly sure the process made the robe slip more than once, but Justin was gentlemanly enough not to mention it. He handed up the pitcher and the goblets and hauled himself after.

"It's easier when you're tall," he pointed out.

"Bah." She lay back on the roof and stared at the sky. "God, it's gorgeous here. Are all games like this?"

"Play some and you'll find out," he teased.

She looked at him with a grin. "Okay. I'll do that if you read some of my favorite books."

To her surprise, he propped himself on one elbow and nodded at her. "It's a deal."

Tina laughed. She'd spent the past few years drifting, worrying her parents with her tattoos and her attitude, but the truth was, she hadn't ever wanted to run off and go on week-long binges or anything like that. Quite simply, she had only wanted them to stop treating her like she was made of glass.

That, and she liked tattoos.

"What do you think you'll do when you get back?" she asked him.

"You mean, besides all the physical therapy I'll probably need?" Justin sounded glum.

"Yes, besides that. Everyone has health problems so don't get self-indulgent."

He smiled at her. "Well… I don't know. I guess I thought I'd talk to my dad."

"What about?"

With a sigh, he pillowed his head on his hands. "What he does for a living, I guess. He's a senator."

"Yes, I know. My parents made a huge deal of it."

"Ugh, I'm sorry. Well, before that, he was in the state senate, and before that—it doesn't matter. But I never really cared. I thought he merely argued for a living and that he wanted an excuse to tell people they were wrong about things."

"And now?"

"Well, you can't really solve problems in our world by running around with a sword. So I have to find something else to do." He shrugged. "What about you?"

"Now, mine seems stupid."

"No, tell me."

"I wanted to open a store," she said. "My grandmother would weave this amazing cloth, and you could make the patterns into rugs, curtains, whatever. I thought I'd open a store where people could buy stuff like that." She sat up enough to take a sip of wine. "It's not exactly on par with saving the world."

"I like it," he said. He hesitated and took her hand tentatively. "I do. I like it. And Tina?"

"Yeah?"

"When we get out of here, could we go out again?" The words came out a little rushed.

Reflexively, she smiled as warmth stole over her. "Yeah. Yeah, I'd like that. Of course, I'm not sure your mother will ever let us leave the house together."

"My mother got me a dragon for my birthday," he said sleepily. "She doesn't get to talk about safety."

"What?"

"Nothing." He laced his fingers with hers. "I...should go. I don't want to," he added hastily, "but I keep thinking about everyone in the lab."

Tina laughed. "You don't have to go straight from this to there. Be grateful."

"You're leaving?"

"I'll be back in the morning," she assured him. "I promise."

She waited as he climbed into the building and left and wasn't surprised when the world dissolved into black a few moments later. When she opened her eyes, the pod lid was raised and she winced when the assistants helped her to sit. Her muscles ached and she had to use the bathroom.

Desperately had to.

Tina practically sprinted through the lab and emerged a few minutes later feeling disturbingly lighter. "How long was I in there?"

"Fourteen hours," Jacob said. He produced a chair out of nowhere as she began to wobble. "Sit. Your blood sugar is very low."

"Eat this," Amber suggested. She brought over a folding table and a bowl of pho. "A little salt protein, some hydration…"

"Do you have any sriracha?"

"No. I'm not crazy. But we'll have some for you next time." She tapped next to the bowl. "Eat up. You're doing great, you know."

"He's beginning to show marked signs of being ready to wake up," DuBois said.

"Oh." She swallowed a mouthful of soup. "What happens if we don't win the tournament?"

The doctor looked offended. "I can't tell you," he said.

"Does it…" She looked at the others. "Does it break the immersion or something?"

He looked at her and almost seemed to bristle. "No. It ruins the fun."

CHAPTER FIFTEEN

"How are we doing for time?" Nick called over his shoulder. He held a large bag of trash in one hand and a sheaf of papers in the other.

"About five minutes," Jacob said. Sweat began to prickle on his skin.

"Fifteen," Amber told Nick in an undertone.

"We want to be ready before they show up," Jacob pointed out. "If they come here and see us cleaning frantically, it won't look good for us."

"The laboratory is already spotless," Anna Price pointed out. "Not that I want to get involved." She looked genuinely amused. After the weird way she had hovered around the area a few days before, he had been worried when she appeared that morning.

However, she had no negative comments on their progress. Instead, she wanted them to allow a news team to conduct an interview. It was a rare occurrence, she'd explained. She was not in the habit of allowing media attention on anything she did, but she was pleased enough with Justin's progress that she had decided to allow this.

There had been an extensive debrief of what they were and

were not allowed to say with regard to patient confidentiality, and they would pretend that Justin was in a different location. Also, they would pretend that he was not the only patient.

Jacob had been leery of agreeing to the interview, but what swayed him was her reminder that this could also help Senator Williams. The PIVOT team had shared articles amongst themselves, horrified by the vitriolic comments toward them and Justin's parents. People had clearly decided that they had hooked the young man up to untested, experimental treatment merely for the hell of it.

He shook his head and returned to scrubbing the bottom of the laboratory table.

"Do you really think they'll look under the tables?" Price asked him.

"No," he replied. "But this calms me."

"Yes. You seem very calm."

Of all the things he had expected from her, a sense of humor was not one of them. He slid out from under the table and gave her a look that drew a small smile in return. She was typing on her phone as she spoke. He had only seen her without extra work once.

Apparently, there was a rumor going around Diatek that she didn't even have a house and slept in one of her offices each night. He had to concede that it seemed likely.

They all heard the door open and everyone looked around. Mary blew out a breath and bounced slightly on the balls of her feet. She had dressed conservatively in a skirt suit and pearls, and a professional makeup artist had come in. The effort had created the very picture of an non-threatening, old-school, classy mother, the kind of person who would always have something for the PTA bake sale and never dropped her kids off for school without having her makeup done. Jacob knew she had been given extensive instructions on how to behave for the camera crew and that she did not like it.

Mary, he knew, preferred to be straightforward.

So did he. Unfortunately, they were in a battle against someone who twisted the truth every way he could.

When the camera crew arrived, he thought his heart would beat out of his chest. He went to shake the reporter's hand.

"Mr. Zachary." The man smiled at him. "David Yang, Johnsonville Chronicle. Thank you for agreeing to meet us."

"Of course." He gestured to Mary and Price. "Would you like to begin by speaking to Mary Williams or Anna Price?"

"Mrs. Williams, I think." David stepped forward to shake Mary's hand. "If that works for you, ma'am."

"Of course." She nodded. "Should I sit, should I stand…"

"Why don't you come here to the seating area?" Yang looked around. "No, one of the desks. You've been here this whole time. I think it's right to show you in the lab."

"If you think that's best." Mary slid onto one of the stools in what was clearly a practiced movement.

"Let me get set up," the man told her. He directed the camera crew into position before he launched into the interview. "Now, Mrs. Williams, can you give us your overview of the treatment Justin is receiving?"

"Of course." Mary swallowed and gestured to the pods. "A comatose patient would normally receive very limited interventions. Feeding tubes, of course, and all the monitors, as well as perhaps a medically induced coma if it was needed, but I think that's only if they seem to be coming out of it too quickly—to slow it, I guess, but I'm not a doctor. But there isn't generally a way to interact with the person. The brain is very complex and there isn't a way to predict when the patient will get better."

David nodded.

"What PIVOT did," she said, "was they gave patients a way to begin to get better while they remain unconscious. The video game that was developed by their team can be interacted with by the patient and will stimulate the brain to heal." She gave a self-conscious smile. "Dr. DuBois, how would you say I did at explaining that?"

The doctor gave a distracted nod. "Very good, yes. Yes. Now, if you'll excuse me…" He wandered away.

Amber edged closer to Jacob. "Where did you hide his popcorn?" she asked out of the corner of her mouth.

"In the ceiling tiles," he muttered. "Let's hope he doesn't think to look at the security footage anytime soon."

She snickered. They had decided it was probably best if no one saw Justin's doctor eating popcorn in the middle of the laboratory but had not been able to convince him of that. Consequently, she had lured him outside while Jacob hid the popcorn.

"So, Mrs. Williams," David Yang asked, "what do you know about the types of stimulation? You mentioned that it was a game. Is it like a logic puzzle?"

"It's a video game," Mary explained. "I've been inside it. Well, in one of the pods. As one of the early tests, I was allowed to interact with Justin."

She described her experience within the game. Although she left out the part about her killing the spider, she was incredibly animated. Her sense of wonder about what she'd experienced would translate well, Jacob thought.

Or, at least, he hoped it would. He noted the way her chin trembled with real emotion while she discussed being able to speak with Justin and send messages.

"Now, one last question, Mrs. Williams," the reporter said. "Early stories about this treatment were very negative and your husband has been pressured to resign. Do you have any comment on that?"

Mary paused and Jacob knew from having watched that this was practiced. She had gone over this several times with the lawyers and publicists as well as her husband. He had also witnessed her ranting about how disingenuous it felt to practice the speech, only to have Anna Price shake her head. "Sincerity isn't enough when it comes to the press," the CEO had said. "Not legally and not in the court of public opinion. We need to be careful."

"I know the stories were scary," Mary said and swallowed. "I guess people must think we're desperate or reckless and if they've only seen the news reports, I can't really blame them. I hope that when they learn the details, they'll think more kindly of us. We feel lucky that we were able to find this treatment for Justin and we hope more families will soon have the same opportunity."

"Thank you, Mrs. Williams. Now, Mr. Zachary…" David Yang gestured around the lab. "Would you like to provide more specifics on the treatment?"

"Of course," Jacob said. "Come with me."

He led them around the lab and allowed his genuine enthusiasm to show when he pointed out the various new pieces of equipment PIVOT had access to as part of the acquisition deal. Finally, he led the team to the pods.

"There's been considerable press coverage of these already," he told David Yang. "Obviously, we didn't originally intend these to be used for comatose patients. What first gave us the idea was my grandmother's treatment. To be frank, my family could not afford to keep her in the hospital. It put us in a terrible position and my parents and their siblings considered draining their retirement funds to help her recover."

"Your grandmother passed away, did she not?"

"Yes." He swallowed. "And I'd be lying if I said I didn't wonder, every day, if she might have recovered if she'd been able to try this treatment. She always loved stories. I remember her reading to me when she was younger. If she'd had a chance to be a hero and go on adventures, I think maybe…" He swallowed hard and kicked himself mentally because he had not wanted to cry. More than anything, he needed to be professional and present a trustworthy image. "I think maybe that would have given her strength," he finished.

"I see. And so your team is now marketing the pods exclusively as a therapy for trauma patients, correct?"

"Right now, that is the only application under development," Jacob said carefully. "However, as you can see, we're also collecting data from healthy patients to understand how their vital signs respond to the game. This gives us a good idea of how brains diverge and we're interested to see those data."

"So these are not patients?" the reporter asked.

"Yes. Obviously, we can't show you any of the treatment as the patients aren't able to sign waivers."

Yang nodded and one of his assistants checked a question off. "Do you see any other uses for these pods?"

"Many," he told him. "There are numerous potential other areas where this could be used. We'll know more when we have a good set of data regarding our patients' recovery. Depending on how recovery is affected, other conditions might benefit from the same treatment. But there are more benefits, too. People can attend college remotely. They can learn combat skills or explore landscapes. Those who have mobility issues could have the sensation of walking again. There are so many ways that this could enhance people's lives."

"Thank you so much for your time." The man shook his hand heartily. "Now, Ms. Price, if you'd be willing to answer some questions about Diatek's involvement in this process."

"Of course," she said smoothly and gave Jacob a tiny nod as she went past him.

"That went well, I thought," Nick said as the team watched her answering questions.

"I hope so," Jacob said. He swallowed. "I hope so but I'm afraid Metcalfe got too far ahead of us."

"Maybe that's the benefit to working with someone who has

defense contracts," Nick suggested. "If Metcalfe tries to screw with her, I wouldn't say it would go well for him."

"That's true." He bounced on the balls of his feet. "Well, we've done what we can. Let's hope this gives the senator enough of a break to hang on for a while longer."

CHAPTER SIXTEEN

"Are you sure about this?" Tina asked.

Justin glanced at her. The roar of the crowd reverberated through the floor and the walls, and all he could think of was home. Only three teams remained from the skirmishes, and with Quartzfire having withdrawn from the final, the Master of Ceremonies had hinted that a grand prize might be on the line for the teams that faced off that day.

The uncertainty had packed the stands. The three teams left were Tayr—the trio of women Justin, Tina, and Lyle had faced off against last time—the Twins, of course, and the remnants of Sephith's Bane. Justin and Tina were the only two to advance without one of their team members. The rules were clear. They could continue without their team member or they could drop out, but they could not sub in anyone else.

He knew she was worried about his choice to keep going. She had argued passionately against it, but he was ready and couldn't remain there any longer. He was ready to wake up and the thought of waiting another few days was torture.

The two of them would win. They had to.

"I'm sure," he told her.

She looked at the floor without speaking.

"Last time, everyone came for us," he told her. "We've had harder fights because we were the unknown. First, they thought we were weaklings and could be easily defeated. Then, they thought we were the big threat. But this time, we're in the arena with the Twins."

"And that doesn't frighten you?" Tina demanded.

Justin thought it over. It should frighten him. He had the sense that he should be worried about this because he had seen the Twins fight and he knew their record. They were clearly resourceful. So was he, though, his mind argued. He'd defeated Sephith—hell, he'd defeated a version of himself in that tower. Thereafter, he'd fought a demon army. What were two humans in comparison to that?

The truth was, though, he was itching for this fight. The others had been quick skirmishes against people who were used to arena fighting and not used to risking their lives. They were more cautious and more frivolous at the same time. The Twins were the ones he had wanted to fight all along.

He shrugged. "I think we can do it," was all he said.

Tina made no reply to that. She swallowed as the lift began to move. The Master of Ceremonies had announced the Twins first and half the stadium seemed to cheer wildly while the other half booed. Surely, with as much noise as there had been, there couldn't be many people sitting silently. Now, Tayr was being announced, and though there was less interest, he could tell that they had their fans.

"Our third team has become a fan favorite after only two matches in this arena," the Master of Ceremonies said. The covering over their platform slid back and light flooded in. Cheers began, along with a few boos.

"Aww, yeah," Justin said.

"What?" Tina looked deeply confused.

"We're being booed," he explained. "That means we've made it."

"I think you may be confused about how humans show emotion."

"No, no, think about it—you see a cool act, someone wins at a sports game, and you get into it, right? It's easy to cheer. But when you hate someone, that's when you've seen them enough to learn about them and care about them. We're not simply some extra team anymore."

"Uh…huh." She looked dubious, but as their platform reached ground level, she plastered a smile on and waved. "That's weird, the countdown hasn't started yet."

"No team has an advantage in this match," the Master of Ceremonies announced. "However, there is one difference between this match and the others…"

The whole arena seemed to hold its breath, and Justin realized he was doing the same.

"Magic is unrestricted in this round," the man shouted.

"*Yes!*" Justin yelled. He pumped his fist in the air.

"You can use magic?" Tina asked him.

"Hell yeah. I can set all kinds of things on fire—and reveal hidden things. And make a sword of fire. Oh, hell yes, I am so here for this."

"Good. That's good." She danced nervously on the balls of her feet. "One more thing, Justin."

"Yeah?" He darted her a glance but he barely paid attention. The countdown had begun in the sky and he scanned the vague outlines of the landscape.

"This doesn't change the plan," she warned him. "Remember that, Justin. It doesn't change the plan. We find a defensible location and we wait. Okay?"

"Yeah. Yes." Justin looked at her and nodded. "Of course. But we have magic once we get there." He held one palm up and made a fireball.

"Oh, shit." Tina's eyes widened. "You actually can make—" She broke off as the walls disappeared.

He had never been to Scotland, but this was how he imagined it. The landscape seemed made half of rolling hills and half of jutting outcrops of rock that were mossy on one side and chalky white on the other. The air seemed to hold mist, cold as it broke against his skin, and he noticed different parts of the landscape appear and disappear.

For a split-second, he wondered if the people in the stands saw the mist or not.

Justin exhaled a breath and did the spell to reveal hidden items. He pictured a wave ebbing away from a beach, leaving shells and sand in its wake, and he was pleased to see several caches illuminate. Three were near his platform and a second-tier one was equidistant between their platform and the one that held Tayr.

"There," Tina called and pointed at an outcrop. "That looks like a place where we will be defended from two of three sides, and it has high ground. You hold it, I'll get the weapons."

"Good. There, there, and there." He pointed to the first, second, and third-tier caches. The third-tier one was close to the first-tier.

They nodded at one another and leapt down from the platform. The ground was surprisingly slick under his boots. He grimaced, regained his footing, and raced forward. As he ran, power coiled in his palms and his magic bar in the top left of his screen, which had been rendered in gray during the past matches, now glowed a steady blue.

Magic, at last. He was excited for this. The question was, which of the other teams had magic users?

He watched from inside the tumble of rocks as the Twins pushed directly toward him. "Tina! We'll have company soon."

Tina called something in return, which he hoped was an agreement. She didn't sound panicked, anyway.

Dexi and Callie looked annoyingly sure-footed on the slick ground. He couldn't make out their faces but he knew it was them. The two figures practically oozed arrogance as they ran. If they had stopped to pick weapons up, he hadn't seen it.

Tayr circled behind the Twins—or, at least, he was fairly sure he saw flickers of people. He leaned forward and wished he had a spell for distance vision. He yelped when Tina arrived behind him with a clatter, and she dropped prone to avoid the fireball he barely refrained from throwing.

"No own goals," she admonished him.

"Right. Sorry." He gestured for her to look. "Tayr's trying to pick the Twins off."

She settled beside him. "Finally, a use for the fact that I can barely see at close range."

He gave her a horrified look. "How do you fight one-on-one?"

"I aim for the blur," she said and failed to reassure him at all. "Okay—Tayr has two of their people trying to flank. They're quick. I'm not sure where the third one is…oh, yep. She's hanging back behind the left flank. Man, if they can pick the Twins off…"

"That would be good," Justin agreed. "So, what did you find for weapons?"

"Fist weapons, a short sword, and a battle-ax with a water potion." She sounded deeply satisfied. "We may be trying a totally crazy thing, but at least I'm well-armed for it."

"It's not crazy," he muttered. "Also, what's going on out there?"

"They're…wait, where are the Twins?" She sounded panicked and scanned hastily behind their hideout. "Shit, shit, shit, where did they—"

"Oh shiiiiiit." He elbowed her. "Tina…Tina, look. Oh, shit. Oh, shit."

"What?" She looked where he gestured and her eyes widened. "Oh, no. Oh, Tayr…"

Tayr was still gaining ground, but the Twins must have known their opponents were there all along. Using the rocky ground and the constant dips and swells as a cover, they had hunkered down and hid to allow their opponents to pass them. Now, the Twins were the ones to creep up from behind, while the Tayr members slowed and began to inch through the mist. They were close enough that even Justin could see them clearly.

He readied a fireball as he watched. He had a unique opportunity in that everyone he could see was someone he wanted to strike. Tayr seemed to have realized what was happening. They spun to look around, while the Twins used every opportunity to close the distance.

When the spell came, it was strong—a gust of wind that knocked all three members of the other team from their feet.

"Well, fuck," Justin said. "I should have known the Twins would have magic. Who are these guys?"

"If it helps," Tina pointed out, "they're probably saying the same about you, what with you coming out of nowhere to get to the final of the tournament."

"That does help, thank you."

Unfortunately, any thoughts of a boost disappeared when the Twins fell on their opponents without mercy. Armed with daggers, they clearly excelled at close range. Callie's style was completely different from Tina's, her strokes shorter and sharper compared to his teammate's swells and powerful movements, but they were equally beautiful in motion. The woman made short work of her first opponent and turned to face the one Justin had fought yesterday who carried the battle ax.

Dexi had eliminated the third member of Tayr with a rush of water that tumbled her with the force of its undertow. She was now encased in shimmering blue and water dripped from her.

The woman he had fought knew she had no chance, but she clearly did not want to surrender. She feinted left and whirled to throw her battle-ax with power that didn't surprise Justin at all—not after seeing her ease with the weapon the other day.

The throw was true. Dexi had to dive sideways to avoid it,

and with the magic-user taken out of commission, she hurled herself at his partner. The two grappled and the stronger woman tried to disarm Callie and get her into a chokehold. Her window of opportunity slipped away with every second as the man had begun to haul himself up.

Justin seized his chance. He scrambled onto one of the rocks and lunged forward to hurl a fireball at Dexi. In his haste, however, he had forgotten how slick the ground was. His boot slipped and the shot went wild. The man whirled and launched a gust of wind at him. It knocked him down, and Callie took advantage of her opponent's distraction to choke the other woman.

"Tayr is out of the match!" the Master of Ceremonies called to the sound of groans.

"Justin!" Tina darted her glance from him to their adversaries. "Justin, are you okay?"

"Yes." He groaned and forced himself to stand. There was no time to waste feeling sorry for himself. The Twins would be there in a moment. He shook himself out, tried to remember his grandfather's stories of marching for days through the forests, and told himself he could sleep when he was dead. "I'm ready. I—"

"Look out!" She flung herself over him as another gust of wind rattled overhead. Unnaturally strong, it swirled around them and began to pick hit points off them both.

"Back into cover!" he called. They held each other up as they limped to their shelter.

The wind couldn't reach them there. It whistled angrily around the stones before it faded. A moment later, a fireball rocketed at the opening from which they'd watched. The friends ducked before they looked cautiously out again.

The Twins now ran to their own defensible position. Justin gritted his teeth and threw a fireball with all the power he had. If he could only land one meaningful strike before the man was out of range.

It hit Dexi and took his health bar down a third, but Justin's magic now needed to tick back at an inexorably slow rate.

He sat weakly. "Fuck, fuck, fuck. What do we do?"

"What do you mean?" Tina stared at him. "We stay here and follow the plan. We have a defensible position and your magic will come back. As long as no one moves, it's you against him. We'll see if it's possible to distract him enough for me to creep out but otherwise, you two will need to chip away at each other."

Half-heartedly, he looked over his shoulder and barely ducked in time to avoid a fireball to the face. He swore. "Cowards."

"They're doing what we're doing," she pointed out. "And this is a compliment, after all. They've never gone on the defensive before. I asked around. They always go straight for the kill. They're scared of you."

"They should be," he muttered. "Because I'll fucking take them out."

"Justin, for fuck's sake. Sit and think for a minute—"

"I am thinking!" he shouted in response. "I'm thinking about the grand prize I need to win to get home. You don't get it, do you? You can go home anytime you want but I can't, Tina. I need that key and if they get it, I'll never get out of here!"

"Calm down." Her voice was fierce. "That is all the more reason to play this safe, Justin. Don't throw away the advantage you have—"

"No." He took a deep breath, remembered the sight of the cache that had nestled between the two teams, and ducked out of hiding to sprint toward it. If he and Dexi had magic, it stood to reason that the Master of Ceremonies would have a magic potion. He needed to get it first.

"*Justin!*" Tina yelled.

Totally focused on the cache, he didn't stop. He ducked incoming gusts of wind with a single-minded determination. No matter what, he would go home. He would win, and he would go home. The key was in his sights and he wouldn't make the mistake of sitting back while everything passed him by like he had so many times before.

She shouted something, but he wasn't listening. He thought he saw movement—Dexi, most likely—but he had proved he could avoid the wind and the man must be running low on magic. He skidded up to the cache, stood to open it, and was hurled sideways with brutal force.

Callie stood nearby, her hands out to throw a spell, and the last thing he saw before the world went black was his health bar flashing red and completely empty.

CHAPTER SEVENTEEN

Anna Price was nothing if not simple and to-the-point, but between the newsworthiness of the PIVOT pods and the potential future applications, the reporter clearly wanted to take his time. After she had finished her interview, David Yang ushered the founding members of PIVOT in for a group interview about their initial development of the technology.

Jacob watched Justin's pod out of the corner of his eye. He wished DuBois was there to oversee what was going on. There was a full medical staff, of course, but the patient's stress levels were climbing steadily beyond where they had been. There was no medical distress but the young engineer hadn't seen him like this since Justin first learned where he was.

He tuned back in time to hear the question Yang asked him. "Were there injuries during the development process?"

At last, he felt he was on solid ground. He shook his head. "We started very small. We worked up from already-used technologies and we tested them on ourselves. I have to say, having never done testing on people before and being the ones who would go into the machine, I think we probably took far longer with it than we needed to."

The others laughed. He didn't need to stretch the truth at all. Not being sure what would happen with the combination of virtual reality feeds, the team had tested each one stringently and had sometimes rerun all their calculations and diagnostics between trials of the same iteration.

"Now, you're laughing," Yang said, with his reporter-smile, "but I think everyone else is probably glad to hear you say that."

"It's good to do things like that," Jacob agreed. "I think we wonder about who we might have had a chance to help if we had gotten this technology online sooner—at least, I know I do—but it really does set my mind at ease to know that it's safe."

"Exactly," Amber added. "We had a few failures in testing but every one of those was running the current too low—never over-loading the system. Besides that, all the testing really gave us a handle on the numbers we should expect to see, and that helped us when we integrated the game."

"Tell me about the game," David suggested. He smiled brilliantly at all of them.

"It's a fairly standard MMORPG," Nick explained. "We really lucked out in our collaboration there. It was a game that was already made and that we really loved. The team had run out of funds to keep the servers online, and we were able to keep the game alive and keep playing our favorite game."

"It's a fantasy world," Amber explained. "The basic premise is very similar to other games—you help people out, get stronger, take on stronger enemies. What makes it so effective as a recovery tool is two-fold. First, it engages social processes in the brain and second, there is a life-or-death component that stimulates the brain to protect itself."

"That was perhaps a poor choice of words," Jacob interjected smoothly. He saw her grimace and hoped the TV crew decided not to show that. "The game isn't dangerous. It's simply that the fantasy combat stimulates the nervous system to behave as if it is conscious and responding to threats."

"So there's no way to die in the game?" David clarified.

Amber opted to keep her mouth shut, for which Jacob was thankful. "Your character can die," he said, using finger quotes on the word, "which will provoke an emotional response due to the immersion. However, in a healthy individual, this is not—"

Alarms erupted behind him and he spun in alarm.

Justin's monitors flashed red and his heart rate flat-lined. A team of assistants had swung into action and DuBois burst through the laboratory doors in the next moment, wiping tell-tale traces of popcorn off his hands.

"What's going on?" he called.

"He flatlined," one of the assistants replied. "Death in-game and his vitals went haywire."

"*Justin!*" Mary ran from the other room, her face pale.

The TV crew looked at the pod in sudden interest, and Jacob was surprised to realize he felt nothing. He didn't care what they thought—not while Justin was fighting for his life. He ushered them to the side as he, Amber, and Nick crowded around the pod. Out of the corner of his eye, he could see Anna Price watching with remarkable equanimity.

"Tell me when we're clear," DuBois called.

"Clear!" an assistant confirmed.

DuBois pressed the button for the defibrillator. Jacob held his breath and watched the jolt on the screen.

Nothing happened and he exhaled, only to drag in another breath.

The doctor's calm demeanor did not change at all. "Tell me when we're clear," he said again.

"Clear," the assistant called. He was pale now.

DuBois pressed the button. Again, the jolt burst across the heart rate monitor.

And, again, the flatline returned.

Jacob turned away and sank onto a crouch. He wanted to

pound his fist against something—anything—but there was nothing safe to punch.

"Tell me when we're clear," the doctor instructed.

"Clear," Jacob heard distantly. A moment later, there was a shower of sparks and several people yelled. Amber and Nick hauled their partner out of the way, and three assistants raced in. They called to each other, panicked, but he pushed them aside.

"You have a loose connection. It's not meant to take that charge so many times at once." He reached in, grimaced, and snapped the piece together, wincing at the jolt. He shook his burned fingers, knowing they would sting soon, and stood to see everyone staring at the heart rate monitor.

With his heart in his throat, he turned and almost collapsed in relief when he saw Justin's heart beating strongly. He met DuBois's eyes and nodded.

"Good work, Doc."

"It looks like he got reckless," the man said. "He—"

Jacob pushed the assistants forward and in the crush, managed to get close enough to DuBois to murmur, "Quietly. I'm doing damage control. They didn't know that was Justin."

"Ah," DuBois said. "In retrospect, that's rather a miscalculation, don't you think?"

"We'll talk about it later." He pivoted to the camera crew.

"Per the agreement," Anna Price said soberly, "I would like to remind you that all footage of monitors must be blurred and that written accounts cannot include any specific numbers."

"Of course," David Yang said. He looked from her to Jacob. "Would either of you like to make a statement regarding the overall safety of the device in testing?"

"Justin!" A red haze came over Tina's vision. Callie laughed, spread her hands, and gave Dexi a bow. His laughter echoed her amusement.

Tina screamed in absolute fury. She didn't take the time to think about what she was doing but simply wound up and let the battle-ax's momentum carry her across the field. Her momentum skidded her toward Dexi so quickly that, as he began to turn, she knew it wouldn't be in time.

She spun as she reached him. The blade of the ax whistled as it cut smoothly into a deadly arc and she felt a moment of complete peace.

Then she realized exactly how much damage the blade would do before the stasis field came down around him. Panic spiked through her. She was furious, yes, but she didn't want blood on her hands—and she couldn't stop turning.

Resisting the urge to panic, she planted her feet but was powerless to stop the skid. At last, she did the only thing she could think of. With all her strength, she wrenched the blade around as she spun. Her muscles screamed in protest, but she held on. Everything narrowed to the point of the blade as it inched slowly upward.

The flat of the blade struck Dexi with bone-crushing force. She thought she heard Callie scream as the stasis field came up around him, and a tidal wave of sound erupted from the stands to crash in on them. Deaf to it all, Tina raced to Justin. She skidded to her knees, felt his neck and his wrists, and yanked his shirt away to press her hand against his chest.

"Someone!" she screamed. "Someone—anyone, *please!*" She could hear the Master of Ceremonies yelling something, and healers ran across the arena toward her.

Her friend's face was pale. His chest wasn't moving and she couldn't think.

"Please," she babbled as the healers reached them. "Please—

he's not breathing. He needs to be revived…his heart needs to be restarted. Please, please!"

They paled at her words but grasped Justin's unconscious body and magicked it onto a stretcher they conjured out of thin air. It hurtled away of its own accord toward the distant door of the arena and she sprinted after it. When hands snatched at her, she made to fight them off but it was only a healer hauling her up onto a moving platform. She held on, suddenly aware of the shouts from some of the crowd and the silence from the others.

Justin.

"Whatever you can do," she implored the AI under her breath, "*please* do it."

"*I can only work within the strictures of this world,*" it told her solemnly. "*The rest is up to you and to Justin.*"

"He's *dead*," she whispered.

"*Then it is up to you.*"

Tina pressed her fingers against her eyes and when she opened them, she was in the shadowy interior of the arena's medical bay.

The chief healer—or so she assumed, given his ornate robes—leaned over Justin with an air of boredom.

"Dead," he pronounced. He waved a hand. "His body should be released to his next of kin."

"Wait just a moment!" She threw herself off the moving platform and landed awkwardly in front of him. Her arms folded, she glared at the man. "Bring him back."

"The rules of the arena are quite clear." He folded his hands inside his sleeves and looked down his arched nose at her. "We are permitted to stabilize the fighters should they be injured and bring them back to a certain level. Beyond that, we do not intervene. Everyone signing on for the arena knows the risks."

"Do you mean to tell me…" Her heart had begun to pound dangerously. "That you can revive him and you won't?"

He sneered and said nothing.

"Listen," Tina said. "Where I come from, you would be thrown out of your guild and strung up in front of a court for this. Where I come from, doctors swear to heal those they can and do no harm. You're no healer!"

"Take her away," he said, his expression one of irritation.

"If a single one of you touches me, you will be sorry," she all but snarled. The other healers backed away as she advanced on man—and the Master of Ceremonies, who had rushed into the room. "Listen. To me. You introduced a new mechanic into this game and you didn't know what would happen. Well, what happened was that one of your contestants unleashed a death spell on my teammate. She played around the rules of the game to kill him when she only needed to incapacitate him to win— and you let that happen."

"Madam," the Master of Ceremonies said, flustered, "rest assured that the recompense for a death in the arena—"

"I don't want recompense!" she screamed. "Do you think I want money? No. I want you to do what you should have done from the second Justin was brought in here. I want you to make him better."

"A revival potion," the chief healer said, "is incredibly valuable."

"So it's about money, huh? It's always about money." Tina grabbed a handful of his robes and pulled him close. "Listen to me, motherfucker. I'm not from this world. I have powers you cannot dream of. If you do not bring him back right the fuck now, I will obliterate everything you hold dear. I will find the piece of your universe that houses you and I will destroy it with a bomb if I have to, but I'll make sure that everything you know and love is not only in hell, it is *gone forever.*"

Whatever he saw in her eyes, he yanked himself back hastily. A quick look between him and the Master of Ceremonies produced a hasty nod, and he went to an ornate cabinet and withdrew a shimmering purple potion. One of the assistants held

Justin's mouth open as the chief healer poured it carefully down his throat.

She twined her fingers with her friend's while her heart pounded. He didn't move and she was terrified that something was wrong. They had waited too long.

Oh, she was not kidding. When she got out of there, she would find the server that ran this snooty healer and she would destroy it with a sledgehammer. The PIVOT team had told her how little Justin could afford to die in the game and now, she was powerless to do anything other than watch over the lifeless body of someone she cared about who should never have died.

Her eyes were squeezed shut when his fingers twitched.

"Justin!" She held him close.

"Can't—breathe—" he wheezed.

"Sorry…I'm sorry." Tina let go of him. "You're here. You're alive. Oh, my God." Tears started but she ignored them. "I was so scared for you. So scared."

"Tina." He wrapped his arms around her. "Uh—well, first of all, thank you. And what's this about you cursing the healer?"

"How did you know about that?" She raised her head.

"The AI told me. It says I owe you big time."

She sniffled and hiccupped.

"If you will rest in one of the suites provided," the Master of Ceremonies said somewhere nearby, "we will summon both teams once a ruling has been made."

"A ruling like throwing that bitch out of the ring and awarding us the prize?" Tina asked dangerously and fixed him with an icy glare.

The Master of Ceremonies flitted away as if he hadn't heard her and she sighed. She was aware of another emotion pressing close now—fury. Her first instinct was to pound on Justin's chest with her fists, but that seemed unwise at this particular moment.

Instead, she looked at him. "What the *hell* were you thinking?"

He let his head drop. "I'm sorry."

"Justin, don't apologize to me. You almost got yourself killed. All you had to do was remember what you told me—that they'd find another way to get you out of here if we didn't get the key." She whirled and put her head in her hands. "Instead, you were so caught up in wanting to leave right now that you...you could have killed yourself. Everything your parents did and all the doctors did would have been for nothing!"

His face looked stricken.

"So you aren't home," Tina continued scathingly. "So everything isn't normal. Well, guess what? You don't get everything you want, okay? I know I'm the last person who gets to lecture you about this. I'll never forgive myself for where you are right now, but you have a chance no one else in the world has ever had. If dozens of people are willing to give weeks and months and maybe even years of their lives to help you recover, goddammit, the least you could do is respect them enough to not do something stupid."

Justin stared at her for a moment before he nodded. "I'm sorry."

Tina sat in a miserable heap. All the other healers had fled, presumably scared out of their wits by the tiny woman in full leathers who yelled threats and curses.

"I'm sorry," she said. "And I'm sorry I couldn't find the words to get you to take this seriously."

"Tina." He moved closer to her and pulled her up. "You can't heal for me."

"So I can injure you but I can't make you better?" she asked bitterly.

"Yeah." He nodded. "You did what you could. In fact, when we get out of here, I'll look up what you yelled at that healer because it sounds impressive."

"Oh, please don't." Her cheeks were burning.

"From here on out," Justin said, "we work as a team. I won't run off and try to do things on my own, and you won't try to fix me. Deal?"

"Deal." Tina took his hand and squeezed. "Okay, we need to get out of here."

"Why?"

"Because I can see them bringing Dexi and Callie in and if I have to see either one of them right now, I'll kill them with my bare hands."

The TV crew stared at him, the recording lights overly bright, and Jacob felt the silence wrap around him like a blanket.

"I do apologize," he said finally. "We wanted to be transparent with you about how the technology worked but we did not feel it was safe to move Justin to another location. We wanted him to be close to all the medical and engineering staff." He glanced to where Mary stood with her palm on her son's pod, her eyes closed against tears.

"You were telling us that the pods were safe," David Yang said gravely.

"If I may," DuBois said. "This has been my area of study for over two decades now. What you have just seen is one of the dangers that faces any patient in a coma, particularly those who have suffered head trauma."

Everyone looked at Jacob, who nodded jerkily.

"The human body is not designed for the speeds we travel at these days," the doctor said. He walked to one of the desks and mimed bashing his head onto it. "Now, if I were to hit my head as hard as I could against this table, I would be injured but my skull could effectively insulate itself against the shock. In a car accident or other impact event, however, that is not necessarily true, and the brain is very delicate."

The young engineer could only hope that DuBois's unusual

calm was helping. He and the other members of the team had gotten used to it, but what if the reporters thought it was a sign that he didn't care?

"At any time during the recovery," DuBois explained, "blood vessels can rupture. It is not uncommon for a slow or quick bleed to cause further injury or death in a comatose patient. It is also not uncommon that normal brain function cannot be restored—at least, within the time frames we've seen." He approached the pod. "What we see in this case is that brain function is being restored. Now, this might happen regardless of our treatment. The truth is, until we have a much larger sample size, we will not know every facet of this. What we can say is that different treatments work for different patients, and what we are doing here is adding another treatment to the repertoire doctors can use."

The crew took notes diligently.

"Any patient using this for recovery would have a full medical team available," Jacob added. "As you saw here and as it would be in a hospital."

"So, what...happened?" Yang asked. "Was what happened related to the treatment?"

"Yes," the doctor said bluntly. The young engineer suppressed a groan of frustration, but DuBois looked calm and completely unapologetic. "Immersion is necessary to activate the nervous system, and it means that if someone 'dies' in the game, their nervous system suffers a shock. Justin has been informed that he should be careful and not take on impossible odds, but combat can have surprises."

"If the treatment is dangerous," the reporter said, "does it make sense to add it to the repertoire?"

"That's a question for individual doctors and families to decide," DuBois said simply. "I would say it is equally dangerous to do nothing. In that case, the brain has no stimulation and no memory of the outside world. Both are a risky choice. It is a logical fallacy to assume that doing nothing is not a choice or that it is not a risk."

David looked puzzled as he wrote that down.

"We have seen multiple 'deaths' in-game from healthy players," Jacob said. "It causes a jolt to the nervous system but it is not dangerous without underlying conditions. As Dr. DuBois points out, the danger of the treatment is due to the same thing that makes it effective. Some families might decide that their family member would do better without this intervention. Other patients, like Justin—who has played video games all his life—show a natural inclination to interact with the game."

"I see." Yang now scribbled furiously.

"The game has provided him with experiences he had always wanted to have," Mary said quietly. She stood beside Jacob and smiled at him. Tears still streaked her cheeks, but she was composed. "He is able to help people in the game and his father and I have been able to send him limited communications. He knows he is not alone. It is a great comfort to us and to him that he is not locked in his own mind."

The reporter finished writing and looked at them. "This is fascinating. Thank you for your input. Ms. Price, rest assured that all drafts will be vetted by our legal team according to your specifications." He went around the room and shook the hands of the PIVOT team members, Dr. DuBois, and the assistants. He nodded and left with his crew.

A long silence followed.

"I think that went well," Mary said brightly. She squeezed Jacob's hand.

"No one cares about the upside when the downside is…" He shook his head.

"Mr. Zachary," Price said, "do you honestly believe you will do anyone any good by convincing yourself that the article will be negative?"

He gaped at her. "Well…I… No."

"Then I suggest you return to work," she suggested. "I feel confident that we can expect both supporters and detractors, whatever the outcome of this article. All that is within our power is to do the best we can. Of course, I speak metaphorically, as I am not participating in this research." She smiled. "I have every confidence in you. Keep working."

She left but paused to scan the records of Justin's fight with disturbing acuity.

When she was gone, everyone stared at one another.

"I cannot get a handle on that woman," Amber said finally.

Every person in the room nodded.

CHAPTER EIGHTEEN

Justin spent a tense quarter of an hour pacing around the emergency suites while the crowd in the arena muttered and shifted restlessly. Everyone wanted to know who would win and the AI constantly offered him a dispiriting account of the odds that were being given for his survival.

When a messenger appeared at the door, the two friends turned quickly. The man who entered beckoned them to follow him, his shoes clicking on the stone floor, and Justin felt a strange calm wash over him. He looked at Tina.

"It'll be okay."

"Easy for you to say," she said but she grinned. "You weren't the one who threatened the chief healer with violent death."

The messenger darted an alarmed look at them and increased his pace.

"I like you two together," the AI told Justin.

"Wait. Really?"

"Yes. She'll keep you on your toes."

"You hope she kills me, don't you?" He rolled his eyes.

"Of course not. Don't be so short-sighted. If she did, I wouldn't get to make fun of you."

He threw up his hands and mouthed "AI" to his companion, who snickered.

In the other room, the Twins waited with the Master of Ceremonies. When they appeared, Callie and Tina locked glances, and it was clear that the two women despised one another. Dexi tried to lounge as if he were bored but he didn't quite pull it off. Apparently, no number of healers could fix every bone in someone's torso in ten minutes.

Having been on the receiving end of a death spell, Justin didn't feel too charitable. Frankly, he hoped it hurt. He hoped the man felt like he'd been kicked by a horse.

"Thank you for joining me," the Master of Ceremonies said. "I am Jaco."

All four contestants looked stonily at him and he laced his hands behind his back with a tense smile. "Very well. As you have seen, there is the small matter of declaring a winner."

"We killed one of their teammates," Callie said. "We're clearly stronger."

"They exceeded any reasonable standards of sportsmanship or necessary force," Tina argued. "They should be disqualified." When she saw Justin staring at her, she shrugged. "What? I was in pre-law for a while."

"Huh." He tried to picture her as a lawyer and couldn't.

"Both teams had one member incapacitated," the official said. "Therefore, the match is declared a draw and both teams will receive a prize of their choosing." He took care to add quietly, "The prizes will be dwarven artifacts of great value from the king's private stores."

There it was—the siren call of his freedom from the game. Justin wanted to sit as a wave of dizziness swept over him. He couldn't think of anything to say beyond a strangled, "Oh."

He looked at Tina and she smiled.

"It seems like you're ready," she said. "Is it time?"

Callie and Dexi were in close-headed conversation. Both

seemed upset and Justin turned and moved to the window. He looked out at the city and the bustling streets and heard the arena crowd singing above him. The thought wouldn't leave him. He could go home. Right now.

"Tina."

She appeared at his side. "Yes?"

"I may be ready," he said, "but there are a couple more things I want to do. I've tried to get out of here so much that I've…I haven't taken time to say goodbye. If I leave now, I'll never see Lyle again, or Kural, or…Zaara." He looked away so she wouldn't see the flush in his cheeks.

His friend said nothing.

"We agreed to do this as a team, though," he said. "And I know that if I stay, I'll make you spend more time here, too."

"Wait—Justin." She looked confused. "What are you talking about?"

"If we walk away now," he said with a grin, "those two won't ever get what's coming to them. Fuck a draw—I want a rematch."

Tina looked at them with wide eyes. "*Oh.*" Her jaw set. "Let's do it."

He turned to look at the Master of Ceremonies. "We've decided we're not satisfied with a draw."

The Twins both stood. Dexi leaned on Callie but he still managed to look intimidating.

"You don't want to make enemies of us," he told them.

"Oh, please," Justin said. "If you only want people to applaud everything you do, start a reality TV show or something."

"Huh?" the man asked.

He shook his head. "My point is this—they didn't win. It was a bad setup and things went sideways. Tayr lost fair and square, but neither we nor the Twins won. A draw? That's a shitty ending to all of this. Do you think that crowd will go home happy? No. They're here to see if the Twins finally get taken down a peg or two, and a draw isn't the way to do that."

He stepped closer to Jaco. "We want a rematch. Us and the Twins."

The official stared at him. "I…allowing teams to appeal decisions would be a very unwise strategy."

"Uh-huh. But you're not, are you? No one won, you said so yourself. Your rules allowed deadly damage and you stopped the match before either team could win. You denied those people out there a winner. If you want to make this right, you'll give them one."

The Master of Ceremonies looked from one team to the other. "This is highly irregular."

"You don't say," Tina said dryly. "Look, you're the MC so you literally make the rules. Let's do it again and this time, you do your part right."

"What does that mean?" Callie hissed. "Do you want them to give you an advantage?"

"Last time, it seems like they gave you an advantage," she said. "No magic wielders on Tayr, one on our team, and two on yours? So be grateful we're not asking for a forfeit from you for your lack of control—or your attempted murder."

Justin stared at the Master of Ceremonies, who swayed worriedly, his frown intense.

At last, the man nodded. "I will announce it. Come with me." He looked at all of them and made a small gesture. Magical barriers sprang up around the two teams and faded to invisibility, and his magic bar went grey again. "Not that I don't trust you," the official said with a raised eyebrow.

The four contestants and Jaco appeared on the dais to the sudden sound of cheering. The man waited while people scrambled to their seats and crowded the railing.

"A unique situation has come to pass," the Master of Ceremonies said. "Each team had one player incapacitated—and, in the interests of our contestants, we paused the match to allow Justin, of Sephith's Bane, to be revived by our chief healer."

"Liar," Tina muttered.

"As the match was halted and no clear winner had been declared, we have decided to stage a rematch between these two teams," he continued. "This will be the conclusion of Season Twelve and will feature treasures from before the founding of Insea."

He raised his hands and the crowd cheered, and he was still smiling when he turned to the contestants.

"Rest," he told them. "Seek out healers of your own, if you can. I anticipate a…spirited match tomorrow, don't you?"

Justin looked at Callie and Dexi and saw death in their eyes. "Yes," he agreed. "I do."

<hr>

Zaara was in her room, studying a book that had come by courier the day before, when her mother knocked on her door.

"Zaara?"

"Yes?" She took care to shut the book before she opened the door as she didn't want her to see arcane rituals and worry.

"A messenger came with a letter for you," the woman said.

"Oh?"

"Zaara…he says you're summoned to the city." She twisted her hands together in anxiety. "To Insea. Promise me you won't enter that tournament."

"Er…" Given what she knew about what was happening, she wasn't sure she could promise that. "Let's see what he wants."

"He's gone." Her mother hesitated, slid her hand into her pocket, and withdrew a scroll. It was tied with a deep blue ribbon, the kind of thing nobles had in abundance but people outside the city rarely saw. "Zaara, promise me you'll be safe."

"Of course I'll be safe," she told her. "No running off anymore. I promised you and I promised Father." She held her mother's gaze until the other woman smiled. "Now, let's see what this is."

She opened the letter and scanned it. At the bottom was a complex rune she had never seen before and another slip of paper held a different rune.

She read the letter again from start to finish. While she had known this was coming, it still hurt to see it. She nodded and rolled the letter again.

"It wasn't a summons," she said, unconcerned that she lied through her teeth. "It's only an invitation, if ever I come to Insea. Someone heard about Sephith. So you see? There's no reason to worry."

Her mother looked warily at her for a moment but nodded. "Very well, then." She looked past her daughter at the candle. "It's late, my love. You should turn in."

"You're probably right." Zaara forced a smile and hugged her. "I'll sleep now. Thank you for bringing me the letter, Mother."

When the woman had left, she shut the door to her room quietly and carefully. She changed her clothes and blew the candle out. Alone in the darkness, she slipped the tiny piece of paper into one pocket, held the letter, and said the words of the spell.

Zaara barely blinked, but between one moment and the next, her room faded around her and she stood on a street of golden stone that glistened faintly in the moonlight. Nearby were the sounds of music and chatter, and she stepped out of the shadows in front of a crowded inn.

She was still trying to work up the courage to go in when a figure emerged, did a double-take, and stopped dead in his tracks.

"*Zaara?*" Lyle asked.

She smiled. "I heard…I heard Justin was leaving soon."

"Leaving?" The dwarf frowned. "I hadn't heard anything about that."

"I had a letter from him," she said. "It gave me a way to teleport here."

"Huh." He shook his head. "Well, I'm headin' to his inn. Come with me!"

"Uh, Jacob?" Nick stared at the screen, his expression one of concern.

"Yeah?" Jacob shoved off and let his chair roll to his partner's desk. "Look, if it's the voice glitch in the barmaid at Riverbend, I don't know how to fix it."

"I—wait. What have you been doing talking to barmaids?" He raised an eyebrow at his friend.

"Nothing." The man cleared his throat hastily. "So, what did you say was the problem?"

"Well, you know how we met after the TV crew had gone and went over the logs?"

"Yep."

"And how we saw that Justin didn't want to leave until he wrapped up all his unfinished business?"

"Yep."

"And then we decided I would go into the game and find a way to get Zaara to Insea?"

"Yep."

Nick looked at Jacob. He was fairly sure he could say anything right now and get the same response. He briefly considered what he could ask that would be the funniest but realized he'd missed the moment. His friend stared expectantly at him.

A raise, dammit. He should have asked for a raise.

Next time.

"Well, I went into the game," he said. "And I brought Zaara up and her asset...isn't in Riverbend anymore."

"Oh?" His friend suddenly looked cagey.

He narrowed his eyes. "Why do you look weird?"

"No reason. Nothing. It's fine. So what's wrong? Do you need me to, uh…take care of it?"

"No," he said slowly. "No, I don't. Because it's already taken care of. She used a teleportation spell she received from a messenger, which brought her to Lyle…who's taking her to see Justin."

"Oh." Jacob smiled.

"And I don't know where the messenger came from," Nick said.

"Right. Well, I'm sure Amber took care of it."

"Amber has been gone all afternoon."

"Maybe…I took care of it?" Jacob tried. "And then forgot? That's probably it. I haven't been sleeping much. Or DuBois—"

"Jacob, what's going on?" he demanded.

His friend sank his head into his hands. "Um. Okay. Look, I'll talk to you and Amber about it over dinner. We…might have a problem. Come on." He locked both their computers and ushered him toward the door. "We shouldn't talk about it here."

In the servers nearby, the AI hummed quietly to itself. It gave Justin a ton of crap but it was pleased that he would get to say goodbye to Zaara. He would be happy, of course, but there was more to it than that. After all, he could leave but it would have Zaara around forever. It didn't want her to be sad that whole time.

Cut off from the rest of Diatek's servers, it didn't know that in her office several stories above, Anna Price was seated in her chair, deep in thought as she stared at the security footage of the now-empty PIVOT desks.

CHAPTER NINETEEN

The inn where Justin was staying was crowded with people trying to catch a glimpse of him. Zaara looked around as Lyle pushed brusquely through the crowd. She noticed that he was limping but there was no opportunity to ask about it over the din.

The innkeeper and his wife were clearly having the time of their lives. They filled orders with cheerful abandon and called greetings to regulars and new visitors alike. She could only imagine how their coffers would overflow by tomorrow.

At the back of the inn, a burly guard stared belligerently at all newcomers. He recognized Lyle but gave Zaara a dubious look until her companion beckoned her through. The crowd made a disappointed noise and shouted questions after them, some of them quite intimate. She blushed a fiery red.

"How are we supposed to know which of those he'd prefer?" she asked in an undertone.

He guffawed. "I'd bet we can rule out a few right off the bat."

She grinned at him. "Are you well, my friend?"

"Ah." He grimaced. "I was injured. The teams are getting desperate an' they'll do anything they can to knock their competitors out. I took an arrow to the knee, I did. I used to be an adventurer too, but not anymore…"

The dwarf was still muttering when he led her out onto the terrace.

Zaara stopped dead. There was more food there than she thought she'd eaten in her entire life, along with a profusion of flowers, enchantments, and gifts. Fairy lights drifted overhead. Of her friend, there was no sign beyond faint noises.

"Justin?" she called.

"Back here!" he yelled. The scraping noise of a chair on the floor was immediately followed by his head popping into view. "Zaara! I thought that was you. Come sit. Help me with the food."

"I don't think any one person can help you with this much food," she said dryly. "Or any two people—Lyle's with me." She clambered over a pile of boxed gifts into an open space filled with couches and a firepit. He held his arms out to greet her.

"Justin." She hugged him and they both looked around when Lyle tumbled over the pile of presents. "I'm glad to see you again before you go."

"How did you know? Some mage trick?" He laughed self-consciously. "I intended to send a letter. I didn't know how to get in touch before I went."

"I thought you'd sent the rune," Zaara said slowly. She shook her head. "It was probably Kural and he forgot to let me know. He persuaded the Master of Ceremonies to offer you the key as your prize, you know."

"Yes, they mentioned it would be a dwarven artifact." He smiled at her. "Zaara…Lyle…I'll miss you both so much."

"Ye can visit, can't ye?" the dwarf demanded. "Yer mother can, so…"

"That's true, but I worry that…well, never mind." Justin sat on one of the couches. "Eat, please."

"Again, I don't think we'll make a substantial difference," she said. She piled her plate with meats and cheese, slices of melon and bread, and some kind of chutney made of a deep-red berry. "So, tell me about you. Tell me about the tournament."

Justin grimaced as he told her about the Twins and their stranglehold on the event. Lyle chimed in once in a while to mention the matches he'd seen and the stories he'd heard. The Twins were revered in certain parts of Insea and feared as well.

"They've trained their whole lives for something like this," the dwarf explained. "I heard their parents are merchants and wanted them to guard the caravans. It's well paying work and it'd mean their caravans would always be secure. That's why they were trained in everything—all weapons, magic, whatever."

"And then they had the chance to compete for prizes like these," Justin said thoughtfully. "And they've trained together their whole lives so they know what the other one is thinking. That explains so much."

Zaara, layering cheese and meat on a slice of bread, did not speak immediately. She took a bite and considered what she'd heard. "I wonder what really drives them," she said finally. "If one of them took a killing shot, there are two things to consider —either they like to kill, or they want to win for a larger purpose."

"A little of both," said a new voice.

Everyone turned to look, but Justin's face was a particular spectacle. He looked like he wanted to drop his plate and run away screaming.

She noticed the woman she'd watched in the Arena. Surprisingly short in person, she was dark-haired and dark-eyed and wore a simple robe. She nodded to Zaara as she came to sit on the same couch.

"I'm Tina. Are you Zaara? Lyle and Justin speak of you often."

"Yes." She tried to wipe chutney off her hands and failed utterly. "I, um…"

"Not to worry. Keep eating." Tina looked at Justin and smiled. "Do you want to hear what I learned?"

"Yes." He cleared his throat. "Yes, of course. That would be good."

"The Twins," she said and drew the word out for effect, "are convinced that a treasure of inestimable power lies at the end of this quest, which will give them the strength to become gods. Apparently, they were sought out by a…well, he calls himself a prophet. He has told them that they are prophesied to rule the entire world—if only they're willing to prove themselves worthy."

"Jesus leaping Christ." Justin put his head in his hands. "So they're deadly and crazy to boot. What now?"

The shawarma joint Jacob found nearby was dirty, noisy, and too full of an ever-shifting assortment of patrons to be bugged. Jacob waited, tapped his toes nervously as his two partners ordered, and explained what was going on in one tense sentence.

They both froze with their sandwiches partway to their mouths. Amber's eyes were wide. Nick looked like he wanted to throw up.

"Aware?" Amber rasped finally. "It's becoming…aware? Are yousure, Jacob? You're not simply messing with us, right?"

"I wish I were messing with you." He shook his head. "Because this is a wrench in the works that no one needed."

"Or is it?" she asked him. She put her sandwich down and looked seriously at him. "We talked about Justin adapting the game to his needs and seeking out what would inspire him to wake up, but what if the game was also adapting to him? There have been story twists we never encountered when we played it, and they've shown up at very convenient times."

"Okay, but that's even worse." He shook his head. "If it can choose to help, then it can choose not to help."

"Yes," Amber agreed, "but so far, it has chosen to help."

"Amber is right," Nick said.

"What makes you say that?" Jacob stared in turns at his most pessimistic friend and his most optimistic one. "Because I've never seen you two agree on something like this before."

"Exactly," the other man said. "Amber is the one who could find the reverse of a silver lining in anything." He saw her look and hastened to add, "No, no, it's one of the things that makes us a great engineering team. We're all good at engineering, and I dream up crazy things no one's done before and you find the ways things could go wrong. Remember that time I struck off on my own and my project literally exploded during finals presentation week?"

She snickered and took a sip of her coke. "That was funny. I have to admit, it was even funnier when mine didn't even turn on."

"See?" He looked at Jacob. "My point is, if Amber says things are going well so far, I believe her."

He considered this.

"I also don't know how aware it is," Amber said.

"It's doing things on its own."

"It was always doing things on its own. That's what procedural generation means." She frowned a little in thought. "You said that it seemed like it was…dreaming."

"Yeah."

"Okay, so here's the playbook. If we have the sense that it's waking up and pulling bad shit, we pull Justin out. He's ready and he's found the keys. Otherwise…we let the two of them do what they've been doing so far. Because, let's be honest, it's helping him."

Jacob hesitated, then nodded. "As long as all three of us agree."

It was the way they had approached most of the big decisions involved in their work together. He put one shawarma-covered hand on the table for a three-way handshake.

"Yeah, I'm not touching that," Nick said. "But I'm in."

"I'm in," Amber agreed.

"I'm in." Jacob grimaced. "Now that we've decided that, do you have any idea what to tell Anna Price?"

His partners looked at one another.

"You're the CEO," they said in unison.

"Cowards," he retorted.

The group ate in silence for a while as they considered the Twins' apparent belief in their divinity.

"It seems to me," Tina said finally, "that it's a moral test."

Justin looked at her in surprise. His mind hadn't been able to settle. He'd been torn between seeing Zaara again, realizing this was goodbye, worrying about the two women being in the same place, and hearing that his opponents were hellbent on his death. His thoughts had simply leapt from problem to problem without addressing any of them.

One of the things he had been surprised to realize, however, was that his feelings for Zaara weren't what he'd thought they were.

Having acknowledged that, he wasn't sure what he felt for Tina yet. He knew she turned his world on his head, infuriated him, and made him question things about himself. Despite that, he wanted to get to know her better. He merely wasn't sure where that was going.

And he was okay with that. With Zaara, things had seemed wrapped up in a nice, neat little bow. She was beautiful and smart, and she made him laugh. Plus, she looked damned good in leather armor and they'd had each other's backs in a fight. He honestly hadn't thought past the beautiful part in a long time. She had been there and she ticked all the boxes. Of course he would be attracted to her. It made sense that she was the love interest. She hadn't taken that first kiss after they defeated

Sephith, but she would fall for him over time. That was the love interest arc.

But that wasn't how people worked. Sometimes, someone ticked all the boxes and there wasn't a spark. He had been so caught up in the way he expected things to go that he hadn't realized he didn't feel that way about her.

She met his eyes now and he saw the same knowledge there. Both knew they would miss each other. They had been through too much not to. But—

He jerked his train of thought to a halt. Zaara was a video game character. He was clearly reading into this. He darted a glance at her and saw her tiny smile.

It was merely a very, very realistic video game. Right?

Justin cleared his throat. Tina had been talking and he tried to remember what she'd been talking about. Oh, right.

"A moral choice?"

"The Twins," she said. "They're willing to do literally anything to defeat you because they want unlimited power. Their motives and their means are cruel and to get the key, you have to defeat them. The question is whether you'll cheat to do it."

"Cheat?" He felt a wave of revulsion. "Bribe the MC, you mean?"

"Or do things like they did," Zaara explained. "Take shots that could kill before the protective field kicks in. Try to injure them." She looked thoughtful. "You could pay someone to slip them poisoned wine—nothing that would kill them, only something that would put them off their game."

"No," he said emphatically.

"Ah," Lyle said. He nodded sagely. "So ye're goin' t'be stupid."

"That's not what this is!" he protested, stung.

"Oh?" Zaara raised an eyebrow. "You have two crazy people who are drunk on power, and the opportunity to eliminate them. Not to mention that they might be considering any of the things we mentioned. They might be trying to poison you."

Justin stood and paced. Eventually, he turned to look at the group. "This wasn't how I planned my goodbye with you two, by the way."

"You didn't plan one at all," she pointed out. "You intended to disappear into another world with only a letter." She seemed more amused than upset.

"Yeah, but I have the chance at one now and I'll take it." Justin made his mind up and sat. "I have almost two days to come up with a plan. *Tonight*, we're going to sit and talk and laugh. We're going to say a proper goodbye. Tina, you've never properly met Zaara. She helped me and Lyle take down Sephith."

"And helped take Justin down a peg or two," Tina interjected.

Justin darted her a look. "Right, because you had nothing to do with that."

"I like to think it's a group effort," she said with a grin and clinked glasses with the other two friends.

"Justin, I have a question for you," Zaara said.

He froze. Tina and Lyle looked on with open curiosity.

"Um…yes?" He cleared his throat awkwardly.

"In Sephith's tower," she said, "you told me you thought none of this was real and that you were dreaming this world." She tilted her head to the side. "Now, you're going home. D'you still think it's all fake?"

Justin felt a swell of an emotion that seemed very close to grief. Something was ending here. A door was closing. He could come back to the game but he would never have these experiences again. This night, with the food and the music from the inn, would only ever be a memory like all his battles against Sephith and the demons and the bandits.

"No," he said. "No, I don't think that anymore. I know it's real."

CHAPTER TWENTY

Tad sat in his office and jiggled his foot with the single-minded determination of someone who both needed to not think and needed to work off the four cups of coffee he had drunk that morning. His bill was up for debate in the house at present, and he should absolutely watch the live feed from the floor.

He couldn't bring himself to do that, though. Quite simply, he had poured everything he had into this and he wasn't sure he could bear to listen to people argue against it. His aides watched in the other room. He could hear the muffled sounds of speeches and knew he should go out there and watch with them.

Instead, he stood and began to pace.

If I lose, I'll lose on my own terms—on my own turf. He wouldn't accept a yes or no vote on a fundamentally corrupt bill as his hill to die on. He intended to champion this bill and show people what was possible.

A sudden shout of celebration from the other room stopped him in his tracks. He turned his head so sharply he got a crick in his neck and had to rub it while the door opened and his aides peeked into the room.

"Sir," Kyle said.

Tad's mouth twitched. "Yes. I heard the cheer."

"Oh. Spoiler alert, I guess." The young man pushed the door open and the group came in with huge grins. "One of two down. Bipartisan support. Are you happy, sir?"

"Ask me again after the Senate vote," he said. He went to sit at his desk before he looked up and saw the awkward expressions on their faces. "What?"

His staff all looked at each other. They seemed to be drawing figurative straws.

"Should I simply choose one of you at random?" he asked finally.

"I'll say it." Kyle swallowed. "Sir, we don't have the Senate votes. We haven't from the start, and we've…well, we thought you knew that."

He frowned at him. "We didn't have the House votes to start with, either. We scraped those together."

"Sir, the Senate vote is in two days and we're so far away that it's…impossible."

"How many do we need?" He stood and leaned over his desk. "Tell me. How many? Six, right?"

"Eight, sir." The young man swallowed. "We had two calls while waiting for the House vote tally to come in."

"And you still cheered?" Tad threw a hand out in the direction of the TV. "Why? Because you were enjoying the idea of watching this get shot down in the Senate?"

"No, sir!" They all looked horrified and Kyle stepped forward. "These things take time. They take years to get pushed through. The fact that you got this through the House at all is incredible. It means there's a base of support and someday, it might actually happen. We were cheering because you clearly changed some minds. You did a good job. Simply having this debated on the floor of the Senate will make ripples."

"So, this whole time…" He struggled for calm. "This whole

time I've talked about this bill and getting votes, not a single one of you thought it would be passed?"

The aides looked at one another. They didn't speak but they didn't have to. Their opinion was clear from their faces.

"I don't believe this." Tad leaned back in his chair. "Is there anything else you want to tell me? Will I be forced to resign? Am I being strung up on corruption charges?"

No answer was forthcoming.

"You know what?" He looked at them, his expression grim. "I have calls to make. I'm sure you all have things to do."

He looked at the papers on his desk until they'd trailed out miserably before he lowered his head into his hands. This couldn't be happening. He'd built his career on the impossible, running without a background or family in politics and against the prevailing party of his district. He'd been tested, but he thought his aides had been behind him.

Now he found out that they'd thought he would fail.

He shook his head once and picked the phone up, punched in a few numbers from memory, and waited. "Addie, yes, hello—it's Tad Williams, is the senator available? Thanks."

He waited for a few seconds before the other man came on the line.

"Tad. Hello."

"Eric." He leaned forward. Eric was on his second term, someone who had made his career bouncing back and forth between Tad's brand of fiery outspokenness and middle-of-the-road, bland moderation. It was always difficult to determine what he would back, but he believed there was a chance here. "I'd like to speak to you about the bill that just passed the House."

"Ah." The man's tone had become somewhat hesitant. "Senator, while I of course respect your passion, I think the bill over-reaches somewhat."

"How so?" he asked bluntly.

So far, he'd had good luck with bluntness. No one seemed to know what to do with it in DC.

Indeed, the senator paused for a moment before he said, "These are some very serious blanket reforms you're proposing. Who can say what necessities might arise in the future?"

"What necessities might arise that make drug companies raise prices past agreed costs?" Tad asked.

"In my experience, forbidding something outright is a sure path to bad feeling," Eric told him.

In your experience? This is your second term. He scratched his head. "So, let me get this straight. First, the problem was that there might be a problem that would require companies who were not in financial distress to raise prices out of the range of acceptable costs. When I asked what those problems might be, you shifted to talking about bad feelings."

No response was forthcoming.

"Thank you for your time," he said as civilly as he could and hung up.

He stared at the phone for a moment. Fiery outspokenness and absolute, bland moderation. When Eric had been elected, he had been far more toward the end of fiery outspokenness, but the bland moderation had become more and more prevalent. He had not, to Tad's knowledge, authored any bills in line with his campaign promises.

Do you think you're the first senator we've dealt with? Dru Metcalfe had asked.

Frustrated, he shook his head again and went back to the drawing board. He'd tried everyone he could think of. Now it was time to call anyone who would speak to him. He wouldn't back down, not yet.

It was an hour later when he put the phone down and rubbed the bridge of his nose. One person had changed their vote. One person.

And they had changed it in the wrong direction.

Tad had learned more than he had ever wanted to know about exactly how many people the drug companies had bought off.

He sighed and dialed one more number. As it rang, he leaned back in his chair.

"Hello?" Mary said quietly.

"It's me," he said. "Do you not have my office number in your phone?"

"I do, but one day I called your aide sweetheart so I've been cautious ever since."

Despite his despondency, he laughed. He had needed to laugh. "Ah."

"So." She had a sixth sense about these kinds of things. "How did the House vote go?"

"Fine. It passed."

"That's fine? Not…good?"

"We don't have the Senate votes," he told her simply. "And, having talked to the better part of the entire Senate during the last hour, I can tell you that it won't have the votes. I don't know what it would take. I really don't, Mary."

"Someone should spill the dirt on those CEOs," she said darkly.

"I won't throw mud, especially when I don't have anything to back it up with yet," he said. "I checked. People have tried that and not a single one of them was re-elected."

"When you got into this, you said re-election wasn't important," Mary reminded him. "You said, and I quote, that compromising your morals for re-election would only give you longer in office to do the wrong thing."

"I really wish you wouldn't listen when I say things. It's very inconvenient at times like these."

She laughed. "Tad, you know you're doing the right thing. And…"

He straightened. "And?"

"Well, I wanted to wait to show you this when you came home, but I think maybe you need it now. Just a second." He heard background noise fade away. "Okay, I'm in the bathroom. Tina is in the game now, you know, and she and Justin are… getting along well."

"Mm-hmm." Tad could not, for the life of him, imagine where this was going.

"Well, the other day, they had a date. I left halfway through but when I got back, Nick showed me an excerpt of their conversation. Tina asked Justin what he would do when he woke up from his game. Do you know what he said?"

"Not a clue, but I'm intrigued." He leaned on his elbows and a smile crept in.

"He said he would spend time talking to you," she said. "Because part of why he never really left his room was that he didn't see a way to help the world like he has in the game. Now he sees that you're one of the people making a difference and bringing the villains down. He wants to know more about what you do."

For a moment, he couldn't speak. His jaw hung open. It had been years since he and Justin were on the same page. He couldn't remember the last time he'd talked about morals without his son rolling his eyes. They'd had everything from silent ice-outs to screaming matches about how to effect positive change in the world, and Justin had usually gone back to his room after those—put off, his father had thought, by a grown-up's assertions that change was more difficult than a young person thought.

And now, Justin wanted to know more.

"Tell him…" His voice was a little unsteady. "Uh. I'll forward something to you if DuBois can get another letter to him."

"Of course." Mary's voice was gentle. "Stay the course, Tad. You know you won't win them all but if I know you, I can tell you that you'll remember forever all the times you let yourself down."

"You're right. You're always right."

"I'll remind you of that," she said fondly. "I love you."

"I love you, too. I'll send that letter along in a moment."

Tad sat down to write. For a long time, nothing came at all and he made several false starts. The letter he finally sent was brief and to the point, the kind of thing his father would have sent. He wasn't very good at the emotional parts. That had always been Mary's realm.

But he remembered one of the last times he and Justin had agreed. It had been years before, and they'd had months of good-natured debates.

He addressed the letter to Aristotle and signed it Socrates.

That done he went into the main room and looked at the aides. "Do you all have a moment?"

"Yes, sir." Kyle stood nervously. "We've been talking—"

"You gave me a realistic assessment, and I had a temper tantrum," Tad said. "I am, therefore, embarrassed and hope we can stop talking about it."

The staff looked at one another as if they wondered if this might be a trap.

"I know we don't have a hope in hell," he said. "We need nine votes."

"Eight, sir."

"No, nine. It got worse." He stuck his hands in his pockets. "But I'll be damned if I simply accept the idea that I don't have enough votes. Jenny, if you'd see what we can scare up for interviews, I'd be grateful. Kyle and Teddy, you're on social media patrol. Anne, I'll send you some talking points and I'd appreciate your once-over on wording. Whatever else you think of, go for it. You all signed up for the off-the-wall junior senator and that's who you'll get."

He walked into his office and left them smiling.

CHAPTER TWENTY-ONE

"**A**re you ready, Jacob?" Amber called.

"One second. I'm trying to get the proportions of this drink right." After a clattering sound in the laboratory's kitchenette, he emerged into the dining area with a full bottle of bourbon. He looked at the startled faces of those assembled. "It kept not being strong enough so I went back to basics."

"Oh, stop panicking." Nick leaned over and patted the couch. "Sit and watch. It'll be fine."

"Says the eternal optimist." He sat with a mutter. "They'll rip us to shreds. I woke three times last night from nightmares."

A few of the others nodded sadly. It had been two days since the TV crew left and yesterday, the PIVOT team had received word that the piece would air tonight—bumped forward due to the vote on Senator Williams' bill. Everyone had been on edge since then, a fact they had tried to keep hidden from Tina when she came out of the pod for food breaks.

Otherwise, they had all thought about little else.

Jacob, personally, was sure that he was about to see his life's work melt away. It was one thing to make a dud company and flame out. That was practically a Silicon Valley rite of passage and had no place there.

Getting thrown out for medical malpractice, though? There was no coming back from that. And he'd have taken all these people down with him. He took a sip from the bottle of bourbon, decided not to half-ass things, and took a gulp. It burned.

Good.

"It's starting," one of DuBois's assistants said.

Amber turned the volume up and the room fell silent.

"Questions have been mounting for weeks about the condition of the senator's son," a news anchor said. "Leaked reports indicated that doctors were using Justin for the trial of an FDA-rejected treatment. The news sparked an international outcry and pressure on the senator to resign his post, while Jacob Zachary, the Chief Executive Officer of PIVOT, was briefly taken into custody at the end of last month. He has been released and charges were dropped, but details have been difficult to come by. David Yang reports."

"Well, if that isn't the bleakest assessment of things," Jacob muttered.

Yang's face came into view. He was outside on a cloudy day and he looked somber. "I'm here at Diatek's Elizabeth Keegan Laboratory," he said. "This lab houses one of the most noteworthy medical trials going on today—the use of an innovative new technology to help resuscitate those in comas following brain injury. While most medical trials do not attract attention, this one has faced unusual scrutiny following the revelation that a senator's son is part of it."

Justin's face and the details of his accident came up on the screen, while Yang's voice continued in voiceover. "This is Justin Williams. A car he was the passenger in crashed. He was flown to a nearby hospital in critical condition, where he was placed on life support in the ICU. While Justin's family is arguably quite affluent, they were shocked by the costs of his care."

The screen cut now to Tad making an impassioned speech before the vote on the bill he had opposed. He spoke of his constituents and his family, recalling the phone call he'd had with the claims representative at his insurance company.

"I was so relieved when he told me that Justin was covered up to five hundred thousand dollars," the senator said. "And then he told me how little that would cover. He told me that the money would be gone within a month, if not sooner. If Justin failed to recover in that time, my family would shoulder the burden alone—and there would be nothing left for his recovery."

"Although the senator did not realize it at the time, his son's accident had been noticed by two people who'd had very similar experiences. The first was Anna Price, the CEO of Diatek Industries."

The camera cut to Price in the laboratory, speaking seriously about her child's accident. "It was only a week away from Mina's fourth birthday when the accident happened. She was an incredible child. She was so inquisitive, so bright." Old footage began to play of a little girl dancing through a tiny backyard and playing with blocks in a small apartment while a male voice told her about the periodic table of elements. "She was also a fighter," Price said. A picture came up on the screen of the little girl in an ICU bed. "Her father and I never doubted that she would recover. We had no idea how much that would cost."

The reporter's voice returned. "As costs mounted, the Price family sold all their possessions and eventually took turns sleeping in their car at truck rest stops near the hospital. They had small donations from their family and a church group, but the costs were too astronomical even for the community to shoulder. Eventually, they had to take Mina off life support."

"I will never forget that decision," Price said. "Because it wasn't a decision. It was out of our hands, but we still had to give the verbal consent for it. It was incredibly cruel, and I remember that the only thing that pulled me out of those years was the determination I felt that no other family should ever have to face that. I started Diatek Industries in order to research treatments for comatose patients. I didn't simply want them to be affordable. I wanted them to be widely available and more effective. I wanted to do what I could to accelerate the research that was happening."

"Another blow came two years later, when David Price committed suicide," Yang said, "leaving a note that he could not live with the fact of his daughter's avoidable death. Still, Price never wavered."

"It was merely another reason," she said. "These costs don't only harm patients, they destroy families. If we'd had other children, how would we have cared for them while Mina was in the hospital? We didn't have to make that choice, but others do. Parents drain their savings and go into debt. People have to choose between providing a good life for their children and helping their community with medical treatment. I don't think it has to be that way."

"Price started acquiring companies quickly," the interviewer explained. "Many of the early experiments were failures, but she does not regret them. She has said in several speeches that each failed experiment has paved the way toward better treatments."

Footage of her was shown which included speeches at commencements and industry luncheons, and Amber elbowed Jacob in the side.

"The music."

"Huh?"

"The music. Do you notice how it's all epic and stirring? That has to be a good sign. Right?"

"Let's wait and see."

"But Diatek Industries was about to find a new collaborator," the reporter said. Jacob's face appeared on-screen, and he hunched in his seat.

"The other person to see the news about Justin Williams was

Jacob Zachary," said the voiceover, "the co-founder and CEO of PIVOT Labs. Only months before, PIVOT faced a critical shortage of funds. Their technology, the virtual reality pod, had taken crowdfunding platforms by storm but struggled to find buyers.

"At the same time, Zachary was facing a personal battle—the hospitalization of his grandmother after a stroke. While her condition improved slowly, the family was staggered by the cost of her care. Zachary and the PIVOT co-founders spoke about his experience to 360 News."

Nick appeared on-screen, seated in the laboratory. "I remember Jacob came into the lab one morning and we could see that something was very wrong. He told us how much his grand-mother's care was costing the family and we couldn't believe it."

Yang's voice returned as a picture of Amber appeared. "Amber Garcia, the third co-founder of PIVOT, was the one who realized that the pods they had developed could be modified to provide life support."

Now Amber was on-screen. She squinted. "They air-brushed me."

"Shhhh," everyone else hissed.

"At the time," she said in the interview, "we didn't think about the fact that the virtual reality component could be used. We only thought about the cost of running the pods and we knew it was so much less than the equivalent equipment in an ICU. As we looked deeper into it, though, we found that someone else had looked at using a technology like ours specifically for comatose patients."

"That someone," David said, "was Dr. Jean-Luc DuBois of American University. In 2002, he had sought approval for the medical trial of a technology that would stimulate a comatose brain. His early research showed that if the subject regained an interest in solving problems or interacting with the outside world, recovery might proceed more quickly and reliably.

"The project was denied FDA testing, which he appealed on the grounds that no credible danger had been proved toward subjects. The FDA was unavailable for comment, but an anonymous source at Bentz & Jay Corp contacted us for this story and reported that several CEOs had lobbied jointly that his treatment not be approved."

DuBois appeared on screen and all the members of PIVOT tensed. If something went sideways, this would be one of the likeliest times.

"The research was incredibly promising," he said. "There is a temptation to be casual when approaching such delicate areas of health because the outcomes are already so bad. I was lucky to work with a team that was wholly dedicated to good outcomes for every single patient."

He explained his earlier research in plain language and with an earnest air that made Jacob realize the man would make an excellent professor.

With a small smile, he leaned over to nudge the doctor, "Hey. This is good. Even I understand the neuroscience here."

DuBois looked up from his bag of caramel corn with a smile. "I worked on that explanation all night," he said. "I practiced many times."

"You did?" Amber asked. Jacob could see she was as surprised as he was.

"Of course," the man said in surprise. "I'm not a natural public speaker and I needed to work hard to find a way that lay people could understand the research and connect with it. I wanted to show the project in a good light."

Jacob gaped. It was surprisingly touching that he had worked so hard on this aspect of things, especially when he had a laboratory with unlimited equipment at his disposal now.

"Thanks," he said.

DuBois merely smiled and offered him some caramel corn.

"PIVOT's treatment went far beyond the original concept of

simple puzzles," the voiceover said. Stock footage of the video game began to play, taken from PIVOT's advertising materials. "The video game was a Massively Multiplayer Online Role Playing Game, akin to World of Warcraft or Everquest, in which a basic character could be leveled up to make it stronger."

"You know, in case you lived under a rock and didn't know what an MMORPG was," Nick said in disgust.

"Remember," Amber said idly, "half the people watching this still think D&D is about demonic summoning."

Everyone snickered.

"DuBois was excited about this development, however," Yang said. The camera panned to show him interviewing the doctor.

"It was the social aspect that interested me the most," DuBois said. "It was something my original research had been unable to replicate. I would describe it as the Holy Grail of coma research —how to get through to patients. This game provided that, and because it waited for player input, the patient could rest and wake without having perceived the intervening passage of time. It would allow patients to interact at their own speed as they recovered."

"The next task," the reporter said, "was to convince Justin's parents that he was a good candidate for the trial. It had not been widely publicized, which meant they were unaware of it."

"I think we were cautious," Mary Williams said. She looked professional, if fragile. Her name was shown in the corner of the screen. "It was a new treatment, obviously, and that was a risk. What impressed us both, I think, was how...how much each member of that team *cared*. Often, in a hospital, it's easy to feel like you're simply another patient. There are so many who live and die that the doctors aren't surprised by anything. The PIVOT team and Dr. DuBois not only knew their technology, they really cared about Justin."

The screen cut to Jacob speaking about his grandmother. With a start, he recognized the background and phrasing. This had been after the camera crew realized Justin was in the pod. The music took on a solemn tone as he explained how much he wished his grandmother had been able to access the treatment.

"It isn't abstract for him," Nick said when he appeared on-screen. "When we first came up with the concept, we wanted the first trial patient to be his grandmother. We knew this treatment could give people a reason to live and remember the best parts of life."

"Jacob's grandmother, Elizabeth Keegan, passed away soon after," Yang reported. "Zachary has said that her death and his inability to help her have spurred his efforts to make sure other families do not go through the same thing his family experienced. The partnership between Zachary and Price could not have been more natural."

Anna Price appeared on-screen now. "As soon as I heard about the treatment PIVOT was using, I knew it might be the breakthrough we had hoped for. I was familiar with DuBois's work, and seeing him come out of retirement to team up with PIVOT meant that Diatek could truly help out."

"There's some confusion about timelines," Yang's voice said to her. "Elizabeth Keegan died on May 2nd, the day after Justin's accident. Now, at that time, there was no record of PIVOT seeking FDA approval, which was part of why Jacob Zachary was arrested in July, a few days before PIVOT's acquisition by Diatek."

Price nodded. "That was a very serious error in communication," she said somberly. "With things happening so quickly between all of us—Diatek, PIVOT, the doctor—and the transfer of the patients, there was an absolutely inexcusable lack of communication with the FDA, who very justifiably believed that there was a danger to the patients in the trial. All of us sincerely regret that Jacob was arrested as part of this confusion, and I have personally apologized. I think our greatest regret, however, has been the fallout suffered by Mary and Tad Williams."

The rest of them had not listened during this part of the initial interview, and they leaned forward with interest.

"Diatek has remained a private company in part because I knew that, as a parent of an injured child, public scrutiny would have been the last thing I could endure while Mina was fighting for her life," she said. "When the news broke of where Justin was and the speculation began about what treatment he was experiencing, his parents were on the receiving end of…truly unimaginable vitriol."

"You've said that the FDA decision was understandable," Yang said. "Do you think the public outcry was also understandable?"

Price paused. "The FDA absolutely has to act when there is a dearth of information," she said. "From their perspective, there was no indication that what was happening was safe. I am… upset, however, by the public reaction. I would have hoped that the press and the public would wait for details, especially once they learned that the FDA had withdrawn the charges."

"Can you comment on Justin's condition?" he asked.

"Details about individual patients are confidential," she responded. "What I can say is that early results are very promising. There are some patients for whom this kind of nervous system engagement would not be the best treatment, but there are also those for whom social interaction is a pathway back to consciousness. We have many rounds of testing ahead of us, of course, but I know that I am sincerely hopeful that we will be able to bring this treatment to the public."

The camera cut back to Yang standing outside the laboratory.

"Justin's parents were able to comment on his condition," he said, "and they report that he has shown considerable improvement. They believe that this would not have been possible without PIVOT's involvement."

Clips of the team in the laboratory began to play, all juxtaposed against uplifting music.

"When I asked the team if they had anything more to say

about the experiment," his voice said, "it was DuBois who summed his feelings up—not with hope, but with anger."

Everyone in the room tensed as the doctor appeared on-screen again.

"It was difficult to see my work dismissed," he said honestly. "Especially knowing that there were no verifiable concerns about safety. I had to put that behind me in order to move forward with my life, and I believed that it was in the past. PIVOT's work has been life-changing, but I have also rediscovered that anger. If we had begun these trials eighteen years ago, this treatment would have been available to the public by now and I cannot imagine how many people would have been helped by it."

He paused, then looked directly at the camera. "We like to think that we leave the schoolyard behind when we grow up, but the truth is that there are still bullies in the adult world. I don't know why my treatment was blocked the first time. I only have conjecture on that and I have no interest in speculation. What does concern me is how many people—how many families— could have been helped with treatments for all kinds of conditions. Unfortunately, those treatments have been lobbied against by industry insiders."

The reporter returned to the camera for an earnest break-down with the news anchor, and they discussed Tad Williams's measure that would go to a senate vote in two days. They mentioned the voting records of various senators and the fact that the measure had, unusually, both bipartisan backing and bipartisan opposition. This was juxtaposed against statements from lobbying groups and pharmaceutical CEOs. The piece did not connect the dots.

It did not need to. The implication was absolutely clear.

Jacob exhaled a breath. "Was it only me, or…"

"No." Amber was smiling. Her eyes were bright with relief. "They completely vindicated us. "Jacob, they…they liked us."

"Or it was profitable for them," he said grimly.

"Stop it," said a new voice and Mary Williams tapped him firmly on the shoulder. "They could be spreading scandal. Lord knows, they'd have the viewership if they did. Amber is right—they vindicated you and your research. After seeing the laboratory and speaking to all of you, they realized that you're not here to make a quick buck or sell snake oil." She squeezed his shoulder. "And Tad and I are only the first parents who will be grateful to all of you for your work."

The group broke apart into hugs and handshakes. The assistants talked excitedly to one another, DuBois moved between groups to offer caramel corn with single-minded devotion, and Nick sniffled suspiciously into a cup of coffee.

Jacob released a breath he felt like he'd been holding for weeks. "The cat's out of the bag," he said to Amber. "And it's okay."

"Yeah." She hugged him. "We did good."

"We did good," he agreed.

A beep sounded from the lab and everyone turned. They knew what that meant. For a long moment, no one spoke.

"Time to go see the fight," Jacob said. "Did someone call Ms. Price?"

"On it," an assistant said.

"I'll be there in a moment," Mary said. She looked quickly at her phone. "The Senate is going into arguments in a couple of hours. I want to see if I can get ahold of Tad before he leaves his office. He should know that at least someone in the press believes him. Hopefully, it will have changed a few minds. Whose, I don't know. But it's possible."

———

In his office, Dru Metcalfe switched the TV off and stared at the black screen in silence. Finally, he stood and buttoned his suit jacket, a reflex from years of business meetings.

He had one move left and it was something he had tried to avoid for years.

On the other hand, he thought with a certain grim humor, he'd made an entire career on doing things he didn't really want to do.

What was one more?

CHAPTER TWENTY-TWO

"*Citizens and visitors!*" The voice echoed and seemed to roll around the vast space. "Welcome to the final match of Season Twelve!" People cheered and stamped so hard that the entire cavern beneath the arena shook.

"Justin survived the car crash," Tina said in a mock-reporter voice, "only to die when a video game tunnel collapsed on him because he was…too popular. Joining him in death was Tina Castro, who had never imagined her life would end this way." She looked at him. "Too soon?"

He laughed too hard to speak for a moment so simply waved a hand. "Oh, God. You're right, though. Holy shit."

The Master of Ceremonies was clearly enjoying this match. He worked to wind the crowd up with descriptions of the two teams, some details of which were a surprise even to Justin.

"I didn't know you defeated a dragon," Tina said. "Did that slip your mind, or…"

"I rode a dragon," he said. "Damn. I forgot that the real world doesn't have dragons. This will be a serious bummer in some ways, I gotta say."

The platform began to ascend. The Twins were being introduced by name and he had a mental image of them waving to the crowd. He could see their smirks in his mind's eye and the same attitude they'd given him on the first day they met.

Now he knew what lay behind them. They believed utterly that they were meant to rule this entire world.

He had to say he wouldn't trust them as gods. They had proven that they didn't give a damn about anyone but themselves. Anyone willing to kill an unsuspecting opponent to gain godhood clearly didn't have a great grasp of ethics.

Tina caught his hand and he jumped. Her hold was so tight that his fingers hurt.

"Are you okay?" he asked her.

"I'm nervous," she said. "Last time, I wasn't fast enough to save you."

"Last time, I ran off like an idiot." He squeezed her hand. "This time…"

"This time didn't have to happen," Tina said. "You knew they would wake you up if you asked. Why are you here, Justin? Why are we still here? The truth now."

The cover slid back and dappled light covered them. He could see the tops of trees swaying above and he suddenly felt oddly calm.

"Do you remember when Zaara asked me if I thought this was real?" he asked her.

"Yeah."

"I…" Justin took a deep breath. "Look, don't think I'm crazy, okay? But I wasn't lying when I told her I think it's real. I don't know if it's only real for people like us—for players or for NPCs too, or what—but I know that you and I have the chance to stop those two from becoming gods and I think that's important for this world. I don't want to leave it with a threat I could have saved it from."

She squeezed his hand again. "You know, I'm really looking forward to seeing what you do when you're awake again." As the platform rose to the arena floor, she pulled suddenly on his hand, grasped his armor, and pulled him down for a kiss. "For luck," she said and her eyes sparkled. "Let's do this. And stick to the plan, Williams."

"Stick to the plan," he repeated. The wall was still around them, but they could see treetops and he pointed urgently. "Zip lines!"

"Oh, this is gonna be as fun as hell," she said as she turned to stand back to back with him. The two of them scanned the area around them for weaponry.

The countdown appeared Ten seconds, nine, eight...

"I'm ready," he said.

Five, four, three...

"I think."

Tina elbowed him with a laugh.

The shield vanished and they stared at an incredible forest, the trees as large as redwoods. Zip lines ran between them and the flat earth covered in a soft blanket of pine needles. With the ground so open, it was easy to see the cache.

Because there was only one—and it was right in the center of the arena.

The two teammates surged into a sprint. He was fast, the legacy of his father's talent in track. It was one of many things he hadn't pursued even when Tad had practically begged him to do so. He wondered if his father was watching now and hoped he was.

The thought of seeing his parents helped him push to an even greater speed. The twins pushed toward the cache with the same determination he and his friend did. He and Tina would reach the area first, but not by much.

"Stick to the plan!" he called to her.

She didn't spare any breath for a response. Her gaze was locked on a battle-ax that protruded from the ground and the tell-tale shimmer of a blue bottle toward the Twins' side of the cache.

Justin burst into the center of the cache when the Twins were still a dozen yards away. He didn't slow as he grasped a sword and went into a spin. A few passes helped him retrieve it fully and he continued to run. If he could eliminate one of them now, it would be incredible. Immensely unlikely, of course, but incredible.

That wasn't his real goal, however. Their adversaries slowed and began to circle outward as he forged forward with the sword. Neither of them was willing to risk decapitation at the start of the match—a pity, that—but they clearly thought they had a chance to defeat him two-on-one.

Idiots. He lunged at Callie and attacked with verve, dragging her partner's attention from where Tina had reached the blue bottle and now spread the water power along the edge of her blade. Out of the corner of her eye, he saw that she snatched as many potions as she could and stuffed them into a pouch at her belt but also threw swords and daggers away from the cache.

The twins realized too late what was happening. Dexi, angry, shouted and attacked him from behind. Justin pounded face-first into the ground and winced when his sword hand made impact a moment later. It stung but he tightened his grasp on it through the pain.

He maintained his hold when the entire sword shuddered. Callie had raced forward to stamp on the blade and pin it down while her partner grappled for a chokehold.

Without a doubt, Justin would have been in a bad way if he had to choose between defending himself from Dexi and retaining his sword, but he didn't have to choose. They'd made plans for a few eventualities, and their one-cache plan had been for him to take a ranged melee weapon and hold the Twins off while Tina collected as much of the cache as possible and threw the rest away. She would then distract them, and the two of them would find high ground while their opponents armed themselves.

Tina held up her end of the bargain now and barreled in with a battle cry.

She disappeared in a cloud of black smoke that stung Justin's lungs. Callie and Dexi both coughed and the weight on his back released. Whether this was what his friend had wanted, he wasn't sure. He only had one goal in mind—to push into the Twins' territory. With that purpose fixed in his head, he pushed to his feet and stumbled. Surely this cloud had to end sometime.

A hand caught his wrist and Tina hauled him along. "Come on!"

"What was that?" he asked. He coughed so violently he almost couldn't speak. "I…can't breathe—"

"We gotta keep running," she said and detoured sideways. "Not this one, not this one—okay, go!"

"Can't…*breathe!*"

"This is not the time for dying," she said succinctly. "You can die later." She hauled him around the side of a tree and up a set of stairs that wound around it. "Come on, come on, come on. One foot after the other. Keep going."

Still coughing and choking while his eyes watered, Justin stumbled up the stairs with one hand in hers and one hand wielding his sword. He held onto it as tightly as he could to keep from screaming at the pain in his lungs, and the metal ridges of the hilt dug into his palms.

When Tina let him stop, he dropped to his knees with a dull thud that shook the wooden planks beneath him. He coughed for a long time until he finally spat out something black that looked malevolently at him and crawled away with a hiss.

"So that's what gremlin-smoke is," Tina said.

"You didn't think it might kill me?" Justin looked at her in horror.

"Nope." She smiled. "And the good news is, it incapacitated both the Twins for a while too."

She pointed and he crawled to look before he gaped at his surroundings. He'd known vaguely that they were going up the side of a tree but he could see now that they were much higher than he'd realized. The forest floor spread below them and he could barely see the movement of their adversaries limping up one of the staircases.

"Whoa," he said.

"Yeah. Also, from the coughing, I learned something important." She pointed at Dexi. "His ribs aren't all better yet—like the healer warned Lyle about his leg."

"Yes, well, it's only been two days since you shattered literally every bone in his torso," he said. He shuddered dramatically. "I keep trying not to think about that."

"It was better than cutting him in half," Tina argued. "I only had the two choices."

"Yes, because you'd started a killing strike." Justin grinned at her. "Okay, breathing doesn't hurt anymore. What's the game plan from here?"

She pointed to the zip lines. "While you and they were out of it, the Master of Ceremonies announced a change. Magic was blocked at the start of the match but it will be available in…well, probably about two minutes now. I'm not sure if either of the Twins heard, so my idea was for you to get on one of those zip lines and throw spells at them as you go. It'll be hard for them to target you in return. I'll follow and we can use the strategy we talked about."

He nodded seriously. This time, they had decided that they would stay on the move, learn about the arena, and not wait for Dexi and Callie to find a hideout. The zip lines had made that a higher-speed game than they had expected, but he was savagely glad about that.

With deft but careful motions, he spread a fire potion on his sword and buckled it to his side. Tina also had a mana potion, which he slipped into the pouch at his waist.

"So, how will the organizers prevent us from dying to magic?"

"Apparently, the arena's spells will automatically reduce the size of any spell so it can't leave you with less than one percent of your health. Each one of us was tagged before the start of the match and that portion of our life force was hidden, I guess? I'm not sure. It must be difficult to do—either that or there aren't any assassinations in this world."

"That's definitely new," he said. "Sephith would have had that if he could."

"Good point."

The two of them strapped themselves into zip lines and readied for the next phase. Tina's gaze was glued on the Twins' hideout, and she reported with a smile that they squabbled over the one potion they'd managed to get.

When Justin's magic bar turned from gray to blue, he made a running leap off the platform before his fear of heights could catch up with him. After a sickening moment when he feared the zip line wouldn't catch him, the harness bounced, the line went tight, and relief spread through him with a tingle.

Still, he had no time to dwell on that. He readied fireballs and hurled them one after another. It was immensely satisfying to see them converge on the Twins' location, and his only regret was that he couldn't take the time to enjoy the zip line. He barely recovered his focus long enough to stop himself from careening into the second tree at high speed—and to get out of the way before Tina came in hot behind him.

They'd divided their tasks at that point too. He would locate their next hideout and look for other caches, and she would report on what their opponents were doing.

"They've split up," she reported suddenly. "Callie got onto a zip line and Dexi didn't. He's going down the stairs. Justin, that zipline—*now*. We have a chance to disable him."

The Twins had run as their platform caught fire. Justin hooked himself onto another zip line and jumped before he realized fully what was happening.

This one led to the ground. He opened his mouth to scream an expletive but fortunately remembered that the element of surprise was necessary. Instead, he mouthed the word over and over until he landed with a clatter and a crash. Thankfully, the impact dislodged his harness and he tumbled free. Tina landed beside him and rolled to her feet, her battle-ax in her hand.

Dexi reached the ground before he saw them. He turned and ran up the stairs with a look of pure panic, and Justin felt a wave of satisfaction.

Surprise, motherfucker. He downed the magic potion in one gulp and lobbed a fireball at the side of the tree. It destroyed the fugitive's next stair and began to burn along the stairway in both directions.

With a curse, the man leapt free. He landed heavily and Justin saw what Tina had meant. He winced when his torso moved. Still, he was a warrior through and through. He'd trained through injury before and launched into motion without missing a beat, wielding two short swords like daggers.

It shouldn't have worked, but Dexi had clearly practiced this, along with magic and claymores and maces. He melded mid-range melee strength with quicks strikes Tina couldn't defend well against. She began to fall back almost at once before she managed to rally.

"Payback!" she called to him. When he ducked, she mouthed, "Gank him," and returned to her attack.

She wouldn't win in the long run but gave a good show of being too emotionally invested to do the smart thing. Her attack was accompanied by shouts of rage and an impressive grimace, and she insulted her opponent's lineage, his morals, and his looks. She spat insults about how little he deserved to win and how he would not even be remembered when he died.

Dexi, hamstrung by his injury, was nonetheless lured in by the slight edge he had over her. Justin remained behind him until he sensed that the man had forgotten entirely about his second opponent.

The timing was perfect when he struck. He raced forward and swung the sword in a powerful slash. Dexi's back arched as he screamed, and the blue shield came up.

"Knockout," the Master of Ceremonies reported. "Dexi has been taken out of the match by Justin."

A scream came from nearby—Callie, he guessed.

"Get ready," Justin told his partner.

"I was born ready." She adjusted her hold on the battle-ax. "Are you ready?"

"Yep." He sighed. "I hate to give her even the momentary satisfaction again, but…" He sighed, winked at Tina, and ran to one of the distant trees. While he dodged and weaved, he also made sure he was seen as if he simply wasn't very good at sneaking.

He located Callie when he was halfway to his target. She sprinted toward him and looked continually around her for Tina. Clearly, she had an idea how Dexi had been eliminated and she was wary as well as furious.

Justin wondered idly if she thought about being a god alone or if she'd let Dexi rule with her.

It didn't matter because she wouldn't win. A thrill surged in his blood. She was a formidable opponent but he'd fought Sephith and the demons. He was no longer afraid and he wasn't desperate. It meant he could choose his time.

The woman cut him off twice. She was armed with a sword identical to his and the two of them parried and clashed. They were close enough at one point for their breath to mingle. She hated him, he could see that.

"You weren't supposed to be here," she snapped. "Only Quartzfire stood between us and the crown."

"Is that what your madman told you?" Justin retorted. "You

know, I could get a pet madman to tell me I'm a god too. Or even a pet dog." He braced his feet and shoved her back.

It had to be done carefully and he wasn't sure he could do it. He was tiring now. His magic was drained and his footwork grew slower each time he danced out of the way. If he could only get under her guard, he could end it.

Unfortunately, that seemed unlikely. He had used swords on the battlefield and he attacked with more strength and brutal efficiency, but Callie had trained for years. Time and again, a little trick of footwork or a tiny twist of her sword would rescue her from what he thought was a winning strike.

She had maneuvered them onto open ground too. The woman knew by now that his partner had no magic and there was no way for Tina to get out from the shadow of the trees before she saw her. It would be impossible to gang up on her.

Finally, Callie tired of the fight. Justin saw her draw on the deepest reserves she had. Her eyes went flat and cold and she launched into a flurry of strikes that he could not begin to parry. He swung his sword as fast as he could but there was no way he could hold out for much longer. Any attempt at offense was impossible and he scrambled back and jerked out of the way of the strikes. He prepared himself to make his own last stand when he tripped.

Justin sprawled full-length and the sword clattered away. A moment later, he felt the kiss of steel on his Adam's apple and looked into his adversary's flat eyes.

He smiled and a tiny flicker of confusion flared in her gaze for only a second.

A moment later, Tina bulldozed into her from the side at high speed. She had daggers now but she didn't need them. The sheer force with which she tackled her opponent catapulted the other woman into a tree. Callie struck the bark a few feet up, slid down to crumple in a motionless heap, and was immediately encased in a blue shield.

The two friends stared at one another, breathing hard.

"Sephith's Bane wins Season Twelve!" the Master of Ceremonies shouted.

The stadium crowd erupted with cheers and Justin let his head fall back with an exhausted laugh. They'd done it. Against all odds, they had finally won.

"Er-hem," the AI said.

"Oh, what now?"

"I only wanted to say one more thing."

He rolled his eyes and waited, panting slightly. When the words flashed up on his screen, he barely had the energy to laugh but he couldn't stop himself from doing so.

CLUMSY, the words read. **MAX LEVEL ACHIEVED**.

CHAPTER TWENTY-THREE

The reporters were gathering. Metcalfe could see them looking for Senator Williams.

He wondered if the man would actually appear. That might be amusing. He allowed himself a small smile before he stepped up to the podium.

"Thank you all for coming," he told them. "I'm Dru Metcalfe. I understand that some details of Justin Williams's care were released to the media in an expose by 360 News yesterday. However, there is a great deal of information that was left out, and I think you would all find it most illuminating."

Tad bowed his head. His hands were clenched on his desk and he took the time to relax them. He wanted nothing more than to head to the chapel but there was no time. He had worked for twenty hours at this point, and only rehearsal and caffeine kept him upright. Even when he tried to sleep, all he could dream of was giving his speech.

Mary's message had come in, telling him that the media coverage was good.

It might help. He had to hope it would soften some hearts and minds so that when he gave his speech, they were ready to listen to what he had to say. He stood, buttoned his suit jacket, and took his briefcase from the desk.

Out in the main room, his aides were clustered around a TV.

"Sir," Kyle said. "You'll want to see this."

"Will it change the speech I'm about to give?" he asked. He paused. "It's not Justin, is it?"

"No," the aide said. He swallowed. "It's not new information for you."

"Then I'll watch it later. I'll need at least one of you with me." He left and made a conscious effort not to listen to the words coming out of the TV. Whispers followed him and finally, Jared came to walk with him. Tad looked at him with a raised eyebrow.

"You said you didn't want to know, sir," the young man reminded him.

"Indeed, I did." He took a deep breath. "I tell you, I'm looking forward to sleep. Oh, I shouldn't have thought of sleep. Oh, dear."

"I'll meet you in the chambers with a large coffee, sir." Jared hurried away and Tad smiled exhaustedly after him.

He only had to get through this speech. He had thirty minutes to prepare—and thirty minutes to not think about why all his aides looked so deeply worried.

***

"A late-breaking news story might change or delay the vote on the pharmaceutical pricing bill up for debate in the Senate," a news anchor reported.

Eric Snelling, surrounded by his aides and several fellow senators, looked up sharply. His heart sank. After yesterday's news story, he had spent hours chipping away at his party's junior senators—the ones most likely, he had to admit, to stand up and do the right thing.

What was happening now?

He went to the TV with the others, only to find another of his colleagues giving him a smug look.

"You haven't been here long enough," she told him condescendingly, "but where there's smoke, there's almost always fire."

He gave her a look that he hoped might turn her to stone.

It didn't work and she shrugged dismissively. "This will not go well for Williams. Whatever dirt there is on him is about to come out."

"How do you know that?" Snelling asked.

"I know because that"—she pointed—"is Dru Metcalfe. Whatever skeletons are hiding in your closet, he'll find them all, polish them, and show them off for the whole world to see. You're lucky, Snelling."

"Why?" He maintained a calm expression although his heart sank even more.

"He hasn't made a demonstration of anyone like this in a couple years," the other senator told him. "In fact, I haven't ever seen him do one in person. Whatever he's preparing to drop, it has to be so big that Williams, his family, and his entire hometown will be a smoking crater by the time he's done."

***

In the main chamber, Tad found a surprising number of people already assembled. Several were clustered around a few at their desks, all of whom held phones. Some looked at him, did double-takes, and glanced nervously at each other.

He sighed. His intention had been to take the time to practice, but it was clear he wouldn't have the chance to practice on the floor.

Disappointed, he headed to his desk and arranged his papers

before he tuned everything else out. His gaze traveled over the first few lines of his speech, and his lips moved as he read:

Nine weeks ago, at 11:15 at night, I got a call from the police about my son Justin...

Dru Metcalf wrapped his hands around the podium and looked at the assembled reporters. Now that it came down to it, he felt sick. He'd done many things over the years that he had to work to forget—the faces of the senators and their children when all the family secrets were dragged into the open were persistent ghosts.

He'd drunk some of those memories away and spent hours in the gym to banish the rest. Every morning, he reminded himself of how the world worked. He'd taken to looking at his bank account when he woke up.

It was all coming back now, though. No amount of zeroes at the end of his bank balance had made him feel better this morning. He'd looked at the latest deposit from Raymond White and wanted to throw up.

Would he actually do this?

Yes, so he might as well get on with it.

"Nine weeks ago, at 11:45 at night, I received a call from my employer," he told the reporters, "a man named Raymond White, the CEO of IterNext Solutions. I've worked for him for the past eight years. He told me that Tad Williams's son had been involved in a car crash and had been transferred to a nearby hospital by life-flight. His prognosis was not good."

The reporters wrote furiously.

"White has worked in healthcare for his entire career," he continued. "He knows intimately how costs have ballooned and how much pressure it can put on a family to face the costs of intensive care. For this reason, he asked me to pass along an offer to Senator Williams and his wife. Mr. White wanted to personally cover the costs of care for Justin Williams."

He looked at his notes and swallowed.

"I met with the senator in person several days later. Justin's condition was stable and Williams was back in DC to attend a vote. I arrived in time to hear Nicholas Ryn and Jacob Zachary pitching him on the treatment developed by PIVOT Laboratories, and I warned the senator that the treatment was untested. I passed along Mr. White's offer to him. In response, he accused me of bribery."

The reporters shifted and a new energy rose in the air. Metcalfe was getting to the good stuff now. This was what they were there for.

"I explained to him that this was an alignment of interests," he said. "There were bills coming to the floor that Williams had shown no particular interest in, and I wanted to speak to him about the negative impact they might have on companies such as IterNext. He disagreed strenuously with my characterization of the situation." He took a deep breath. "So I showed him doctored photos I had made of him with a mistress."

Total silence fell over the group.

"Williams was a junior senator," he continued, "and so I had not worked with him before. He was shocked by the photos I showed him. In response, I told him that...he was not the first senator who had been determined to not play ball with my clients. I told him that the choice was his—either he could have all Justin's medical bills paid, or not only would the bills not be paid, he would also be embroiled in scandal.

"I've checked my records. Tad Williams is the forty-second senator I have had a similar conversation with. Thirty-eight were persuaded, either by the initial offer or by similar methods of blackmail. Four, I made sure were not re-elected. I have been immensely successful in my line of work."

The reporters' jaws hung open.

"I leaked the story of Justin's treatment to the media," Metcalfe said bluntly. "I was the one who began the recall petition for Senator Williams. I told a reporter where she could find PIVOT's original laboratories and tipped the FDA off that there was unapproved human testing being conducted. At each step, I offered Senator Williams the chance to end the game. At each step, he refused.

"Yesterday, I saw the piece on 360 News regarding Diatek's creation and PIVOT's treatment technique." He looked up and focused on those present. "I have contacted federal prosecutors with the information that I can provide regarding why the FDA blacklisted the treatment pioneered by Jean-Luc DuBois, as well as information regarding the senators I have blackmailed. At this time, I cannot share specifics of any of those cases or confirmation of their names. However…"

He looked unwaveringly at one of the cameras. "I can tell you that several of them will be in the chamber today when they take their votes. I urge them to follow their conscience on this bill. The information I had on them is no longer in my possession and much of it was manufactured. They may consider themselves free of the chance of retribution. I will not be taking questions."

He walked away through the din of demands to a car waiting for him at the base of the steps.

"Mr. Metcalfe," a Federal Marshall said.

"Hello," Dru told him. "I assume we need to go to the station?"

"We do." The man held the door open and took a set of handcuffs from his belt. "You'll also need these."

Dru Metcalfe held his hands out and smiled as the words began. *Dru Metcalfe, you are charged with…*

Tad had hardly noticed the chamber filling. When he stood to speak, low murmurs rippled through the ranks. They were probably talking about how the junior senator was about to have his ass handed to him in the votes, he thought as he made his way to the floor.

In all honesty, he no longer cared. All that mattered was the speech and looking them in the eyes and telling Justin's story. In his hands, a piece of paper crackled—the draft of the first letter he had sent to his son in the game. His wedding ring gleamed when he looked at it.

"You'll never forget it if you let yourself down," Mary had told him.

She was right.

The speech passed in a blur. Tad knew he choked up at one point, a fact that would have mortified him mere weeks before. In some ways, he hardly recognized the man he'd been then. He told the stories of the constituents who had reached out to him and shared Anna Price's story. With quiet affection, he spoke about going into the lab to see Mary sleeping with her head resting on Justin's pod.

When he finished, he expected only silence. Instead, senators rose to their feet and applauded. Tad stared at the group.

"Okay, what was going on with that press conference?" he asked over his shoulder.

The Senate Majority Leader, a man who had never liked him in the slightest, shook his head. "You picked a hell of a time to tune out."

CHAPTER TWENTY-FOUR

The landscape of the arena faded away and Tina pushed to her feet and offered Justin a hand. He let her pull him up and became vaguely aware of the noise beating at his consciousness in waves. The crowd continued to cheer.

Somehow, even his eyes could see Zaara and Lyle in the crowd. She was crying openly, while the dwarf harrumphed and tried to hide the sheen in his eyes. Both clapped enthusiastically and leaned against each other.

I'll be back, He told them silently. *Someday.* He took his friend's hand. "Shall we?"

She walked with him, her shoulders set.

"Are you shy?" he asked her.

"Shy is being in front of a dozen people. I don't think it's unusual to be unnerved by this many people cheering for you. It must be twenty-thousand or more." She looked around. "I guess I only thought nothing like this would ever happen to me in real life."

"You never know," he said. "Maybe the world will start a live Battle Royale tournament."

"I'll be one of the hosts," Tina said, "not a contestant. With really high heels."

"That's good. You'll come all the way up to my sternum that way." He dodged out of the way of a kick and laughed.

The Master of Ceremonies waited in front of the dais and smiled at them. He inclined his head as he walked closer in the dust and when he spoke, his amplified voice seemed far away and they could hear him speak as one person to another.

"I promised you an artifact of unimaginable value," he said. "And now, I am pleased to present it."

He held the final key out and Justin's breath caught. He slid his hand into the pouch at his belt and retrieved the other two, placed them in his palm, and took the third. For a moment, he was afraid that he would fumble and be unable to put them together and it wouldn't work, but the keys seemed to know one another. They slotted together perfectly and the seams between them vanished. He held it out to Tina, who put her hand over his so they held it together.

"They key between the worlds," the Master of Ceremonies said. "The king has chosen his champions, citizens—champions to find us allies so that Insea will always prosper. Champions to end all threats and safeguard us against all foes." He turned to them again. "Sephith's Bane, are you prepared to be the Champions of Insea?"

In answer, the friends exchanged a glance before they lifted the key high. It gleamed in the sunlight as the official stepped back to gesture at the stone wall behind him. Now that Justin looked more closely, he could discern the pattern etched there, complete with a tiny, triangular hole for a key.

He looked at Tina. He couldn't seem to think anymore. His head buzzed and the stadium seemed to fade.

"Are you ready?" she asked.

"I'm ready." He walked to the stone and slid the key into the lock until it clicked in place. With a creak and a rumble, the stone doors opened into blinding white light. "It's a little on the nose, don't you think?" he asked.

He blinked reflexively and Tina was gone.

And a white light usually meant something else. Justin stared at it. He wanted to live. For so much of this, he hadn't cared. He'd tried to avoid danger, stepped beyond that fear, tried to escape this place, and stepped beyond that, too.

Now, more than anything, he wanted to live. It was time to find out if that would be his future. With one last breath and his heart pounding, he stepped into the light.

Tad stared at the ceiling. He had told himself that all he cared about was the speech, but he now realized that wasn't exactly true. With that stress now removed, he was desperate to know what had happened outside, and he was equally desperate to know what would happen inside.

Jared sat beside him and shifted from side to side. When he looked at the kid's face, he could see that the aide hadn't taken his eyes off the vote screen.

The Senate Majority Leader stood, and Tad leaned forward. His breath seemed to shudder in and out and he swallowed.

"The votes are," the leader said, "sixty-eight aye, and thirty-two nay. The bill has passed."

Buzzing swarmed in Tad's ears. "Sixty-eight?" he managed to say. "*Sixty-eight?*"

Jared looked like he might cry as he nodded. "The press conference, sir—it was Metcalfe. Remember when you said it would really help you out if he told the truth?"

His jaw dropped. "You have to be kidding me."

The young man shook his head. "You took the high road and now everyone knows that."

"Holy shit." Tad breathed in and out a few times. He pressed a hand over his mouth, aware that he might be under scrutiny, and startled when his phone rang. It was Mary's number and he answered the call to the sound of sobbing, barely audible over the cheers and chatter in the Senate chambers. "Mary? Mary! What's going on?"

"It's…Justin," she managed to say.

Tad sat hard. The phone slipped out of his grasp.

He'd been too late, he thought brokenly. Against all odds, he'd done all this and it was too late. None of it would matter for his son.

Regret was agonizing. He should have been there. All the times he'd left to come back here, and for what? He should have been at his son's bedside or gone into the game with Mary. At least that way, he'd have had a chance to see his son again and hug him, and he hadn't taken it.

Jared picked the phone up and listened. Tad couldn't hear him talking but gradually became aware of the young man shaking him. "Sir? Sir? Your wife needs to speak to you, sir."

He focused on his aide's face.

"Justin woke up. Sir? Did you hear me? Your son is waking up."

Tad had no recollection of moving but he suddenly realized he was taking the stairs three at a time to get out of the senate chamber. His aide was hot on his heels and called for a car to the airport. Senator Snelling jumped out of the way and pressed other colleagues back as he flashed Tad a thumbs-up.

"Thanks!" he called over his shoulder and only barely missed the door as he barreled out of the room. He blazed past a group of protesters with signs too quickly to know if they were supporting him or wishing for his violent death and skidded onto the steps outside. The car was already pulling up and he had to resist the urge to throw himself head-first down the stairs.

Remember, Tad, that won't actually be faster. He ran, wishing he was in better shape, wasn't wearing a damned suit, and that he was already back in California.

His son was waking up.

Justin was aware of the light first as a wash of red. He hadn't noticed any time passing since he stepped through the door. In fact, he'd forgotten about the door entirely. A little concerned, he squeezed his eyes shut and noticed that they ached.

Experimentally, he flexed his fingers.

That hurt too. His eyes opened again and he shut them again hastily when the light stabbed through him like a spear.

"Ow."

Talking also hurt. Good Lord, was anything working? His throat felt like it had been hollowed out with sandpaper.

"He's talking!" an unknown voice said. A sudden hush followed—he hadn't realized until that moment that he could hear low-voiced conversation—and the sound of footsteps grew louder.

Justin opened his eyes again slowly. At first, there was only brightness but he gradually saw shapes resolve. White...and a triangle. A dark triangle. He squinted and allowed his eyes to open a little wider. What was he looking at?

The inside of someone's nose, he realized. He sighed.

Two more faces swam into view—or, rather, two very blurry shapes that he was very sure he recognized.

"Mom? Dad?"

"We're here." His father's voice sounded choked and his mother gave a little sob. "Apparently, you're not supposed to try to sit up on your own for a while."

He immediately and completely wanted nothing more than to sit. Unfortunately, he only managed to raise one shoulder off the bed before he fell again, trembling.

"And that," said a male voice, "is why I recommended that you didn't tell him not to." A hand pressed on his shoulder. "You'll be able to sit up soon, Justin. Right now, your muscles are still waking up."

"Uh-huh." He regretted the words as soon as he said them. His throat still felt terrible.

Justin realized he must have grimaced because the doctor continued quickly. "You've just had your feeding tube removed. Your throat will feel very sore for a while. On the plus side, the time spent in your coma has allowed several bones to heal fully."

"Goody," he managed to respond. He looked at his parents. "You're…both here."

"Your mother has hardly left," his father said.

"And your father has flown here more times than most people will get on a plane in their life," his mother said fondly. Her voice trembled as she said, "It's good to see you again."

"Yes." He felt the bed shift. "What's…"

"They're sitting you up," she said. "Just-"

Exhaustion claimed him, and he laid his head back and drifted into unconsciousness for a while.

When he woke again, voices held a conversation nearby. With a start, he recognized Tina's—and, in an even bigger surprise, she was speaking to his mother. It wasn't even a fight. Justin listened, bemused, as they discussed a book they had both read. It was only a few minutes, however, before his father said,

"I believe he's awake again."

Warily, he opened one eye but was able to focus better this time. He stretched one set of fingers and his father squeezed his hand gently.

"Hi," Justin said.

"Hello." His father nodded at him. He clearly hadn't shaved in a couple of days and wore what looked like borrowed sweats.

"I've missed you."

"I've missed you too," Tad agreed. "I look forward to having you home."

"Until you move out and get a job, anyway," Mary said. She was teasing, but there was a moment of worry in her eyes.

Justin understood now, though. He had seen the way she fought for him.

He was also not above teasing her in return. "Oh, don't worry. I have it all planned. Just gimme some knives and I'll hitchhike around and do exorcisms."

Tina appeared behind his parents. She was smiling. "Can I come along?"

"Absolutely," he said. "After all, I need someone to come in on a zip line and eliminate assassins."

"I have to watch those videos," his father muttered. He looked at the edge of the room, then back. "When you're feeling better, you can meet the care team—those who made the game and the...pod. They're off sorting through applications. Tons of people want their family members to have the treatment you had."

"And you know, if you need a job," a voice called, "we could really use a spokesperson."

"Who wuzzat?" Justin asked muzzily.

"That was Nick, dear," his mother said. She patted his hand. "Don't worry, you'll meet them all soon enough. Focus on staying awake for now." She stood.

"Where are you going?" he asked.

His mother looked embarrassed for a moment before she shrugged. "I have an appointment. Didn't Zaara ever mention who her new magic tutor was?" She strolled away and he stared incredulously after her while his father laughed hysterically.

The story continues with *Accept No Attitude,* book four in the P.I.V.O.T. Lab Chronicles.

Coming soon to Amazon and to Kindle Unlimited

www.ingramcontent.com/pod-product-compliance
Lightning Source LLC
Chambersburg PA
CBHW070633100726
47907CB00007B/1971